THE LAZARUS JOURNALS

Wilderness

Book #1 of the *In the Beginning Series*

To Dick & Sandra

David L Beeler

David Beeler

Bridges to Tomorrow Publications

The Lazarus Journals: Wilderness
Book #1 of the *In the Beginning Series*

Copyright © 2016 by David Beeler
www.authordavidbeeler.com

Bridges to Tomorrow Publications
Chattanooga, Tennessee

Requests for information should be addressed to:
Bridges to Tomorrow Publications
425 Shadow Parkway
Chattanooga, TN 37421

To schedule David Beeler to speak to your group or church or at a conference or event please send an email to: authordavidbeeler@gmail.com
Please include contact information including phone number.

All scripture references are paraphrased and fused by the author from various biblical passages and are not direct quotes from any particular translation. Furthermore, these references are in some cases composites of things Jesus is reported to have said, and are removed from their biblical context and order of presentation.

Cover Design by Heidi Lyons
Editing by Barbara Maples and Cynthia Beeler

ISBN: 0997802405
ISBN 9780997802405 Paperback Edition 978-0-9978024-1-2 ebook Edition
Library of Congress Control Number: 2016913502
Bridges to Tomorrow Publications, Chattanooga, TN

Dedicated to my children:
Daniel, Andrew, Gabriel, Justin, and Emma
You keep me believing!

PROLOGUE

Point of reference: Revelation, Chapter 12

The entire universe was about to change forever, because nothing like this had ever been done before, and nothing like this would ever be done again! The plan had been laid out over hundreds of years, and now the time had come. The die would be cast, and no one would be able to take it back. The players would take the stage, and all would watch with bated breath.

If all went well, the age of sacrifice would be abandoned, and the religions of Earth would be transformed by an age of faith. For humanity, what had been a season of darkness would become a season of hope, for those who called themselves "The chosen people of God," what had been a winter of despair, would now become a spring of hope.

However, if things didn't go well, there would be an entirely different outcome. Not everyone agreed with the plan, and rebellion was breaking out at the highest levels. Now everything hung in the balance, as Heaven, the great abode of peace and tranquility, became a place of war.

It was the last of times; it was the first of times. Yes, everything was about to change . . . forevermore!

A young boy is looking out an elaborate window at the ramparts of what appears to be an ancient castle. Only, this bastion is surprisingly surrounded by nothing but the dark void of outer space, or perhaps, some other space altogether. Stars twinkle in the distance, but so do other celestial orbs. They glimmer and shine like precious jewels in every color ever known.

In the distance, he sees a waterfall cascading from the skies above to form a beautiful river that runs through the center of the city surrounded by the castle walls. He smiles as he thinks of the many times he's stood on the fringes of that great waterfall and allowed its magical waters to pummel his body.

The lad appears to be about 12 or 13 years old, just on the verge of pubescence. Intense intellect sparkles in his bright eyes, one of which is green, and the other blue, as he watches the activity unfolding outside the window. His long dark hair, which has never been cut, falls freely on his shoulders and down his back, in luxurious curls. His handsome, sharp features are softened by his innocence, yet there is a regal wisdom in his countenance that belies his youthfulness.

As he stares raptly out the window, a glowing presence approaches and lays a strong hand on his shoulder. "My son, what do you see below?"

The young boy takes a deep breath and speaks in a lilt and tone that's delicious to any ears that may hear, "Gabriel has blown his horn, and the angels gather from near and far, as if they're preparing to do battle. Even now, Michael is directing them to take up defensive positions on the ramparts. Also, down by the River of Life, and throughout the city, people are running around in a panic. What's happening, Father?"

"I'm afraid we're about to go to war, son."

"How can that be? Who would dare come against us here? We designed this refuge as a place of absolute harmony and serenity, and besides, aren't all our subjects under your complete control?"

"No, son, I chose long ago to allow all my offspring throughout my creation the freedom to make their own choices. Even here, in this sacred sanctuary, the angels can choose to be faithful, or to rebel against my authority. I have given them life, and all I ask in return is that they love me.

"As you know, you and I have been preparing for a possible mission to the planet Earth. Unfortunately, our various experiments with redemptive covenants haven't turned out as we'd hoped with this particular world. The people we chose to implement our last covenant, have selfishly kept our teachings and precepts to themselves, and cut the rest of humankind off from being able to know us. It's time we took a more universal approach to invite the people of Earth to partake in our bounty.

"Since everything that was made on Earth was made through you, it just makes sense that you should be the one who undertakes this mission. I could go myself, and believe me, I've considered it, but you *have* to be the one to do it. I would rather go myself, and it would be easier for me if I did, but this mission requires the ultimate sacrifice, so only you will do."

The Father tightens his grip on his son's shoulder and continues, "You're my only true son. You are the blood of my blood, and flesh of my flesh, so you're the most precious thing I've ever created in the entire universe. Giving you up, in this way, is the hardest thing I could ever do. Your suffering will be the basis of the new covenant I will make with the people of Earth, for there can be no redemption without sacrifice.

"As you know, there are some among us who fervently disagree with our plans. One in particular would like to take your place, but only because he thinks it would elevate him to be equal with us. He has no true affinity for the well-being of humans, and is only acting out of greed and conceit. Unfortunately, there are many who have been led astray by him, so I believe an attack is imminent. If you're still willing to carry out this mission, the time is short. Are you ready to make the transition?"

The young boy lifts his head and looks up into the glowing face. "Father, I have always been faithful to do what you tell me, and if this is what you say we must do to redeem our children, then I am willing to be the sacrifice. I will be a shepherd to our sheep, I will teach them of your love and mercy, and I will lead them in The Way that leads to life eternal."

The face of the Father glows even brighter, as he answers, "You make me proud son, but you always have, and I believe you always will. However, I must warn you, not only can the angels go against my will, but you, also have that capacity. You're free to make your own choices in life, so just because you choose to go on this mission today doesn't mean you have to see it through to the bitter end. You can choose at any time to withdraw. Just say the word and 10,000 angels will come to bring you home at any time, and no matter what you decide to do, I will always love you forevermore!"

"I'm ready Father; just tell me what I need to do."

"Very well, but before you go, there's something you need to see and some information you need to etch into your psyche. Follow me."

The glowing visage of the Father turns, and the Son follows his billowing robes down enormous hallways until they come to an ornate door. They stop and the Father says, "As you know, while we are here, you and I are not bound by time and space. We can travel anywhere, and anytime, in our creation to see what's taking place. Of course, when we travel forward in time the events we see are somewhat fluid, because the final outcome of each stream of time can take many paths, according to the actions of specific agents and beings. Yes, I know, it's complicated.

"The point is, if all goes according to our plan, we know how things will turn out. Already many pieces of the puzzle are in place, and many more will come into play in the years to come. You're about to be transitioned into a human seedling, and before the day is over you'll be implanted in a holy woman on Earth who will serve as your earthly mother. From the time of your birth, until the end of your time on Earth, you will be bound by time and space, but right now, you have one final chance to peek into the future to see what your sacrifice may mean to the people of Earth over time.

"I have something to show you inside this room. It's a record compiled by a man who will become your dearest friend on Earth if everything goes according to plan."

"What kind of record is it, Father?"

"It's the personal journals and stories your friend will compile about your final days on Earth, and the ongoing sacrifices he, and others, will make in the future in response to your own sacrifice. When the day of reckoning comes, you'll be tempted to stop the suffering, my son. I want you to quickly absorb all the records in this room. Hold them in your heart and ponder them in the years to come. Then, in your darkest hours, you should cling to them with all your might, so you can find courage to do what must be done."

A battle horn sounds outside the castle, and the Father says, "Once we step through this door you'll only have a few moments to process the information inside before we must begin your transition, so be quick about it."

The Father pushes the heavy door open and they step into a room lined with thousands of books and parchments. Some of them are so ancient they look as if they may fall to pieces if they are touched.

The boy whispers, "Father, what are all these books?"

"Jesus, these are the Lazarus Journals!"

CHAPTER ONE

²⁰ Peter turned and saw the disciple whom Jesus loved was following them. (This was the same one who had leaned back against Jesus at the supper and said, "Lord, who is going to betray you?") ²¹ When Peter saw him, he asked, "Lord, what about him?"

²² Jesus answered, "If I want him to remain alive until I return, what is that to you? You must follow me." ²³ Because of this, the rumor spread among the believers that this disciple would never die.

John 21: 20-23

The time has come to tell my story. I've decided I should make better use of my time since I never sleep (No . . . really. . . I NEVER sleep). It's the beginning of the 21st century, and we have these wonderful things called personal computers, so typing and recording the events of the past is a breeze now. I can sit here in the "Memories Room" and blaze away on my keyboard undisturbed for hours at a time.

I have all of my journals going back nearly 2,000 years, so my plan is to copy all my journal entries so they're easy to identify. Then I'll fill in the blanks between each entry, and tell my story to the best of my recollection.

I'm probably going to be a little fuzzy on some of the names, so I'll reserve the right to make up some of those as I go. I may also be a little iffy on some of the events and dates, but I'll do my best to tell the story as truthfully as possible, no matter how painful or embarrassing it may be. Also, to keep things simple I'm abandoning the yearly, monthly, and weekly names used in the first century, and substituting the names we use today.

When I'm recounting conversations from the distant past, don't expect to find anyone using language like, "thee, thou, thy, or thine." My mind just doesn't work that way anymore, so I'll be reconstructing even the most ancient of conversations in modern vernacular.

I don't know why I've felt compelled to keep a journal for all these years, and I can't say why I feel it's important to tell my story in greater detail, but if no one ever reads my musings, it doesn't really matter. I'm doing this for myself. I've carried around a lot of stuff for a long time, and it's time to download my soul, so here goes. . . .

March 19ᵗʰ (33 A.D.)

If only I can stop trembling I'm going to try and write what happened today.

They say I was dead for four days, but I don't remember dying. I remember being flogged to the point of death by the Romans. I remember my sisters, Mary and Martha, worrying over me, day and night, as they tried desperately to nurse me back to health. I remember the awful smell of my festering wounds and the pain that made me hope to die. And then . . . well, I'd rather not spend a lot of time right now describing what I experienced next.

Let's just say, I went to a very bad place and saw a lot of really horrible suffering, along with some terribly frightening beings (I'm not sure any of them would qualify as people . . . at least not living people).

I've heard some folks whispering today, when they think I can't hear, that they think I went to Hell.

In the past, I've heard people speculate about what happens when we die, and most of us Jews believe there is no life after death; but a few believe there's a place called "Hell" or "Hades," where the wicked dead go after they die. And even fewer still (like my cousin Jesus), believe our spirits live on: either in a good place called Heaven, or a bad place called Hell.

I'm not sure where I was for those four days, or if I was just dreaming, but it wasn't a good place, that's for sure!

One moment I was running for my life in this incredibly scary place while I tried to maintain my sanity, and the next moment I was hearing Jesus calling my name. At first, it sounded like he was far away, and I thought I had finally lost my mind entirely. I stopped running and looked all around, and then I realized the voice I was hearing was coming from inside me.

That's right, it was inside me. That's the only way I know to describe it. It was like a force was inside my chest, and when he called my name the next time something seemed to turn me inside out. I heard him say, "Lazarus, come out!" and suddenly I was falling. I felt like I fell forever into a deep well of darkness. I tried to scream as I was falling, but I couldn't draw any air into my lungs, so I couldn't scream. Finally, I hit bottom and almost simultaneously sucked into my empty lungs the largest volume of air I've ever inhaled with one single breath. Curiously, the air I consumed smelled strongly of flowers and . . . burial spices.

I was already frightened out of my wits, but that endless inhalation scared me even more, and once it was finished, I heard myself screaming. But my screams were muffled by something covering my mouth. I tried to sit up, but something was wrapped around my body.

I struggled for a moment to free myself from the bindings, and finally loosened things up enough to stand up and shuffle across the floor. I still couldn't get my hands free, so I couldn't tear the bindings off my face, but I could see a light through the cloth, so I hobbled towards the light until I felt a breeze blowing. Then I heard a voice I recognized saying, "Take the grave clothes off him."

That voice was the voice of Jesus, and as my friends and neighbors unwrapped the bindings from my body, he stood and watched me with big sad eyes. I saw I had been wrapped up like a mummy, and the grave clothes gave way reluctantly. At times, it was as if they were tearing away my skin as they pulled and tugged at the wrappings that had held me tightly in a rotten cocoon. As the bindings fell away I saw bits and pieces of my favorite flowers from my gardens entangled in the cloth, and I wondered to myself, "Who would wrap be up like a dead person and cover me in flowers and burial spices?"

Then I looked back at the place I had just walked out of, and it hit me that I had been left for dead in a tomb. It didn't quite register with me that I had actually been dead; I just assumed it had been an accidental case of someone mistakenly thinking I was dead, when in fact, I wasn't. In any case, I wondered why Jesus was looking so sad when everyone else appeared to be so happy for my rescue.

My sisters certainly looked happy, but they weren't rushing up to hug me. Instead, they were looking disconcertedly at my midsection with reddened faces. I looked down and realized, with a good deal of embarrassment, I was standing there before God and everyone completely naked.

Someone quickly came to my rescue and took off their outer robe and wrapped it around my shoulders to cover my nakedness and the grotesque scars on my back. Once I was covered up my sisters, Mary and Martha, hurried forward and simultaneously embraced me.

Just then, the whole multitude parted to let Iris come running up to leap into my arms. When she kissed me, a roar of applause and approval ripped through the crowd that some claim was heard all the way in Jerusalem. I thought our romance had been kept under wraps, but I guess we weren't quite as clever as we thought.

Then the crowd parted again to let her father, Darius, come striding through to where Iris and I stood in an awkward embrace. Darius is a giant of a man. He's 6 feet 7 inches tall and all muscle. At that moment his dark Egyptian countenance was obviously contorted with raging emotion, and I thought he intended to break me into little pieces.

He spread his huge arms apart, ran the last few steps towards us, and grabbed me up in a bear-hug while lifting me off the ground and spinning me around in a wild circle. Then he bellowed, "So, it appears my master's son has not only come back from the dead, but he's also finally claimed my Rainbow Girl as his own. Hah! Hah! This is the happiest day of my life!"

With that, the crowd roared its approval again.

Then my friends hoisted me on their shoulders and carried me back to my home here in Bethany, with Iris walking by my side. Along the way I gathered that everyone thought I had been dead for four days. I also figured out everyone was convinced Jesus had performed some kind of miracle by resurrecting me from the dead.

When we arrived back at our home, the whole village broke out into an instantaneous celebration that lasted until late into the night. My sisters tried to get me to eat and drink, but I didn't have any hunger or thirst, which everyone thought was really weird, since I had been in that tomb for four days, but I marked it down to the excitement of the day's events. However, as the day wore on, I began to notice some other bizarre things about myself.

The first thing that everyone noticed was that while I had come back from the grave, and appeared fine in every way, the scars on my back hadn't healed at all. It was as if I had been in suspended animation while I was in the tomb. I came out just like I went in. The second unusual thing was that I felt great. One would expect that someone who had presumably died, and then lay in a tomb for four days, would be a little groggy at least, but I felt more alive than ever in my life. I felt like I could run and never get tired. The third thing I noticed was that I seemed stronger than before, and my reflexes were sharper and quicker. Then I realized I was hearing whispered conversations between other people that I shouldn't have been able to hear. And if I really concentrated I could even hear an individual's heart beat!

And now . . . the crowd has finally thinned out. Jesus and his followers are staying here for the night, and some of them are still hanging out by the bonfire. Iris has gone to her quarters, and my sisters have retired for the night, so I've finally been able to bathe and put on fresh clothes. And most importantly, I'm finally able to sit down and write these words in my journal.

I guess I should be elated, but actually, I'm trembling with fear. There's something seriously messed up going on! Not only am I still hearing things I shouldn't be able to hear, I'm also smelling things I shouldn't be able to smell, I'm seeing things too clearly, my mind is racing with information, and I feel incredibly strong and vibrant.

What's right with me?? Now that's funny . . . and if I wasn't so scared I'd laugh, but I'm afraid if I start laughing right now I may lose my mind completely and never stop.

So, what should I do?

I looked back over the words I'd just written, and then I lay down my quill, and gazed out the window of my room into the night. I recalled how Jesus had seemed to always be watching me through the day with those big sad eyes, and I wondered if he might be able to shed some light on the strange things I was feeling. After all, none of this would be happening if it weren't for him. I decided to seek him out first thing in the morning and see what he could tell me about my condition.

But for now, I had no desire to sleep, so I decided to go to the gardens and enjoy the night air while I contemplated my predicament and tried to calm down. Strangely enough, for a warrior such as myself, I had always enjoyed growing plants. Whether it was colorful flowers or common vegetables, I just liked gardening, so my estate reflected my hobby with the many gardens that dotted the landscape. Right now, escaping to my plants seemed like the perfect distraction.

I arrived at the balcony overlooking the gardens, and was headed for the stairs, when I suddenly realized someone was standing there with his back to me and gazing up into the stars. Unexpectedly, it registered in my mind that it was Jesus, and I knew it was him because I recognized his heartbeat.

It was strange enough that I could hear his heartbeat so distinctly, but it was doubly strange that I could identify him by his heartbeat. I was so flabbergasted by this discovery, and so afraid of myself at that point, that I quietly turned to slip back inside.

Before I could even take a step, I heard him say, "Where are you going, Cousin? I've been waiting on you, and I was beginning to think you'd never come."

I slowly turned back to see that he was still standing there with his back to me and still looking up into the sky, so I asked, "How did you even know it was me?"

He replied, "I recognized your heartbeat." He let those words hang in the air for a moment, and then he turned and said, "Surprised? No, I didn't think so. It's an ability that we both share now. I suppose you're wondering what has happened to you and what you've become."

He motioned to the stairs that led down to the gardens and said, "I'd suggest we take a walk in your gardens where we can have a private conversation if that's all right with you."

I nodded my agreement and then followed him as he led the way down the stairs.

We walked in silence until we reached the center of the exotic plants and flowers that populated my gardens, and then he stopped and turned to face me again. The skies were clear that night and the moon overhead was bright, but I was still shocked at how well I could see his face and all our surroundings. Everything was crystal clear to me. It was almost as if we were standing in the light of day. I gazed about in wonder and amazement.

And there I was with my wonderful cousin, Jesus!

For a moment the whole world seemed to stop, and I saw Jesus as though I'd never seen him before. I marveled at the magnificent specimen of humanity that stood before me. His skin tone was naturally dark, but the last three years of living mostly in the elements, as he roamed the countryside had left him well-tanned. Growing up as a carpenter had hardened his arm muscles to the point they were ridiculously large in proportion to the rest of his body. Not that there was anything soft about him, as he had lived the life of a common laborer and he had the scars and physique to show for it. He was a tough man in many ways due to the difficulty of the life he had lived. This toughness caused hardened men to respect him, and the band of mostly fishermen who followed him wherever he went were a testament to this fact. But underneath his hardness was an undeniable gentleness and gracefulness that was emblazoned in every feature of his countenance. From his long hair and well-kept beard, to his chiseled features, he seemed regal in every way.

He was an undeniably hard man; he was an undeniably beautiful man. He was bronze and steel, he was night and day, and he was sunshine and rain. His appearance and character seemed to touch on every extreme point known to man, but one thing was undeniable: he was everything that was good!

When he opened his mouth to speak, words of wisdom and encouragement were sure to be heard. When he taught the masses, those who had the privilege to hear him came away feeling profoundly blessed.

He had always been a little above average in size and height, and most people had to look up to him. But since I stood at 6 foot 2 inches, I could almost look him in the eye, and that's what I did now as I patiently waited for him to speak.

Finally, he broke the silence between us as he said, "Lazarus, do you love me?"

I hesitated, but only because his question caught me off guard. I thought he had brought me out here to explain the crazy things I was feeling and experiencing, but now the first words out of his mouth were mushy words about how I felt about him. I was a businessman, thanks to my father, but first and foremost, I was a warrior, both by upbringing, and by choice. I would rather wrestle a worthy opponent than talk about my feelings any day. After I had a moment to absorb his question I managed to stammer an answer of sorts. "Well . . . uh . . . of course Jesus, you're my cousin. We're family . . . and, uh . . . well, we grew up together . . . and I've always looked up to you and admired your wisdom . . . so um . . . I'm very fond of you."

He looked me in the eye with those big sad eyes and pressed the issue, "Yes, I know you're very fond of me, but do you love me?"

I swallowed hard and somehow managed to force myself to say the words he apparently wanted to hear, "Well sure . . . uh . . . if you put it that way . . . I, um . . . I love you."

A look of satisfaction softened the sadness in his eyes for a moment, and he continued. "I love you more than anyone I've ever known Lazarus, but that's not why I came to Bethany when I heard of your death. I came here and raised you from the dead because my time of trial is at hand, and I'm going to need your help and protection to accomplish my mission."

"I'm not sure I know what you mean."

"Do you remember when we were younger how I would react when bullies would want to fight me?"

I paused before answering because this was not a subject I was particularly comfortable with. "Well, yes, I remember you refused to fight, and wouldn't even try to defend yourself."

"And how did that make you feel about me?"

"Well, honestly I was a little disgusted with you on those occasions because you were always big and strong, so I just couldn't understand why you wouldn't stand up for yourself."

"And do you remember how you reacted towards those that picked on me?"

"Yeah, I kicked their butts usually, but sometimes I got my own butt kicked while trying to defend you." I looked down and forced myself to continue, "Frankly, I wasn't too happy with you on those occasions. Most of my memories of growing up with you are good memories, but those are not so hot."

"Do you remember asking me why I wouldn't defend myself?"

I nodded, "Yes, I remember asking, and I remember you telling me that you didn't need to fight because you had me to defend you. In fact, you said you would always have me to fight for you."

"And you would then reassure me, that while you couldn't understand my reluctance to fight, you would always 'back me up,' as you used to say."

"And that's true. I'll always watch out for you. Nothing's changed in that regard, and it never will."

Jesus placed his hand on my shoulder and looked me directly in the eye before speaking again. "The words you just spoke are completely true, and if you knew how true they are you might not be so quick to speak them because something has changed, my friend. You have changed! When I raised you from the dead today, your body came out looking the same, but on the inside, a wonderful transformation had taken place.

"What happened to you today was not a mere resuscitation of a body that was on the verge of dying. You had been dead for four days. I intentionally waited for two days when I heard of your death because you needed to spend some time in a state of death for your transformation to be fully effective.

"I raised you from the dead today by the powers endowed on me by our heavenly father, and I didn't just resuscitate you so you could die again later in life. I gave you the gift of eternal life. Lazarus, as long as this world we call Earth exists, you will never die!"

CHAPTER TWO

I slapped his hand from my shoulder when he announced I would never die and nearly shouted, "What do you mean I'll never die? That's impossible. Do you know how crazy you sound right now?! Please, just tell me what you've done to me?"

"I know this is a lot to take in, but please listen while I try to explain. By now, you've noticed that you're hearing, seeing, and smelling things that would have been impossible before. You've probably also figured out that you're stronger and quicker than before. And like everyone else at your celebration today, you're probably perplexed by your lack of appetite and thirst. These are all permanent changes in your body.

"Your ability to see, hear, and smell have been vastly improved. Your ability to feel things with your skin has been elevated. Even your sense of taste has been raised to the highest level possible, but that's of small consequence because you no longer need food or drink to live.

"You are now stronger than any man alive, and your reflexes are quicker than anyone could imagine.

"Once you get a chance to try out your new body, you'll find that your stamina is now unlimited, so you can stay active indefinitely. And speaking of being active, you're about to discover that you no longer need to sleep. In fact, you can't sleep, which may seem like a curse before long, but it goes with the job."

I shook my head in bewilderment. "Job? What job?"

"Lazarus, you've chosen the path of a warrior in life, and now you've been chosen by God to be an eternal warrior for good! From now to the end of days you will devote your life to defending the weak and innocent from evil. This is your destiny, this is your blessing from God, and some would say, this is your curse.

"I should warn you, that as time progresses, the influence of evil will grow stronger and more apparent in the world. While this is taking place, the people of Earth and the spiritual forces behind the scenes will be drawing closer to a final battle between good and evil. When that battle comes, you will play a major role"

I shook my head more violently. "No! This can't be happening. There's no way this can be real. I never asked for any of this."

"No you didn't ask for it, but like I just said, it's your destiny. It was all decided a long time ago, and now that my time of trial is at hand, it's time to bring you into play. You want to see me succeed in my mission, don't you?"

These last words really caught my attention. The reason the Romans had flogged me was because they were told I was working with the Zealots to start a rebellion and install Jesus as the new King of the Jews.

The Zealots were a group of nationalists who desperately wanted our people, and our nation, to be free from the oppression of Roman rule. We believed God would send a Messianic savior who would lead our people to rise up in rebellion and overthrow the Romans for good. We thought the Messiah would be a fulfillment of our ancient prophecies and would serve as our new king in a new age of glory for our nation.

We thought the peculiar birth of Jesus was direct evidence of his fulfillment of our ancient prophetic scriptures. We also thought his life and teachings were further indications he was the Messiah we had been waiting for.

The decision to install Jesus as our king was made by me and my compatriots without consulting Jesus himself. He had said plenty of things in his teachings to encourage us to believe he saw himself as the Messiah. If he wasn't completely onboard with the idea, we figured we could nudge him in the right direction when the time came.

Now, with the words he was saying, it seemed he was aware of my aspirations for him and looking for assurances that I would back him in 'succeeding in his mission' as he had just put it.

If he really had raised me from the dead, and if my new body had half the capability he had just described, then surely he really was the Messiah. And, with powers like the ones he possessed, even the Romans would be powerless against us. When I thought of it this way, it seemed maybe this eternal warrior role I'd been given wasn't such a bad thing after all.

I had turned away from him while I was thinking things through, but now I turned back to him and asked, "I told you I would always have your back, so if everything you've just told me is true, how am I supposed to help you fulfill your mission?"

"The leaders of the Jews are afraid the people will clamor for me to lead them, which would displace them as the rightful rulers of our people. They're threatened by my popularity. Also, they're afraid if there's any more talk of me being the new King of the Jews, the Romans will round them all up and slaughter them, since they're supposed to be keeping such talk in check.

"What I've done today in raising you from the dead will cause a huge commotion among the common people and among those that wish me to take on the title of Messiah. So, mark my words. When the Pharisees and Sadducees hear about your resurrection they will call a meeting of the Sanhedrin and that esteemed body will order my arrest, and probably yours as well.

"I need to wait until the Passover week before I allow that to happen because Jerusalem needs to be full of our people when everything is set in motion. As you know, Passover week is only a week and a half away, so in the meantime, I'll need protection from anyone who may want to arrest me or even kill me. My followers are brave men for the most part, but they aren't warriors. So that's where you come in. Can I count on you to protect me until my time comes?"

I thought about what he was saying, and it made perfect sense. Passover week would be the ideal time for Jesus to allow himself to be put forward as the Messiah. With Jerusalem overflowing with Jews it would be much easier to start an uprising and kill the Roman soldiers quartered there. Then the Zealots could encourage their people to stay in Jerusalem instead of going home after Passover, so they could man the walls and participate in turning back the Roman invasion that would inevitably result from their rebellion. The town would be overflowing with extra provisions to take care of the thousands of pilgrims who came to town for Passover, so they would literally have enough food to feed an army.

I nodded my approval and replied, "I think you're exactly right, and I'll be right there by your side to see that no one harms you before you're ready to make your move. And I'll continue to be by your side while you rule."

"I'm glad to hear that you're so willing to pledge your allegiance to me, but I should warn you now, I will eventually die, and you will be left to carry on your fight without me."

"Not as long as I have anything to say about it!"

"Your bravado is admirable, but I assure you I will die before you, and when that day comes, you will need to learn how to meditate to seek direction for your actions. Since you ʻ   ᷉

you'll find that meditation is a welcome relief from never-ending activity, and a wonderful way to find focus for your life."

"Please stop with all this talk about dying. We've hardly agreed to work together, and already you're talking about busting up our team by dying on me. Enough already!"

Jesus smiled broadly, and only a hint of his earlier sadness shown in his eyes as he spoke this time, "So we're in agreement. That's wonderful! I know you're going to have more questions for me in the days to come, but do you have any last questions before we retire for the night?"

"Well, yeah, kind of, I guess. . . ."

"Go ahead, what's on your mind?"

I hesitated, but finally formed the question in my mind, "While I was dead, I either dreamed I was in a horribly scary place, or my spirit really *was* in a horribly scary place. Do you know anything about that?"

He replied in a hushed tone, "Your spirit visited Hell, which is the abode of the wicked."

"Well, I'm having a hard time shaking off some of the memories of that place, and I was wondering . . . will I ever have to go back there again?"

Jesus looked at the stars and said, "That's not for me to say, but for your sake, I hope not!"

CHAPTER THREE

March 20ᵗʰ

    It's sometime after midnight and I've just finished an unexpected meeting with Jesus. Earlier tonight he took me into the gardens so we could have a private conversation that wouldn't be overheard by any of our lingering guests.

    I'm still reeling from what he's told me. It's too much to comprehend, and I'm afraid to write it all down here for fear that someone may find what I've written. Let's just say, for now, that he claims my body and my life have been miraculously transformed in ways that are almost unimaginable.

    I've not had time yet to check out everything he's told me, but if half of what he said is true, then my life will never be the same again.

    The good news, if there is any, is that his intentions for the future are exactly what I'd hoped they would be. Again, I'm afraid to be perfectly frank here, but I'm encouraged to believe my efforts and my suffering may not have been in vain.

I'm sure much will be made clearer in the coming days as we approach the Passover week, since he told me that's when he will make his intentions known. Until then, I will stay as close as possible to his side to make sure no evil befalls him. Also, I'll need to somehow re-establish contact with Barabbas to make sure I still have his support.

So much to do and so little time to do it; maybe it's good that I can't sleep!

✦ ✦

I finished my journal entry and wondered what I should do with myself until morning. I was fully awake and effusively aware that Jesus had told me I would be unable to sleep. I recalled he'd told me I should begin practicing meditating in place of sleeping, so I decided to give it a try.

Some of the fighting masters I had trained under had tried to teach me to meditate, but it had never really appealed to me. I sat on the floor and crossed my legs. I closed my eyes and tried to concentrate on my breathing, but I still felt like I was about to explode with stress. Then I recalled that one of my masters had advocated staring at one's image in a mirror to induce a state of meditation.

I got up and stood before a mirror made of heavily polished copper and looked at myself. I was pretty pleased with what I saw. While I wasn't as good looking as Jesus, I was blessed with the same dark skin tone, dark wavy hair, and chiseled features. My arms weren't quite as muscular as his, but overall I was more balanced in my athleticism and body type. While he somehow managed to be regal and rough all at the same time, I was more just plain rough for the most part. Living on the road with the caravans was tough, and the men I rode with were tougher, so I had long ago left behind most of the frills of growing up as a rich man's son. While

Jesus was bronze *and* steel, I was just steel. Not that I was above having compassion and sympathy, but I certainly didn't let my feelings show very often either.

There was one way, however, that I looked completely different from most of the men of Judea. Jesus and nearly all of his disciples wore the customary beards that were prevalent at the time. I, on the other hand, had adapted the Roman style of keeping a clean shaven face. I had found that when traveling on caravans, or when living in close quarters on ships, a beard tended to get grimy and was prone to becoming infested with lice. No, thanks!

As for meditation, well, I wasn't having any luck meditating while looking at my overall image, so I began to stare into my own eyes. For a while, nothing happened.

Then. . . .

I was walking on a dusty trail between Jerusalem and Bethany. I sensed Jesus was there with me, and when I looked over at him he was a young teenage boy. When I looked down at my own body I discovered I was a boy again, also. Coming towards us was a small group of other young boys. Leading the pack was Barabbas.

Now, Barabbas was bigger than any of the other boys in our village, and truthfully, bigger than any boy had a right to be. He was also meaner than any boy had a right to be, and he was a bully. Usually, he would have given me a wide berth, and not done anything to rile me up because he had seen and experienced my fighting abilities on more than one occasion, but today was different. Today, he had his little gang of knuckleheads to back him up, and today my cousin Jesus was with me, and Jesus didn't have a reputation for being a fighter. However, he also wasn't known as a coward. He would bravely take a beating, but that was the problem; he would *only* take a beating, he wouldn't offer to give one back.

I quickly surmised that there was no way to keep from having to cross paths with Barabbas and his cohorts short of turning tail and running in the other direction, and I was never one to run away. So I reached over with the walking staff I was carrying and placed it in front of my cousin's chest to bring him to a halt. We stood uneasily on the trail and watched warily as the group of boys grew closer.

Barabbas whispered something to his friends as they drew nearer, and they spread out and encircled us, as he himself came and stood within striking distance of Jesus. After a brief moment of tense silence he said, "Well Jesus, I see you've decided to come and visit us again."

"Well, of course, Barabbas, I always enjoy your company."

"Huh, I thought I warned you to stay away. I don't like it that we share the same name. Most people call me Barabbas, or son of the father, but my first name is Jesus, which is the same as yours. It makes me sick to think that I have the same name as a wimp like you. I'm surprised you Nazarene riff-raff can even find your way out of your hovels in the hills. After all, you're all so stupid, you'd rather kiss each other on the rear than on the lips, or at least, that's what my father says."

This claim brings nervous laughter from the boys who are standing in a menacing circle around us with their walking staffs held like Roman spears.

"In fact, I've seen the way you look at me, and I think you'd like to kiss my butt now wouldn't you?"

He broadly smiled at his fellow persecutors and began to untie his pants.

As he did, I growled a warning, "I wouldn't do that if I were you, Barabbas."

Without looking at me, he dismissively replied, "Well you're *not* me, and besides, I can tell Jesus really wants to kiss my butt."

He continued to undo his pants and then turned away and lowered them below his waist to reveal his hairy buttocks. "Come on now. Kiss it!"

As he looked back over his shoulder to see the reaction of Jesus, he was shocked to find Jesus lunging forward to kiss him on the cheek. Before he could react, Jesus gushed, "There. How was that?"

Barabbas turned a searing shade of red, as he hurriedly buckled his pants and screamed to his pubescent henchmen. "Get 'em!"

As our tormentors moved in, Jesus just stood there with an amused look on his face. I knew from past experience, he would be of no help to me in what was about to transpire, so I sprang into immediate action. While Barabbas had been talking, I'd been looking over the group of five boys who had encircled us, and I'd picked the two who looked most capable, for instant elimination. I swung my staff at the one closest to me, and rapped him in the head before he saw it coming. He went down like a rock, and I focused on the second boy. I started a long sweeping swing that seemed to be headed for his head, but as he scrunched down to avoid it I lowered my swing at the last moment and walloped him soundly on his knees. As he went down howling, I thumped him on his hindquarters and sent him diving into the dust. I sensed another boy coming at me from behind, so I stopped in my tracks and reversed my stick in a sharp jab to the rear. This blow caught my would-be assailant in the gut, and he went down frantically struggling just to breathe. Then the other two boys and Barabbas were upon me with their own staffs.

They had already made short work of Jesus, and now they showed no mercy as they pummeled me from all sides. I took at least two solid blows to the head and saw my own blood falling on my staff. In a desperate move to get out of their circle, I held my staff overhead like a spear, and charged at Barabbas, as if I meant to jab him in the face. He reacted by raising his staff to block my thrust, so I abruptly stopped and kicked him in the gonads. He instantly exhaled all the air in his lungs in a huge grunt and rolled to the ground.

I wiped the blood from my forehead, and spread it on my cheeks like war-paint. Then I grinned at the two remaining boys and began to whistle an old tune my father used to whistle. It was something I did in tense moments without even realizing I was doing it.

The two boys who remained on their feet looked at each other like they thought I'd lost my mind.

I stopped whistling, and motioned with my staff to the two boys who still remained standing. "You can come and get what I've given your friends, or you can help them up, and run home to your mommies, before you get your asses beat. I'll leave it up to you, but I'd suggest you run."

Without bothering to confer with each other, they quickly helped their fellow hoodlums up, and they all shambled away in a stumbling trot in the opposite direction of some adults, who were yelling at us to stop, as they approached.

Before Barabbas joined the retreat, he painfully groped his testicles, and gave me a murderous glare while struggling to croak, "I'll get you one day Lazarus. Just you wait and see. I'll get you!"

I helped Jesus up, and we briefly spoke to the adults to assure them we were okay. Then they left us to fend for ourselves and went on their way.

I couldn't look at Jesus at first, but after we had assessed our wounds and cleaned ourselves up to the best of our ability, we started back down the trail for home, and I finally stopped him and looked him in the eye. "Why'd you do that?"

"Well, when he told me to kiss his rear, I did what he told me and kissed his face. Who can tell the difference? Come on now . . . you've got to admit that was priceless!"

I couldn't help but smile as I replied, "You're right, that was priceless, but that's not what I'm referring to. I want to know why you did something you knew would lead to a fight and then refused to defend yourself. Just help me understand. Why won't you fight?"

"I'm not cut out for it, and besides, I don't need to fight; I have you for that."

"What if someday I'm not around to fight for you?"

"I'll always have you Lazarus. *Always. . . .*"

He suddenly stopped and began to speak excitedly, as if he'd had a huge inspiration. "You know what? We should make a secret pact right now, to always be there for each other. We can even have a top-secret motto that we'll repeat to each other every time we go on an adventure together."

"What're you talking about? Have you lost your mind?"

"Oh, come on now, it'll be fun. Just do as I do, and repeat after me."

He jumped in front of me and put his right hand over his heart before continuing, "First, put your right hand over your heart."

I was trying to pay attention to him, but I was distracted by a huge dust devil that had just formed near us. It was kicking up the dry Judean soil and looked as if it was on course to come near us. I absentmindedly put my left hand over my heart instead of my right hand, as I watched the dust devil out of the corner of my eye.

Then I heard Jesus saying, "Your other right hand, dummy."

I put my right hand over my heart as instructed and Jesus said, "Now, repeat after me."

"Now, repeat after me."

"Very funny. Now, can you please try and humor me for a second? Just say what I say. I hereby solemnly swear to always defend the weak and innocent in alliance with my friend Jes. . . No. That's too long and complicated. We should keep it simple. I've got it! Repeat after me. *For the weak.*"

I repeated as instructed, while noticing, that now, several dust devils had become active around us, "*For the weak.*"

"*For the innocent.*"

"*For the innocent.*"

He gushed the last words, "*Forevermore.*"

And I enthusiastically replied, "*Forevermore.*"

We both looked around at the strange phenomenon of the dust devils that had formed all around us, and I whispered without looking at him, "I've heard that when a pair of gladiators are about to enter the arena they make a sign of their allegiance to each other by holding up two fingers and then touching them together. On that last part I think we should make the sign of the gladiator's to each other."

Jesus said, "Yes, I like that idea. Let's do it one more time and add that on the end, and this time, say it with me."

We faced each other, as the dust devils rose to a fever pitch around us, and placing our right hands over our hearts, we shouted in unison into the whirlwind, "*For the weak, for the innocent, FOREVERMORE!*"

Without moving my right hand from my heart, I lifted two fingers on my left hand, and when I reached out to touch the fingers of Jesus, while we shouted "forevermore", a bolt of energy seemed to pass between us, as a battle horn went off inside my head. . . .

With a start, I found myself still staring at my reflection in the mirror. I rubbed my eyes and saw to my amazement the morning light seeping through my windows, which led me to wonder just how long I'd been standing there in my trance. Outside in the courtyard, the Captain of the night guards was blowing his horn to signal the end of the night watch, and the call to inspection for the day guards. In the distance, a rooster echoed the call of the battle horn, by crowing at the rising sun.

I quickly began preparations to begin my day, as I reflected on the dream I'd just experienced. Jesus said in the dream that he would always have me to fight for him, and last night he said I'd been transformed and would live forever. So it seemed to me that this would be the first day of finding out just how much of that was true. It was time to leave dreams behind and start facing the reality of my new life, and something told me it was going to be more interesting than any dream I could ever dream.

CHAPTER FOUR

So now you know about the big event that reshaped my life forever, and I've told how Jesus explained everything to me that night in the gardens.

It occurs to me that, in all fairness, I should take the time to give you at least a small part of my background information before I go any further with my story.

I was born near the beginning of the first century. My parents named me Lazarus in honor of an ancestor.

My mother, Rachel, sadly died within a few days of giving birth to me, so I have no memories of her at all. But I'm told she was a fine woman who loved me very much.

My father, Josiah, hired a widow to come and take care of my older sisters, but he felt I needed the influence of a father figure in my life, and his business kept him away from home most of the time, so he sent me to be raised by my Aunt Mary, and her husband, my Uncle Joseph of Nazareth. They were living in Egypt at the time, due to their fear of King Herod, so for a few years, I too, was raised in Egypt. The nice thing about this arrangement was that I got to grow up with my cousin, Jesus, who had been born on the same night as me. Then, after the death of Herod, we moved back to Nazareth, which was the original home of my aunt and uncle.

I didn't get to spend much time with my father during those early years, but when I was 12 he decided it was time to have me come and live with him, so he could begin training me to take over his business when I was older.

My father and his brother, Joseph of Arimathea, operated several business ventures together. One of their more prosperous undertakings was a mining business that was centered in a place that would later be called Cornwall, England. The mines in Cornwall produced a wide spectrum of minerals, but they were primarily tin mines.

In order to transport the tin and other minerals from the mines to their far away destinations, my father and uncle needed naval transports and land caravans they could trust, so one of the offshoots of the mining business was a distribution network, which also required a veritable army of guards and sailors to make sure everything got where it was supposed to go without being stolen by pirates or marauding hoodlums.

My father's main contribution to the business was to run the distribution network, which meant he spent a lot of time traveling with the naval transports and land caravans to make sure the proper men were in places of leadership throughout the organization. He wanted me to assume his role someday, so he spent liberally from his vast wealth, and used his far-reaching influence, to make sure I was trained by some of the finest warriors of my time in many forms of combat.

He and my uncle were also members of the Zealots, so he was hopeful if a serious rebellion against the Romans ever came to pass, I could use my fighting skills to aid our people in their uprising.

I often traveled with our trade caravans and naval transports, and while we were on the move, I'd pick the brains of the guards, soldiers, and sailors about fighting techniques. Then at night they'd demonstrate their skills, and we'd practice what they had taught me. Some of my best training in the art of hand-to-hand combat came in that school of hard knocks. Fortunately, everyone agreed I was a gifted warrior and had natural instincts for warfare, so most of the time I gave out more beatings than I took, even when fighting older men who had much more strength and experience.

After I came to live with my father, I didn't get to see as much of my cousin Jesus because we lived in different towns. However, even as a teenager Jesus had a ridiculous fascination with the temple, so every time his family traveled to Jerusalem for feast days, we would spend as much time as possible together. His family also allowed him to come and spend weeks at a time with us in Bethany.

On those occasions, Jesus would inevitably enthrall the crowds in Jerusalem by openly debating the rabbis who taught on the temple steps. I always treasured those visits because I was amazed at the wisdom and cunning wit of my beloved cousin.

I felt proud just to be in his presence when we would visit the temple because he seemed to know and understand things that were mysteries even to most adults. And when he would debate the Rabbis and other learned men at the Temple, it seemed as if he were speaking on behalf of God himself. He often challenged the way people were used to looking at things, but his love and respect for others caused him to be loved and respected in return.

Besides coming to visit with us in Bethany, there was one year when Jesus was allowed to accompany my father and me on a voyage to Cornwall. We stopped along the way at various exotic ports, and spent nearly six months together that year. That was the longest continuous time we ever got to spend together as teenagers, and I grew to love and admire him more than anyone I knew in the process.

As we got older, his father needed him to help out more in his carpentry business, and my father insisted that I spend more time traveling with him, so our time together diminished, as we both began to take on the roles of young men in a hard world.

Traveling with the caravans was a fascinating adventure for a young man, but it was also highly perilous at times. We were often forced to fight off bandits and pirates, and eventually my father was killed in one of these battles, even as I fought by his side.

I was heartbroken to be all alone in the world without parents, but there was no time to truly grieve. I was only 18 at the time, so I became a wealthy man with a lot of responsibility at a very young age. My obligations kept me away from my homeland for the most part over the next several years, but I occasionally got to spend some time in my home in Bethany with my sisters, Mary and Martha, and the rest of our extended family.

When I would come home from my adventures, I would track Jesus down to see what was going on in his life. However, I soon found that our worldviews had begun to move in different directions. He was teaching love, peace, and harmony, and I was dreaming of ways to overthrow the Roman oppressors.

I still spent as much time as possible with him because I was enthralled with his insight and advice, but our core interests often caused us to argue, and when that happened, he usually found a way to make me look foolish.

When he reached the age of 30 and put himself forth as a teacher of the scriptures I wasn't surprised. Nor was I surprised when many of his followers began to advance the idea that perhaps he was the long-awaited Messiah. I could easily see him having the wisdom to be a king. The only thing that concerned me about him taking on such a role was his complete lack of military training. He didn't have even the slightest interest in the art of warfare.

The story I'm telling here, took place when I came home for a visit in 33 A. D. At that time Jesus was 33 years old, and at the height of his popularity with the common people of the land. But to be honest, the main attraction for me on this trip wasn't Jesus. The main attraction was Iris!

⊨+ +⊨

Iris was the daughter of my most trusted Captain of the Guard. His name was Darius, and he was an Egyptian. My father discovered Darius on one of his many excursions as he journeyed to far-away lands in search of new customers for his minerals and other trade goods. He brought Darius and his family back to Bethany, and they had remained a part of my father's household for as long as I could remember.

Darius had become my father's most trusted advisor in matters pertaining to overseeing the many soldiers and guards in our employ. He and his son, Horus, were able warriors, and both led caravans. Darius's wife, Nida, served as the chief cook in our home, and his daughter, Iris, aided her in this endeavor as she grew to be a young lady.

I was nearly nine years older than Iris and had always viewed her as a thin- limbed, stringy-haired, cactus-skinned, tomboy of a girl. But somewhere around the age of 20, something changed dramatically. The girl became a woman; and the thistle became a flower!

I had been gone for several months on a lengthy excursion, and when I came home I took a walk with Horus to inspect the grounds and guards. As we were walking together I saw a beautiful young lady with a flower in her hair walking in my courtyard. I was so entranced with watching her movements, I stumbled over a bucket someone had left in my path and fell painfully to the ground.

As Horus helped me up and dusted me off, I strained to see where the mystical apparition I had just seen had disappeared to.

Finally, I saw her walking on the other side of the courtyard, so I grabbed Horus, twirled him around, and pointed at her, as I nearly shouted, "Who is that?"

He turned back to me with a knowing smile and dismissively replied, "Oh that's no one sir. It's just Iris."

"Excuse me. I thought you just said that's Iris. Is there someone else living here now besides your sister with the name of Iris?"

Horus nearly laughed as he replied, "No sir. No one lives here with the name of Iris but my sister. And yes sir . . . that's Iris . . . the one and only Rainbow Girl."

"Rainbow Girl . . . why did you call her that?"

"That's what the name Iris means in our native language. It's the word for rainbow. And, as you can see, my little sister has undergone a transformation lately that would indicate a promise from the gods of a bright and colorful future. In our culture that's what a rainbow signifies, so my father has taken to calling her 'his Rainbow Girl'."

I muttered as I continued to watch her movements, "Rainbow Girl . . . well I'll be."

I continued to watch Iris from afar with wonder, when I would visit my home in Bethany, until one day I gathered the courage to approach her and clumsily express my admiration. After some playful back and forth banter and good natured flirtation, we eventually escalated our interest in each other to holding hands and a couple of shy kisses. But all of this was done out of sight of everyone else because there were complications.

First, there was the issue of our differing religions. Her father, Darius, was not an overly religious man, but he and his wife quietly paid homage to their Egyptian deities. My father had carefully explained the Jewish faith to them, but he had been respectful of their own faith and traditions, and never demanded they convert to Judaism. This had caused a good deal of ridicule from many of the Jewish ruling party, and such ridicule was not to be ignored, unless one was willing to risk forfeiting their good standing in the community, or perhaps, even their lives.

My uncle, Joseph of Arimathea, had used his standing on the Great Sanhedrin to keep the most hostile critics at bay, but I knew that having an open relationship with a pagan woman would only exacerbate the problem. So my affection for Iris was a forbidden love.

Second, there was the issue of her father, Darius. He was a proud man, who had served my father faithfully until his untimely death. Since that time he had switched his devotion to me without missing a beat. The problem was that he thought no man was worthy of his daughter Iris. I had personally witnessed him violently beat a couple of would-be suitors and send them packing when they tried to strike up a relationship with his daughter without his approval. There weren't many men I was afraid of, but wisely, I *was* afraid of Darius.

Then last, but certainly not least, there was one other person whom I feared even more than Darius when it came to Iris. That person was her mother, Nida. Ever since I came home to live with my father, Nida had been cooking the meals of our household, and for as long as I could remember, she had been trying (mostly in vain) to keep me out of her kitchen. As a young lad, I would sneak in at every opportunity and help myself to her delicacies. Her son Horus and I grew up like brothers, and the two of us were notorious for stealing her pastries and cakes before they could make it to the dining table. She would chase me with a huge steel spoon, or anything else she could lay hands on, and curse me in the names of her foreign gods. She would chant strange spells, some of which, Horus claimed could change me into a frog, or something much worse. She would give me the evil eye and make other threatening gestures, but it was all to no avail. I was a young boy, and I had a sweet tooth that wouldn't be denied. And besides, she was a marvelous cook!

As I grew older my sweet tooth declined, and I grew more respectful of Nida's kingdom in the kitchen, but I swear there were still times she spat in the plates of food she would serve me. I'd be eating and notice something in my food that seemed out of place, and when I'd look up I'd see her watching from the kitchen with a wicked smile of contentment on her face.

Iris was the apple of her eye and her most precious treasure in all of life. If stealing her pastries could make her mad, I could only imagine how she would react if she knew I was stealing kisses.

So while I came home primarily to see Iris, I was dedicated to being discreet for the time being, and besides, I was somewhat distracted by other events that were unfolding at the time.

As I've pointed out, my uncle, Joseph of Arimathea, was a member of the Great Sanhedrin council in Jerusalem. This was a group of 71 elders who had the final say in ruling the people in religious matters. He and some of the other sages on the council were secret followers of Jesus, and some of them were also Zealots. They, along with many others, including myself, thought that Jesus was the Messiah, and we also believed he was on the verge of declaring himself as such and leading an uprising of the Jews.

I was working behind the scenes with the primary leader of the Zealots to prepare the coming insurgency, when an unknown traitor revealed my involvement to the Romans.

I was arrested and would have been crucified, but the influence of my uncle barely saved my life. Instead of crucifixion, I was sentenced to 39 lashes with a Roman cat-of-nine-tails. That's a whip with nine pieces of metal attached to nine appendages at the end of the whip. Each time the whip lashed a person's back the metal pieces jerked out hunks of flesh. Forty lashes were considered a death-sentence, so I was sentenced to be whipped *nearly* to death.

The initial flogging didn't kill me, or at least it didn't kill me right away. My sister Mary had been traveling with Jesus, but when she heard of my arrest she came home immediately, and after I was flogged, both of my sisters took me to our home in Bethany to try to nurse me back to health. At first, it seemed their efforts would not go in vain, but then my wounds became infected. In those days, we didn't know anything about infections or antibiotics, and the primitive means we used to treat such wounds probably only made things worse. The end result was that I got deathly sick and died.

Upon my death, my sisters had me wrapped in a traditional death shroud. They entombed me in our family's sepulcher, covered me with a heap of my favorite flowers, and left me alone for three days. On the third day they opened the tomb and checked to make sure I was really dead. This was customary at the time because sometimes people were mistakenly entombed when they weren't even dead. Seeing that I was, indeed, dead, they spread some perfume and burial spices on my body and resealed the tomb to let me decompose in peace. When Jesus arrived for the big event I had been dead for four days.

So that's the story before the story . . . and here's the rest of the story. . . .

CHAPTER FIVE

As soon as I had made myself presentable after waking from my dream, I rushed from my room. I desperately wanted to spend time with Iris this morning, but before I could do that there was someone else I needed to see. I hurried through the house and made my way to the door outside our kitchen. I had carefully rehearsed the words I wanted to say as I was on my way here, but as I pushed through the door all my words escaped me, and I found my mind had gone completely blank when I saw Iris' mother, Nida, standing before me.

I had wanted to speak to her privately the day before, but in the hustle and bustle of the celebration, no opportunity had presented itself. Now we stood and looked uneasily at each other, and I didn't have a clue what to say. At first she just looked me up and down without giving a hint of what she was thinking. Then her face broke out in a huge smile, and she opened her arms wide to embrace me.

She hugged me long and hard before stepping back and exclaiming, "There were many days I know you think I hated you for your thievery of my delicacies, but the truth is, I was always flattered by your determination to steal my food."

"So are you saying that all that aggravation you exhibited was just a show, and I shouldn't have been afraid?"

She answered with a sly smile. "Well maybe not all of it. Were you really scared?"

"Yes I was, but not scared enough to stop stealing your food." I laughed and she joined me.

Wiping the laughter from her face she said, "You should remain scared of me. We'll probably get along better that way, but Iris tells me I'm going to have to get used to treating you better."

"Oh, she does? So, how much better will you be treating me, and does this new treatment include pastries?"

"I don't know about that, but according to Iris I'm going to have to start treating you like a son-in-law. Is that true?"

I realized I had stumbled into a neatly prepared trap, and I struggled with a proper response. Iris and I had expressed our mutual admiration for each other, and we had shyly and discreetly flirted with each other, but there had been no formal marriage proposal. Now Nida was clearly probing to find out if my intentions toward her beloved daughter were noble.

I finally managed to speak haltingly, "Well, uh . . . yes . . . I'd say that's probably . . . pretty . . . uh . . . true. But. . . ."

Nida bristled, "But what? Are you serious about being with my Iris or not?"

This time I spoke confidently. "Yes, ma'am. Yes, I am! It's just that I haven't formally asked her to marry me yet, and it doesn't seem hardly fair that you should know my intentions before she does."

"Well, what's been holding you up?"

"Nothing, except I had a little problem with getting arrested and dying before I got the chance."

"Then I suggest you get on with it. That poor girl was heart-broken when it seemed you'd died. I didn't think she'd ever stop grieving over you. Everyone had picked up on how you two were making goo-goo eyes at each other, even though you tried to hide it. But when they closed you up in that tomb there was no way she could hide how she felt. We all thought she would lose her mind. Your sisters were supportive and encouraging to her, thank the gods, but even that couldn't console her.

"But now you're back, and she needs to know she hasn't made a fool of herself by letting everyone see how much she loves you. You need to make your intentions known to her, and you need to make them known to everyone else around here."

Before I could respond, a deep voice boomed from behind me. "I agree, it's time for you to let her know what you intend to do." As he spoke, Darius stepped from the shadows where he had apparently been listening to us talk.

I smiled and replied, "Seeing that you have me surrounded, I guess I have no choice."

We all nervously laughed, and I continued, "In all seriousness, I'm glad we had this chance to talk, and I'm glad to know I have your blessings in asking for the hand of your daughter in marriage. As soon as I leave here I'll be seeking her out."

Nida nodded knowingly, "I think you'll find her in your favorite meeting spot down by the well. She just so happened to tell me she was going there."

"Oh, so, 'she just so happened to tell you' that, huh? Why do I feel like I'm being led around on a leash?"

Darius bellowed, "Get used to it! You're in love with a woman, and all women have a way of leading us men around like fools with their mysterious powers. My Rainbow Girl is no exception."

Nida waved her big metal spoon menacingly, "Don't make me come after you. You had better treat her well."

I called out as I walked away, "I'll always treat her like a queen. After all, she's my Rainbow Girl now!"

⚊⚊

I stepped into the courtyard and was headed toward the gates when I sensed a couple of powerful forces rushing at me from behind. I whirled, dropped to my knees, and spread my arms wide to absorb the shock I knew was coming. And with a laugh, I embraced the loves of my life, my hunting dogs, Samson and Delilah.

Samson was a heavy Molossian and was capable of tearing a man's arm off if agitated, but his only goal at the moment was to drown me in dog spittle, or so it seemed. Delilah was a slightly lighter and significantly swifter Laconian or Spartan breed. While also capable of mauling an enemy, the only thing he ever wanted from me was my affection. Of course, he might not have liked me so much if he knew I'd given him a feminine name, but if he ever figured that out, he never mentioned it.

I playfully wrestled with them as Horus came running up. He yelled, "Samson. . . Delilah. . . heel."

They obediently, but clearly, reluctantly, stopped playing with me and trotted over to sit beside Horus. "Sorry sir, I was walking them, and they saw you before I did and broke from my grasp."

I grinned as I got up and knocked the dust from my robes. "It's okay Horus, I'm always glad to see my children. But I've got to go for now, so go ahead and finish that walk."

I hurried through the gates of my estate, declining to take a guard for my protection. The Romans had administered their punishment, and I had survived (with a little help from Jesus). They had no reason, or right, to arrest me again, as long as I didn't draw attention to myself, so I saw no reason not to go into the village alone.

The well Nida had directed me to was a common well on the outskirts of Bethany that was used mostly by travelers who were just passing through. Most of the homes in our village had their own personal wells, which were actually just cisterns that were replenished when rain fell on our dwellings and drained into the crude tanks we each maintained.

This well was called Josiah's Well in honor of my father, and it was an actual well that tapped into an underground stream. Iris and I had agreed to meet here on a few occasions, so we could talk away from prying eyes, but apparently, we weren't as crafty as we thought. Now, it seemed that everyone knew about our feelings for each other, so I was determined to let her know I was ready to proudly tell the world how much I loved her.

When she saw me coming she jumped up and started toward me, and I thought she was going to break into a run and leap into my arms, as she had the day before, but instead she drew herself up, turned back to the well, and sat back down on its edge.

She swung her head in a slight arc and threw her long dark hair over one shoulder, and I was so stricken with her beauty I nearly tripped and fell on my face. I had traveled the world and seen many striking women in my life, but in my eyes, there was none more beautiful than my Iris.

She was blessed with the same exotic dark skin tone that was strikingly particular to many of the people of Egypt. Her majestic face was framed by a wild and luxurious mane of dark curly hair that suited her perfectly. Her eyes danced with stunning brilliance like the finest green emeralds the world had ever seen. And most importantly to me, she always seemed to be quick with a smile. I had never met anyone with a more positive outlook on life, and this above all else drew me to her in ways I couldn't describe. I often seemed to carry the weight of the world on my shoulders, but when I was with her, my worries melted away like snow in the desert.

I slowed down as I drew near and enjoyed the view before reaching tentatively for her hand, "When you first saw me just now I thought you were going to run out to greet me." I said, "So why'd you turn back?"

"I've run after you long enough Lazarus, now you will have to come to me."

"So that's how it is, huh?"

"Yes. That's exactly how it is." She said, "I fear I've made a fool of myself by grieving over you so openly when you died. And I probably didn't help matters by leaping into your arms yesterday and kissing you in front of everyone in Bethany. So now, there's no turning back for me. Either you will publicly acknowledge that you are also in love with me, so the world can see I'm not crazy, or . . . or. . . ."

"Or what?"

She didn't hesitate this time. "Or I'll go back to Egypt on my own."

"Whoa! Slow down!" The thought of her leaving me shocked me to the core, and I couldn't find words to respond for a moment. Finally, I seemed to find the right words to say. "Please don't ever talk about leaving me, Iris. Our affection for each other has only just begun, but already you're the most important thing to me in all the world. I can't begin to imagine living without you.

"I've been reluctant to let everyone know how I feel about you because of how I thought it might be perceived by the Jewish elders, and because I wasn't sure how your parents would feel about me being in love with their daughter, but I'm done worrying about what other people think when it comes to how I feel about you. The only thing that matters is how I feel about you, and the truth is I love you above all else. If Jesus hadn't raised me from the dead, I'd never have had the chance to do what I'm about to do, and that would have been a shame."

I got down on one knee while still holding her hand and choked out a few more words, "Iris, will you honor me by becoming my wife?"

She coyly smiled and looked about disinterestedly, "Well, let me think about that." Then she abruptly jumped into my arms as I still knelt there on the ground. The impact of her leap nearly sent us both rolling in the mud surrounding the well. I lifted her in my arms and struggled to my feet as she screamed and giggled, "Of course I'll marry you, you idiot! Of course, of course, of course!"

Then she stopped her crowing and frowned, "Now what did you get me to show your intentions?"

I frowned back and replied, "I'm not sure I know what you mean. Was I supposed to get you something?"

She freed herself from my grip, jumped to the ground, and put her hands on her hips looking as if she might throw a fit, as she cooed, "Remember, I told you it's customary in my culture for the man to give the woman a piece of jewelry to show he's sincere in his intentions when he proposes betrothal. So what did you get me?"

"I thought you were making that up."

"Enough already. I've explained to you that this is an important part of our culture, so you'd better have something in your pockets, mister."

"Well, since you put it that way . . . lucky for me, I do have a little something here." I reached into my pocket, and drew out a heavy pouch. Reaching inside, I drew out a substantial silver necklace with an odd symbol hanging from it. I let it dangle in the light so the exquisite emerald in its upper loop could reflect the rays of sunshine that seemed to intensify as we embraced. "I believe you'll know what this is."

She whispered, "Yes, by the gods . . . it's an Ankh! It's the symbol of eternal life among my people."

"Yes, it represents eternal life among your people, and for me it represents the eternal love I'll always have for you. Unfortunately, it also looks something like the crucifixion crosses the Romans are so fond of, so to soften it up a bit I had the emerald placed in the upper loop. The jeweler who sold it to me said emeralds have mystical powers that aid us in growth, reflection, peace, healing and balance. He also said it represents fertility." With this I rubbed her belly lightly.

She grabbed my hand and said, "Whoa big fella. Simmer down now. You're still in the proposal stage. There'll be plenty of time for all of that soon enough."

I laughed and held it out to her and she slipped it over her head and let it hang from her neck. She looked down at the emerald, as I asked, "Well, how'd I do?"

She purred, "It's perfect."

I reached into the pouch and revealed an exact replica of her necklace and ankh with a significantly sturdier silver chain. "I also thought it would be nice if we had identical necklaces, so I bought one for myself as well."

She clapped and exclaimed, "I love it!"

"And that's not all. Watch this." I gripped the emerald in the upper loop of the symbol and pulled up. The upper part of the symbol separated from the bottom cross-piece and a small two-inch blade was revealed.

I held the tiny blade up for her to see and said, "Go ahead and try it with yours, but be careful. The edges are razor sharp."

She tentatively gripped the ankh and carefully lifted the blade out of the sheath of the cross-piece. Waving it about playfully, she chuckled, "You'd better think twice about calling off our wedding now, buster."

"There's no chance of that happening, and there's probably no chance you'll ever have to defend yourself, but it'll give me a degree of comfort to know you have a weapon if you should ever need one. Of course, the main reason for giving you this is to demonstrate that my intentions are sincere."

She beamed, "It certainly does the job of showing that your intentions are pure, but I also kind of like it that I have a secret weapon hanging around my neck if I ever need it."

"You'll need to practice with it to get the blade into action quickly, but once you've tried it a few times you'll be fine. Now let me show you how to put it back. All you have to do is reverse your movements and let the blade fall back in its sheath. Then just press the blade the rest of the way in until its firmly seated and, voilà."

She gave me a questioning look and asked, "Voilà. What does that mean?"

I laughed. "It's a word I've heard used in a foreign country that simply means *"there,"* or *"there you have it."*

She looked at me suspiciously and frowned. "You and your exotic foreign countries . . . you probably have beautiful women stashed away in every town where you travel."

I replied in a serious tone. "But none of them are as beautiful as you, my love."

She playfully reached for her ankh and started going through the motions of releasing her blade. "That had better be a joke, mister."

I said, "Of course it's a joke. They're all much prettier than you."

This time I wasn't sure she was playing when she went for her blade, so I wisely skipped away, and that was probably the first time my super-human speed saved me from sure and certain death.

CHAPTER SIX

I ris and I walked hand-in-hand back to my estate while making plans to call everyone together to make a formal announcement of our engagement. But as we approached, I realized we may have to put our plans on hold because something peculiar was going on. A long line of people had formed up in front of the main gate to my fortress, and it stretched for at least 200 yards. I could see others coming in the distance to join the throngs who had already assembled. As we drew closer, many of the people began pointing at me and talking amongst themselves in an animated fashion.

Upon seeing us, Darius came rushing out to meet us and began explaining excitedly. "Lazarus, I don't know what to do. It seems that word of your resurrection has spread across the countryside, and now people are coming from all over and bringing their sick and afflicted to see Jesus. Some are even offering large sums of money if he will perform miracles for them. Even as large as your grounds are, there's still no way we can accommodate all of them. I've told them they can't come in, and they can't see Jesus, but no one is listening, and they refuse to go away. What should I do?"

Since Darius was nearly 50 he was considered an old man in our day and age, so I had pulled him off caravan duty, and put him in charge of managing my estate in Bethany. Normally his duties consisted of overseeing the activities of my well-paid servants who tended the gardens and grounds, and of course, making sure the walls of the fortress were well guarded. Over the years my father and I had made more than a few enemies in our business dealings, and some of them were wealthy and cunning enough to be capable of trying to attack my home to pay back old grudges and to steal my wealth. Darius was well prepared to deal with a military siege, but he wasn't sure what to do with a deluge of civilians at his gates.

I tried to put his nerves at ease. "Calm down, I'll go in and talk to Jesus and ask him to address the crowds from the walls and advise them to go home. Just ask the people to be patient."

I hurried to the gate, but before I could get inside, several people rushed toward me in wonder, exclaiming that I was the one who had been resurrected. Darius, got between me and the crowd and lifted his staff in a threatening manner. The sight of such a gigantic man waving a staff was enough to deter anyone from getting in my way. Once I was inside I saw a group of Jesus's disciples who were loosely congregating around a small fire in the center of the courtyard. It was only around 50 degrees at this early hour of the morning so many were seeking out the warmth of the flames.

I approached one of the men and spoke to him. "Say, if my memory serves me, you're the one they call Simon, is that right?"

He nodded, "That was my given name, but Jesus gave me a new name. Now everyone calls me Peter, but can I help you?"

"I'm looking for Jesus. Can you tell me where he is?"

"Yes, he's in your gardens."

"Oh, is he with someone?"

"No. He's alone. He likes spending time alone."

"Oh, thanks. You and your friends help yourselves to some food."

I turned to Iris, "Please forgive me, but for now we're going to need to delay our announcement until we can deal with our little crisis. I promise I'll call everyone together as soon as possible."

She smiled and gently pushed me towards the gardens. "It's okay my love. I should probably go and help my mother in the kitchen. It looks like we've got a lot of mouths to feed today. I'll see you after a while."

We went our separate ways and I soon found Jesus sitting on a bench among a section of wildflowers. I spoke as I came close, "I'm sorry to disturb your serenity, but we have a bit of a problem at the gates."

He answered, "Well, before we get mixed up in problems I have a little gift I want to give you. I wanted to give it to you the other night, but there was just too much excitement after you came back from the dead. It's not much, but I hope you like it."

He held out a leather satchel and I opened it to find writing utensils. "Oh, wow, thanks, I can really use these." I held up some sheets of material that looked similar to vellum and asked, "Is this vellum? I don't think I've ever seen anything like this. Usually, I use papyrus when I write, but this looks really interesting."

"It's a new kind of writing material. It's very popular in some places, but I wouldn't let anyone else know you have it. It's very valuable."

"Well thanks! It's nice to know you think about me when you're not around, and like I said, I can really use something like that."

"Then I take it you're still keeping your journals?"

"Oh yes, I write a new entry nearly every day. I can't imagine why anyone but me would ever want to read them, but I feel compelled to do it for some reason."

I slung the bag over my shoulder and continued, "Now about that problem at the gates. . . ."

Before I could go on he interrupted me, "There are always problems in life, Lazarus. You should take a moment to enjoy the sunshine. Just sit back and bask in its majesty and mystery. It's positively refreshing, and I promise it will empower you in ways you never dreamed possible."

I glanced up at the sun and impatiently replied, "I wish I had time to sit around and get a tan, but we've really got some pressing matters to attend to."

"Really? You've got a lot to learn my friend, but apparently you're not going to relent until you ruin my day, so go ahead and tell me what's troubling you."

"News of the miracle of my resurrection has spread far and wide, and now many people are gathering outside and demanding to see you. Apparently they've brought many of their sick to you seeking healing. Some of them are even offering to pay you for your services if you'll heal their friends and family."

"If I needed money to achieve my purposes it would fall from the skies, but what would you have me do?"

"Well, I thought maybe you could address them from the walls of my fortress and offer some kind of blessing, and then ask them to go home. We certainly don't have room for them inside the gates."

He paused and looked up at the skies for a moment before answering. "To be honest, I'm weary of the crowds. They follow me everywhere I go these days unless I travel by night when no one is aware. They've even followed me by the thousands into the wilderness and desert at times. Always it's the same with them. They clamor for me to heal their sickness and disease, they ask me to pronounce a blessing on their children, and they demand that I cast out demons from those who are troubled in spirit. If I were willing they'd have me empty every cemetery in the country by raising the dead. And, of course, they want me to announce myself as their king. Lately, that seems to be on their minds more than anything else."

"I understand. Look, if you don't want to deal with them I'll take to the walls myself and just demand they disperse. If my guards go out and give them a little nudge, I'm sure they'll get the message and go home."

"No. I'd like to have a chance to be alone, but I can't turn them away. They need me, and I'm going to need them for what's to come. I'm their shepherd, and they're my sheep, you see. And while I'm weary at the moment, I truly love them. I'm going to have to go out among them, so you need to figure out a way for me to do that safely since the Jewish elders may have spies, or even assassins scattered in the crowd. Also, we need to do it without causing a riot. Can you do that for me?"

I thought for a moment, and then replied. "My father built this fortress on a hill overlooking the rest of Bethany because it's an easily defensible location. We can put you on an oxcart just outside the main gate where no one can get to you easily. That way we can simply wheel you inside if things take a turn for the worse. We'll have the crowds take a seat in rows on the hillside looking up to where you'll be. I'll array your disciples directly in front of you, and I'll sprinkle in some of my guards in a discreet fashion, and from our vantage point above the crowd we'll be able to see if anyone looks like they mean to do you any harm. How does that sound?"

Jesus nodded, "That sounds fine. You set it up, and I'll do the rest."

⊨⊰╋ ╋⊱⊨

After some frantic maneuvering of the multitude, we managed to get most of the people to sit in orderly rows on the hillside between my fortress and the village below. We wheeled the oxcart outside the main gate, and I motioned from the wall for Jesus to make his way outside. When he came within their view, shouts arose from the people gathered below, and many of them got to their feet and cheered wildly.

Jesus serenely walked up some makeshift stairs we'd arranged by the oxcart, and stood in its center facing the crowd. He raised and lowered his hands to signal the people to cease their cheers, and a hush immediately fell over the assembly.

His disciples had followed him out along with a few of my guards, and they now filed in front of him and turned to face him. My sisters, Mary and Martha, also followed him out and stood nearby. He waited until he had everyone's attention, and then he spoke compellingly, "I know many of you have come here today because you heard of the great miracle of my friend Lazarus being raised from the dead." He turned and motioned to where I stood on the wall. "That's him standing there and I assure you he's very alive. In fact, I'm told he proposed marriage today to his beloved, Iris, the beautiful flower everyone here calls, the Rainbow Girl. Oh, and there she is, too."

Out of nowhere Iris appeared by my side, and I wondered if I was the only one who didn't see this coming. I guess someone was going to make sure I didn't back out of making a formal public engagement announcement.

I put my arm around her, and halfway raised my hand, and halfheartedly waved at the crowd, while wondering how she had managed to pull this off without me knowing. I wanted to give her a playful swat on the tail to acknowledge my admiration of her craftiness, but I had to settle for a stealthy pinch of her side since everyone was watching.

By now the crowd was cheering enthusiastically, so there was no danger of them hearing as Iris waved at them and softly crowed to me, "There's no backing out now, mister. Everyone knows you're mine now."

I stepped up my waving a bit, and spoke to her out of the corner of my mouth as I gently applied a little pressure on the small of her back. "Oh, I don't know about that. All it would take is one little shove. It's a long way down from here, you know."

She smiled and ceased waving to turn and embrace me. As she looked up into my eyes she fingered the ankh hanging from her neck and whispered. "I should warn you, I'm armed."

"While I am obviously helplessly in love, and completely at your mercy, my dear." And then, to the pleasure of the crowd, we kissed.

The crowd went wild for a moment, but when they calmed down, Jesus resumed speaking. "I know that many of you brought sick and afflicted family and friends in need of healing, and I promise I will attend to as many as possible in a few moments. But before I tend to your temporal earthly concerns, I would first minister to your eternal souls. So open your ears and hearts and hear the Word of God."

The crowd became so quiet I believe you could have heard a baby's sigh, and then he spoke:

"Blessed are the poor in spirit,
for theirs is the kingdom of Heaven.

Blessed are they who mourn,
for they shall be comforted.

Blessed are the meek,
for they shall inherit the Earth.

Blessed are they who hunger and thirst for righteousness,
for they shall be satisfied.

Blessed are the merciful,
for they shall obtain mercy.

Blessed are the pure of heart,
for they shall see God.

*Blessed are the peacemakers,
for they shall be called children of God.*

*Blessed are they who are persecuted for the sake of righteousness,
for theirs is the kingdom of Heaven.*

*Some say, 'Love your friends and hate your enemies.'
But I say, love your enemies and pray for excellent things to happen to those who persecute you!
In that way you will be acting as true children of your father in Heaven.*

For he gives his sunlight to both the evil and the good, and he sends rain on the just and the unjust.

If you want to live a life that pleases God, then you should do this: love God with all your heart, mind, and soul; and love others as you love yourself.

By doing these things you will fulfill all the expectations of the scriptures.

But beware! For if you say you love God, while in your heart you hate your fellowman, then you are deceiving yourself. For no man can love God, and hate his brother.

So today, I give you a new commandment; love others as I have loved you."

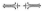

When Jesus finished speaking everyone remained frozen for a moment as if in a trance. Then he moved to the end of the oxcart and hopped down to the ground. I was alarmed when I realized he intended to go out into the crowd, so I ran down the stairs, pushed and shoved my way to his side, and muttered in his ear, "You can't go out into the crowd. I can't protect you there."

"But the sick need me."

"Then stay here among my guards, and we'll bring the sick to you."

Iris appeared by my side and added, "Yes, let us bring them to you. I'll help"

Mary and Martha came up to stand with us and they chimed in simultaneously, "We'll help too."

I was so proud of Iris and my sisters in that moment!

Jesus smiled at us and nodded his agreement with my plan, so I had Iris and my sisters begin bringing those who sought healing to where Jesus stood. I was busy watching the crowd for signs of danger, so I can't provide many details of how he ministered to the supplicants who were brought to him that day. But I can tell you, that by all accounts, miracle upon miracle was performed. The blind saw the light of day, the deaf heard the cries of their children, the sick were relieved of their suffering, and those who had troubled minds were restored to sanity. As the day wore on, there was an outpouring of emotion that moved us all to tears.

After the better part of the afternoon a shout went up from those in the closest proximity to where Jesus was standing, and I whirled to find him lying on the ground. My hand went to the sword at my side as I looked about desperately for an assassin and shouted, "What happened?"

Mary and Martha were bending over him, and Mary said, "Nothing happened, he just fainted."

Iris was gently patting his head with a wet cloth and looking at me anxiously as I came closer.

I took his hand in mine, and he smiled weakly as he softly spoke. "I'm afraid that's all I can do today. Please help me inside and assure the people I'll still be here again tomorrow."

"Tomorrow!? You expect us to do this all again tomorrow? You've lost your mind. It's probably going to be freezing cold tonight, and by tomorrow any food these people brought with them will be gone. I hope you don't expect me to feed all of them. You alone, brought over 100 people with you when you came here. You have your 12 principle disciples, and 72 other disciples, and numerous other followers. I can barely feed all of you until Passover. It's March for goodness sake. We've put a serious dent in our stores just getting through the winter, and we're far from any harvest that would allow us to restock."

"Has anyone ever told you that you worry too much Lazarus? No? Well . . . you worry too much." He staggered to his feet and shuffled toward the gate speaking to me as he walked away. "Just tell the people I'll be here again tomorrow."

I shouted indignantly at his back, "You think I'm going to let you do this again tomorrow. Yeah . . . when Hell freezes over!"

So I told the people. . . .

CHAPTER SEVEN

After I made my announcement, the crowd began to make camp in the fields outside my fortress. Some families, who had received the healing miracles they had sought, departed for their homes. But for every one that left, it seemed that two more arrived. Thankfully, the temperature was not as cold as I had predicted. Normally, at this time of year a temperature of around 45 degrees would have been normal at night, but tonight it was a balmy 55, which was tolerable if one snuggled under a good blanket.

I was in the courtyard with some of Jesus's disciples listening to them relive the events of the day, and contemplating how to spend another sleepless night on my own, when I saw Iris's brother, Horus, motioning to me furtively from the shadows.

I had sent another man to relieve Horus from his duties of leading one of my most important caravans, and called him home for my visit because I was anticipating the unfolding of some serious events, and he was one of my most able fighters. If he was seeking my attention in such a discreet manner, then he probably had important news for me.

I casually excused myself from the company of the disciples and nonchalantly strolled after Horus until we were in complete shadow.

He immediately whispered in my ear, "*The Ugly One* has sent his lackey to talk to you."

"Take me to him."

Horus led me to a remote corner of the gardens and I recognized the smell of the man before I could even see him. It was Uriah, the slave-trader and pimp, and as usual, he was accompanied by a couple of brutal bodyguards, and a thin whisper of a man everyone called, Fishbone. I had no idea what Fishbone's real name was, nor did I care. Truthfully, I had no desire to know a great deal about anyone who spent most of their time in the company of Uriah.

I thoroughly detested the man, but for the moment I put my feelings aside. "Uriah, why are you here?"

"What? You don't seem very happy to see me, and I've been waiting in the wings practically all day to get a word with you. What's all the hubbub about around here today anyway?"

"Sorry to keep you waiting, but it's been a crazy day. As you've probably noticed, we've got thousands of people camped outside our gates."

"Yes, and I believe I heard Jesus announce you got engaged today as well. That makes it a crazy day for sure. Any man as wealthy as you who gets married must be insane. You should let me fix you up with some of my girls, and then you could have all the women you want without the bother of having a wife. You could even buy a couple to keep you warm at night."

I felt the heat rising from Horus, and I heard his heartbeat begin to gallop with the insult to his sister, so I reached out my hand to restrain him. "As you know Uriah, I don't approve of slavery or your pimping practices. Everyone who works for me in any capacity is treated with respect, paid a generous wage, and free to come and go as they please at any time. If it were up to me slavery would be completely abolished, and I believe one day it will be."

"Well, have it your way. That's not the reason I'm here, as you know. The fact is, *The Ugly One* sends word that he wishes to meet with you at the usual place just after nightfall."

"Then I'll go immediately."

Uriah turned to Fishbone and said, "Run and tell *The Ugly One* that Lazarus is on his way."

Fishbone grunted and trotted away without saying a thing.

I started to turn to walk away, but then I turned back to speak to Uriah. "In the future you should tell your friend he should send someone else if he has a message for me, Uriah. You're no longer welcome in my home."

He just stood there looking at me, and then his temper flared and he yelled, "You can tell him yourself you bastard. You're about to go meet him, but first let me give you a little something to chew on." He angrily reached for his dagger, but before he could unsheathe it, I pulled the tiny dagger from my necklace and held it to his neck, as I grabbed his beard in my other hand to keep him from backing away. I had moved so quickly he and his bodyguards were temporarily so shocked they didn't know how to react.

Before they could recover their wits, we all heard a couple of deep growls from the darkness.

Uriah and his bodyguards hesitated, and we all watched as Samson and Delilah crept into the moonlight with their teeth bared. They were crouching down and growling as they kept a transfixed glare on Uriah.

I whispered, "Samson. . . Delilah. . . hold."

Then I pulled on Uriah's beard to draw him closer to me as I applied just enough pressure with my small dagger to start a trickle of blood flowing down his neck. When we were face to face I said, "Are you still here? I thought I told you to leave and never come back. Now get out of here! My dogs will see you to the gate."

I roughly pushed him away and said, "Samson. . . Delilah. . . follow."

Uriah backed away and began to trot toward the gates with his guards while looking over his shoulder at my dogs and holding his hand on his wounded neck.

Horus chuckled, "He's lucky the dogs showed up when they did. I was about to split his skull."

"Me and you both." I held my small dagger up for Horus to see and then put it back in its sheath, as I said, "I despise what he does and what he is, and I hope I never have to see him or smell him again."

Horus steered me back to the business at hand. "Will you require a guard for your trip tonight?"

"No, I've already been betrayed once. The fewer people who know about this meeting the better off we'll be."

Horus nodded, "Then may I suggest you disguise your appearance. Many of the people outside the gates will recognize you after your appearance on the wall tonight. Your resurrection is the talk of the town and all the people who've traveled here."

"Just give me your cloak, and I'll drape it over my head and tie it around my face, so my features are obscured."

I hastily covered my face and continued, "Now take me to the back gate and let me out that way. Most of the people are camping in the vicinity of the front gate, so I should be able to slip out unnoticed. And let's grab Samson and Delilah as we go. They'll be delighted to go on a midnight walk with me."

I slipped out the small back gate with my trusted hounds and slinked into the night. No one paid me any attention, and as soon as I was free of the crowd I quickened my pace in the direction of the Well of Josiah. Only this time I wasn't going to meet Iris there. This time I would be meeting the person Horus and others liked to call *The Ugly One*. Yes, tonight I would be meeting my old childhood nemesis, Barabbas!

The Well of Josiah was our usual meeting place for the same reason I met Iris there. It was on the outskirts of town and mostly used by people passing through, so no one was likely to notice us, or know us. At this hour of night, no one would even be around.

It occurred to me that this was the first opportunity I'd had to really check out the new powers Jesus said I'd been given, so I stepped up my pace to a quick trot and I glided so effortlessly across the land that I decided to really put the spurs to it and see what I could do. I was flabbergasted to find myself moving at a faster pace than the fastest horse I'd ever ridden. I looked over my shoulder and saw that even Delilah wasn't able to keep pace with me, and poor Samson was quickly falling behind. Amazingly, after running several hundred yards I didn't feel the least bit winded or tired. I felt like I could run forever!

I slid to a stop and waited for my dogs to catch up. They were breathing hard, so I decided to give them a brief rest before continuing on. I picked up a smooth palm sized rock from the trail and hefted it in my hand. I'd always been pretty good at throwing rocks as a kid. The other boys and I would often have competitions to see who could throw a rock the furthest or with the most accuracy.

With my enhanced night vision, I could see clearly all around me, so I took aim at a tree in a nearby field. I thought that if I was truly stronger now I should be able to hit the tree branches from where I stood. I leaned back and threw the rock with all my might, and was shocked to see it go sailing completely over the tree and landing instead in a stall of livestock several yards beyond the tree. The animals brayed and ran about their stall, and I worried the owner might come out to check the disturbance, but no one appeared.

So I picked up another rock, and this time I decided to see if I could hit the tree trunk, which appeared to be about 50 feet away. I could see a dark place in the center of the tree that made a nice bullseye so I aimed for that. I threw the rock directly at the tree trunk and was rewarded with a loud "thunk." I walked up to the tree to see if I could determine where I'd hit it, and I was wonder-struck to find my rock halfway buried in the tree's bark right in the middle of my chosen target.

The owner of the tree, and the livestock, now stood in the doorway of his home holding a candle and barking irritably, "Who goes there?" I silently slipped into the darkness and bolted away in the direction of the well.

Just before I came into sight of the well, I slowed my pace to a brisk stroll and looked around to make sure only one person was in the vicinity.

Barabbas was sitting silently in the shadows of a nearby tree where he probably thought no one could see him.

I could see him clearly, and I could hear his heart beating, so I added his particular heartbeat to my growing catalog. Apparently he was enjoying the idea that I didn't know precisely where he was, so I pretended I didn't know he was there, and began whistling my favorite tune.

I didn't get far with it before he yelled, "Stop that infernal whis-tling. I couldn't stand it when you did that as a kid, and I can't stand it now. And why'd you bring your mongrels?" He watched Samson and Delilah with a wary eye and continued, "Where'd you get those beasts, anyway?"

"I got them on one of my journeys to another country. They're practically puppies, they're so young."

"Puppies? They're nearly as big as a cow!"

"Yes, aren't they great?"

"If you say so . . . just keep them away from me, will ya?"

"Certainly. Samson. . . Delilah. . . guard."

The dogs trotted a few feet away and peered into the darkness watching for any signs of danger.

"Hope I didn't keep you waiting."

He grimaced, "Keep me waiting? I barely had time to walk here after Fishbone told me Uriah had delivered my message to you. How did you get here so fast?"

"You're just getting old, Barabbas. I swear I didn't break a sweat getting here. Now let's get to it. Why in the world would you risk calling a meeting so soon after my arrest and flogging?"

"Well first, let me say I'm glad to see you walking the Earth again. We may not have always seen eye-to-eye on some things in the past, and we certainly weren't the best of friends growing up, but I do value our current alliance. I was upset when I heard about your death, but apparently, reports of your demise were premature, unless the rumors of Jesus raising you from the dead are true. So, fill me in. What really happened when Jesus showed up here the other day?"

He was right. We were sworn enemies as children and teenagers, but in adulthood, the fates had conspired to force us into an uneasy and unholy alliance due to our common interest in overthrowing the rule of the Romans.

Barabbas's father had been the leader of the Zealots in our region of Israel since the beginning of the freedom movement instigated by Judas of Galilee in 6 A.D. Upon his father's death, Barabbas assumed his mantle, and my father, my Uncle, Joseph of Arimathea, and I were members of the group. It was a loose organization of Jewish theocratic nationalists who were dedicated to sending the Romans packing. But with Passover week approaching, and the popularity of Jesus soaring among the common people, the Zealots in the area surrounding Jerusalem were quietly conspiring to start an uprising. Proclaiming Jesus as the Messiah would be the catalyst for an Earth shattering revolt.

I responded to his question. "I really died, and Jesus really raised me up from the dead. Don't ask me how he did it. He just did. And now, you'll be glad to know, I'm better than ever before."

"Well that wouldn't have required much improvement, but it's too bad he couldn't do something with your face though," he quipped.

"You're one to talk. Most of my men call you *The Ugly One.*"

"Your men are not only incredibly stupid, they're also obviously blind."

We both chuckled at that, and then his voice took on a serious tone. "I took the risk of meeting with you tonight because I've received some bad news. The Great Sanhedrin has called an emergency meeting for tonight. In fact, they may be meeting, as we speak. The elders of our faith are concerned that this miracle of raising you from the dead in such close proximity to Jerusalem will get Pilate and his superiors all in an uproar.

"Your arrest and flogging had everyone on edge just by itself due to your standing in the community. It was embarrassing to the Jews that someone like you could be treated so cruelly by the Romans. Your uncle Joseph being a part of the Sanhedrin didn't help things, but at least he was able to use his influence to spare you from crucifixion, which was something, I guess. Pilate, of course, had the gall to act like he was doing us all a favor by flogging you instead of nailing you to a cross, but everyone knew you had virtually no chance of surviving either way.

"Now, with Passover week being so close, some are pushing to have you and Jesus both arrested under charges of conspiring to install him as King of the Jews."

I smiled. "Well, the funny thing is, we *are* conspiring to install him as our king, and some of the Sanhedrin *are* conspiring with us, especially my uncle Joseph of Arimathea, and Nicodemus. In some ways, they're leading the pack. So if they issue an arrest warrant for us, what do you think will happen? Do you think the Romans would dare come for us?"

Barabbas shook his head. "No. I don't think the Romans are going to come after you so soon after your flogging. That almost caused an uprising by itself. And they certainly won't come against you while you're inside your home. They've allowed you to keep your small fortress because, until recently, you were perceived as being a loyal subject of Rome, and they need the supplies and trade goods you supply them with by way of your caravans. That's true not just here, but throughout their empire.

"The temple guard would have to arrest the two of you and bring you to the high priest for trial. Upon your conviction they could then turn you over to the Romans for punishment, which would almost certainly lead to your crucifixion. But the temple guards aren't going to come and try to drag you out of your stronghold. Your guards are far superior fighters, and you have the added advantage of fighting behind your walls. They'll wait until the two of you go into Jerusalem and scoop you up when no one is looking. Frankly, I wouldn't put it past Caiaphas to put a bounty on your heads and let an assassin take you out quietly. I think he's afraid he might end up on a cross himself, if he doesn't quell this talk of Jesus being the Messiah."

I nodded in agreement. "I think you're right on all accounts. So what do you suggest we do?"

"Keep Jesus inside the gates of your estate, and don't let him out of your sight if he insists on going outside. We've got another week before Passover week and we need more time to prepare our plans. Besides, we've got our fellow Zealots traveling here for the festivities, and we're going to need their help to accomplish our goals. We need to wait until everything, and everyone, is in place before we let him go into Jerusalem. If he's arrested then, it won't really matter because we'll have our people in place to bust him loose. And for that matter, if he announces he's the Messiah we won't have to lift a finger. The people themselves will take matters into their own hands at that point.

"And that's where you come into play. He loves you more than anyone, and he listens to you. Over the next few days you need to feel him out, and make sure he's got his head on straight about all of this. We can nudge him in the right direction if we need to, but it would really simplify things if he took the lead in all of this. We're ready to follow him wherever he leads. All he has to do is proclaim himself as the Messiah, and he'll have an army at his beckoning."

"Well, the good news is that he really does seem to have his head straight about all of this. Just last night he was telling me he wanted me to help him fulfill his mission by keeping him safe until Passover week, and it seemed like he almost knew what we were planning."

"Great! Then all you have to do is keep him inside for the next week or so until Passover starts."

"You want me to keep him inside?" I said, "You've obviously forgotten how impulsive and hard-headed my cousin can be. Don't you remember the time he kissed you on the cheek when you tried to get him to kiss your butt? And he had to know you were going to thrash him for it."

Barabbas smiled ruefully. "Yeah, that was a pretty brash move on his part, and pretty ballsy for a future rabbi, huh?"

I laughed. "It was fabulous. I'll never forget the look on your face that day."

"Yeah, well I made him pay for it, and the Sanhedrin will make him pay, if you can't control him. Seriously, it's up to you to keep a handle on his activities for the next week. I've got my job to do getting all of our people and resources in place, and your job is to keep Jesus out of the limelight for a few days while making sure his head is on right. Can I count on you for that?"

"Sure. How hard can it be to keep a traveling rabbi confined to his quarters for a week or so?"

Barabbas frowned and gave me a stern look. "Seriously, Lazarus. Don't let me down. If you screw this up, there's going to be hell to pay!" His heart was beating extra hard as he uttered these last words.

"Why, Barabbas, if I didn't know you better, I'd think you were threatening me."

"Sorry. I didn't mean to come across that way. You know me. Sometimes my temper just gets the better of me, and I can be a bit of a hot-head."

"Oh, I'm well aware of that, and I've got the scars to prove it." I lowered my voice, "But just to be clear . . . don't ever threaten me again."

Even in the moonlight, I could see the redness of his face as he fumbled for words, "Like I said, it's just my temper getting the best of me. I didn't mean it really. I'm just worried is all."

I turned and started back to my home while calling over my shoulder. "Don't worry. I've got this. Oh, and see you soon, *Ugly One!*"

⊷ ⊶

While Barabbas and I were meeting by the well, an emergency meeting of the Great Sanhedrin was taking place in Jerusalem. The group of 71 sages typically met in the daytime, but this was not a normal meeting. They had been called to this meeting by the high priest Caiaphas, and many of them were not happy with the break in protocol.

They took their assigned seats in the Chamber of Hewn Stones inside the Temple and murmured angrily among themselves, until their *Nasi*, or Prince, called them to order. Beside the Prince of the Court stood the *av bet din*, or Father of the Court. They functioned as a kind of president and vice-president of the council. Tonight, to the right of the Prince of the Court stood the High Priest Caiaphas. While the High Priest technically wasn't a part of the council, he often met with them, and in the case of Caiaphas, he held sway over most of their more important decisions.

The sages sat in a semicircle facing their leaders and waited for the meeting to commence. Finally, the Prince of the Court spoke, "My brothers, it has come to our attention that the traveling teacher known as Jesus of Nazareth has reportedly performed an amazing miracle just outside the walls of Jerusalem in the little town of Bethany. The people are claiming he raised Lazarus from the dead."

Upon hearing this, the sages began to speak excitedly among themselves.

The Prince motioned for order and continued. "As you all know, it caused quite a stir among the people when the Romans arrested and flogged Lazarus, and everyone is aware he's the nephew of our own esteemed member, Joseph of Arimathea. We all love Joseph and his family, and we all hated to see what happened to Lazarus. When we heard news of his death we were appalled and deeply saddened. If he has indeed come back from the dead, then we are elated for his family and for all those who love and admire him. But ascribing his good fortune to a miracle performed by this Nazarene scoundrel is obviously nonsense."

With these words more anxious muttering broke out among the sages.

"Furthermore, we have been told that Jesus is now encamped at Lazarus's home, and is offering to perform more miracles for the people. We've been told the people are claiming many sick and afflicted were healed there today. It's reported that multitudes of people are coming from all across the country to see him, and with Passover week nearly upon us, there will be huge crowds coming here who may be swayed by his followers. As you know there's a great deal of talk among the common people that he may be the Messiah, and this isn't the first time this council has discussed the repercussions this could have for our nation."

Now the muttering rose to a higher level, and some of the sages looked as if they may come to blows with one another.

The Prince and the Father both called for the sages to cease arguing, and he continued, "If we can't stop this talk about a new King of the Jews being put forth by the people, the Romans will have no choice but to make examples of us by removing us from our places of leadership. As you all know, in most of the providences where Rome has taken control they have installed their own systems of governance, but up until now, they have allowed our country to be governed by our own people. Amazingly, they've allowed us to keep our councils and left us in control of deciding our own legal and religious issues. Yes, it's true they have their own regional governors who oversee their individual territories, and yes, they have garrisons of soldiers who make sure our people stay in line, but for the most part, we are allowed to govern ourselves. However, all of that could easily change in an instant if Pilate becomes convinced we're not doing enough to stop a potential rebellion."

With that, Nicodemus stood and shouted, "I demand my right to address the council on this matter."

Some of the others sages attempted to shout him down, but the Prince motioned once again for order and said, "It is his right to address the council. Let Nicodemus be heard."

Nicodemus gripped the folds of his robe and said, "Brothers, we have been waiting for a Messiah, and who are we to say that Jesus is not the one we've been awaiting. There are numerous accounts of him performing great miracles. Too many to count really, and they can't all be the fabrications of a bunch of Nazarene ruffians. To be honest in the matter, I have spoken to him myself."

This caused more murmuring, so Nicodemus paused, and then continued, "I met with him in secret one night for fear of what you might have thought of me. I'm ashamed to admit how I behaved, but I'm telling you openly now because I'm convinced there's something special about this man. We need to proceed with caution lest we become enemies of God out of our fear of the Romans."

Until this point, Caiaphas had been standing by idly, but now he stomped in front of the Prince and yelled, "Enough!! Is this a council of fools?! You have no idea what I have to go through on nearly a daily basis to keep the Romans happy with our arrangement. Yes, they let us govern the minor ins-and-outs of our peoples' religious and legal affairs, but make no mistake; it's they who rule Israel. And if you need to be reminded of who's in control here, just go and take a look at Golgotha. Even now there are bodies of our people hanging there from today's crucifixions. If we don't stop this madness of people wanting to proclaim Jesus as the Messiah, we'll all be hanging on crosses together, and the Romans won't stop there. If there's an uprising of the people, Pilate will call for reinforcements and entire legions of troops will descend upon us, so that our streets will run red with Jewish blood!"

Someone shouted from the group, "What would you have us do?"

"There's only one thing we can do. We've got to see that Jesus dies."

Many of the sages jumped to their feet now and demanded to be heard, but Caiaphas held his place, and they soon relented. He stalked back and forth in front of them for a moment and then roared, "Don't you get it? Jesus may be a good man, and a wonderful teacher, and even a legitimate worker of miracles, but it's better for one man to die for all the people than for our whole nation to perish!"

Now most of the sages took to their feet and began shouting. "Yes! Yes! Let him be the one to die, not us. Arrest him! Arrest him!"

And from that day forward they began to plot the death of Jesus. . . .

(John 11:53)

CHAPTER EIGHT

March 21ˢᵗ

It's after midnight and the Sabbath has begun, so today is supposed to be a day of rest, but I have a feeling there'll be no rest for me today. Certainly there will be no sleep, I fear. Once again, I feel no need to sleep, and believe me; I've had a full day of activity. I'm starting to believe Jesus may have told the truth about me not needing to sleep anymore. Anyway...

Yesterday morning, I proposed to Iris after receiving her parents' blessing. Then, just when I thought I might enjoy a relatively quiet day after the hubbub of my resurrection from the dead, everything just got crazier around here. Thousands of people arrived here today when word of my rebirth spread through the countryside. Now it seems as if everyone with a nosebleed wants Jesus to heal them. And to the amazement of everyone, that's just what he's doing. He must have healed hundreds today before he finally gave out.

Now the problem is that the multitudes are camping out in the fields outside my gates, and Jesus won't allow me to send them away. Luckily, a freakish warm wind blew in from somewhere, or they'd all be freezing, but the real problem is going to be tomorrow because tomorrow they're going to be starving, and I don't have enough provisions to feed even a fraction of that many people.

To top it off The Ugly One called a meeting tonight and informed me the Great Sanhedrin were meeting to consider arresting Jesus, and possibly me as well. He wants me to keep Jesus confined inside my fortress until Passover week and that's going to be next to impossible.

Honestly, I'm starting to wonder if the uneasy alliance I've formed with my childhood nemesis may blow up in my face. If he can't learn to control his temper, I'm afraid it could eventually cause us trouble. But, I guess for now, I need to stay the course and hope I can figure everything out.

Maybe if I can find a way to spend more time with Jesus some of his wisdom will rub off on me. Then again . . . maybe not. . . .

⤐ ⤏

I t was another night without any desire to sleep. I spent my time pacing in my gardens alone while thinking of creative ways to get the multitudes to depart. I was also dreaming of ways to keep Jesus inside the walls if we received word of the Great Sanhedrin moving against him.

I knew my sisters would be in a panic over what to do about feeding the people camped outside our gates because they were by nature gracious hostesses and of a nurturing inclination. If it was left up to them, they would empty our storehouses with no thought of how we would feed our own household until the next harvest. I also knew they would be up at the break of dawn, so I was waiting when they exited their quarters and stepped into the courtyard.

I intercepted them before they could start giving orders to our servants to feed the people. "Ah, my lovely sisters, you're just who I was hoping to find."

Martha looked at Mary and deadpanned, "Did he just call us lovely?"

Mary said, "Yes, he did. He has to be up to something."

"No doubt about it. Yesterday, we had to learn of his engagement when Jesus announced it, instead of from our own brother, and now that same cold-hearted, selfish, and egotistical brother comes strolling up to us as if he never slighted us, and has the audacity to try to flatter us. He's definitely up to something, and I say we ignore him."

Mary nodded, "You mean you want to ignore him today, just like he ignored us yesterday?"

"Exactly."

"Agreed."

Mary slipped her arm through Martha's arm, and they began to stalk away from me with their noses held stiffly in the air.

I trotted ahead of them to cut them off and began trying to apologize. "Come on now ladies. I never meant for you to find out from someone else about my engagement. I proposed to Iris yesterday morning, and had planned to make a formal announcement to everyone myself, but things got a little crazy with all the people showing up here yesterday, and then Jesus beat me to the punch. Please forgive me. Please!"

My sisters pulled to a sudden stop and Martha exclaimed, "Mary did you hear something?"

"Well yes, but I think it was just the wind."

"Oh yes, it was definitely something windy that's for sure . . . but I thought I may have heard a plea for mercy in the midst of all that bluster and commotion."

Mary looked right through me and said, "You know that may have been a plea for mercy. Let's listen and see if we hear it again."

They both put a hand over one ear and directed that particular ear towards me.

I shook my head, and after a brief pause, I gave them what they wanted. "Okay, I'm sorry you had to hear about my engagement from someone else, and I humbly ask for your forgiveness. Please allow me to return to your good favor."

They replied in unison, "AND?"

"And you're the finest sisters a man could ever have, which makes me the luckiest man alive."

They looked at each other beseechingly, and Martha said, "I say we forgive him."

Mary nearly yelled, "Agreed!"

They rushed to my side and begin dancing around me, while chanting, "You're engaged to be married! Hooray! You're engaged!"

We all laughed and embraced for a moment, and then I addressed them sternly, "Now that you've had your fun with me, I need to talk about some serious issues. I know you two all too well, and that leads me to believe you're already making plans to try to feed all those people camped outside today."

Martha pouted and said, "Well if we were, what would be wrong with that?"

I said, "Because we've got to think with our heads, and not our hearts. Even if we completely emptied our storehouses, we couldn't feed that many people, and once they left we wouldn't have enough food to last us until harvest."

Martha protested, "But over half that crowd is made up of women and children. You can't expect us to let them go hungry."

I shook my head and said, "You're not listening. If we feed all of them, we'll all go hungry ourselves."

Mary chimed in, "But we're wealthy. Surely we could buy enough food to replenish our storehouses after we've fed the people."

"No. No. NO! You're talking about spending a fortune on a bunch of strangers, and besides, there's no food to be bought right now."

From somewhere nearby Jesus spoke from where he had apparently been listening, "Lazarus, didn't I tell you last night you worry too much?"

I turned to him and ruefully replied, "Yes you did, but this is a serious problem and someone has to worry about it."

Jesus said, "I will need some time in your sunny gardens to prepare myself for what must be done today. In the meantime, prepare the oxcart and the people as you did yesterday, and let me address them this afternoon. I believe we can solve your little problem."

As Jesus walked away, I began barking orders at guards and servants and they jumped to the task of arranging the people in rows on the hillside below my home. Once I had everything in motion, I ascended the walls again and found to my amazement there were many more people assembled in the fields than the night before. Apparently, they had been arriving all night, and I could see even more approaching from the distance.

Iris joined me on the wall just after noon, along with her parents, Darius and Nida. We all stood there in wonder as the huge crowd of people continued to arrange themselves in rows on the hillside below us.

Iris asked, "How many do you think there are?"

I replied, "I just counted at least 400 men in the first row and there's at least 10 rows of people. So that's at least 4000 men, and that's not counting women and children. There must be somewhere close to 10,000 people. There has never been this many people gathered in our little village at one time in all our history."

Nida asked, "What do you think he's going to do?"

I said, "I really have no idea, but it looks like we're about to find out. Here he comes now."

We watched Jesus make his way through the gates, followed by my sisters, Mary and Martha. Once again, he walked regally up the wobbly stairs and took his place in the oxcart.

His disciples followed him out along with a smattering of my guards, and I noticed his followers were each carrying empty baskets. The disciples spread out in front of him and turned to face him.

A few cheers arose from the crowd, but the people were not as animated as the day before. If was painfully obvious the weather and lack of food had drained them of much of their enthusiasm.

Jesus motioned for silence and then spoke, "Our hosts and I are concerned because we realize most of you are probably out of food after traveling to get here, and then spending yesterday and last night in the fields. I know there's probably not a lot of food left at this point, but I was wondering if anyone might be willing to share what they have. Anyone?"

I looked at Iris and my sisters and said, "If this is his idea of how to feed the people, we're doomed. There's no way there's enough food left among this crowd to feed everyone, even if they *all* agreed to share."

Iris pointed and said, "Look!"

I looked back and saw one small boy making his way through the crowd toward Jesus.

As the boy came forward, Mary ran to meet him and she and the boy had a brief conversation before she took him by the hand and led him up the hill. Jesus stepped down from the oxcart and came to meet Mary and the boy as they reached the apex of the hill. The boy lifted up a small basket and Jesus peered inside.

He lifted the basket above his head and proclaimed, "This young lad has offered us two fish and five loaves of barley."

The crowd began to murmur, but Jesus lifted the basket even higher and asserted, "It's enough! Let us give thanks for what our father in Heaven has provided for us this day."

Holding the basket high above his head he lifted his eyes to the heavens and prayed, "*Our Father who is in Heaven, we honor your holy name. May your kingdom come, and may your will be done on Earth as it is in Heaven. Thank you for giving us our daily bread, and for forgiving us our sins, just as we have forgiven those who sin against us. When we are tempted, give us wisdom to do the right thing and avoid doing evil. For yours is the kingdom, and the power, and the glory forever. Amen."*

Jesus motioned for his disciples to come forward with their baskets, and as they passed by him he broke up a meager portion of the fish and bread into each basket and then instructed them to begin feeding the crowd.

We watched in amazement as the people kept reaching into the baskets that had been nearly empty a moment ago, and pulling out whole cooked fishes, and whole loaves of bread. Soon, all the people were busy stuffing themselves with food. I hurriedly called my remaining guards and servants and had them begin carrying water to the people in buckets. In just over an hour all ten thousand people had been completely fed. When everyone was done eating, the twelve principle disciples of Jesus came back to the top of the hill and set twelve full baskets of food at his feet.

Those of us watching from the wall had been observing these proceedings in mostly reverent silence while only rarely speaking in hushed tones, but now Iris broke the spell by proclaiming, "By the gods . . . what sort of sorcery have we witnessed here today?"

Without speaking to anyone in particular I responded, "This wasn't sorcery. We've just witnessed a miracle from God himself by way of Jesus. If anyone had any doubts of him being the promised Messiah after he raised me from the dead, surely they will see it now."

I took Iris and Martha by the hand and said, "Come with me. I want to get closer."

By the time we made our way outside the fortress, Jesus had resumed his place in the oxcart and began to once again speak to the hushed crowd. "Today this little boy came in faith and humbly offered up his fishes and loaves to feed the people. You witnessed me lifting up this offering to God and then breaking the fish and loaves so they might be sacrificed for your hunger. Listen closely now, for I must tell you of things to come. . . ."

The crowd became completely quiet as he spoke....

"For just as Moses lifted up the serpent in the wilderness on a pole for all to see, so must the Son of Man be lifted up in like manner so that whoever believes in him may not perish but have eternal life.

For God so loved the world that he gave his only son, so that whoever believes in him should not perish, but have eternal life.

For God didn't send his Son into the world to condemn the world. He sent him so the world might be saved through him."

When he finished speaking someone who appeared to be a scribe or Pharisee yelled from the fringes of the crowd. "Are you saying you will be lifted up as a king or as a sacrifice?"

Jesus answered simply, *"You have eyes to see don't you? So how is it that you don't see? And you have ears to hear, so why don't you listen? Have you already forgotten what was said and done here today?"*

This seemed to agitate the man who had yelled, and his fellow scribes and Pharisees were stirred to a frenzy of muttering and yelling. Such men had much to lose if Jesus were proclaimed King of the Jews because much of what he taught seemed to contradict their own convictions concerning the religious laws that governed the lives of the people. For now, the scribes and Pharisees held sway over the peoples' beliefs, and perhaps more importantly, their tithes. If Jesus were made king, they could lose their power and prestige, as well as the ability to line their pockets with the peoples' gold and silver.

Just as it appeared the temple elders might rush the place where Jesus was standing, a small contingent of boys and girls came out of the crowd and approached him. As they drew near they uncovered their heads and faces to reveal enlarged facial features and horrible sores and lesions.

The crowd gasped and pulled back from them and the cry went up from all quarters, "Lepers! Lepers!"

The disciples and guards stood unflinching in their way and blocked them from coming closer to Jesus, but he quickly dismounted the oxcart and came rushing to stand with the children.

He motioned for the crowd to hush their murmurings and then he spoke to the children, "Who are you, and why have you come here today?'

One of the older children spoke, "I am Stephen, and I'm the leader of this band of orphaned lepers. We heard of the many miracles of healing you were performing here as you touched the sick and afflicted, and although we knew you wouldn't want to touch us in our condition, we thought if we could just touch the hem of your clothing we could be healed."

Upon hearing this, the scribes and Pharisees, who had made their way nearly to the front of the crowd, pushed everyone aside and their spokesman began to shout. "Are you going to heal on the Sabbath? Don't you know that's against our laws?"

Jesus glowered at them and then spoke compellingly, "*Is it lawful on the Sabbath to do good deeds on behalf of others or should we do harm. Should one save life or destroy it?*

If one of you had a single sheep fall into a pit on the Sabbath would you not take ahold of it and lift it out of the pit? Of course you would! Well, how much more valuable is a man than a sheep?

Be careful that you don't despise one of these little ones, because their angels are always in touch with my Father in Heaven.

For the Son of Man has come to seek and to save that which was lost.

What do you think? If a man has a hundred sheep, and one of them goes missing, doesn't he leave the ninety-nine and go to the mountains to find the one that's gone astray?

And if he should find it, I can promise you he'll rejoice more over that one sheep than over the ninety-nine that never went astray.

In the same way, our heavenly Father wouldn't want one of these little ones to perish or suffer."

The scribes and Pharisees slowly retreated as Jesus rebuked them, and the people pushed them back to the fringes of the crowd.

Jesus glared at his detractors one last time, and then walked boldly into the midst of the leprous children, and began to lovingly caress each of them on the head. As each one was touched, they were immediately healed of all signs and symptoms of leprosy. They threw off the rags that had hidden their afflicted flesh and looked with astonishment at their perfect complexions. They felt of their faces and stroked the faces of their friends while laughing with joy to find they were no longer swollen and disfigured. I was amazed to see Iris and my sisters frolicking with the children and also touching their unblemished faces. Then, like a flock of birds responding to some unheard signal, the children joined hands with one another, and the leader of their band led them laughing and rejoicing as they ran through the crowd and retreated into the distance.

Iris looked back at me and gave me a longing look that made me think she might bolt after them and attempt to bring them back, but the spell was broken when a huge burst of laughter erupted from nearby.

It was Jesus. He was laughing almost uncontrollably as he watched the children running in the distance.

Then he lifted his eyes to the sky, held up his hands, and proclaimed, "Bring me your sick and afflicted!"

And they came. . . .

CHAPTER NINE

For the next few hours Iris and my sisters lovingly lined up the sick and brought them one at a time to be healed by Jesus. As the sun began to set in the Western sky I saw that Jesus seemed to be fading in exuberance, so I called an end to the healing and reminded the people there were 12 baskets full of food for them to share for their evening meal.

Before I could get Jesus back inside the gates, there was a stirring among the people, and someone shouted. "Don't you all see? We should make Jesus our King! Behold, he has raised Lazarus from the dead, he has miraculously fed us, he has healed our sick, he has stood up to the religious leaders who berate us with every jot and tittle of the Law, and who attempt to tithe and tax us to the bone. All that remains is for him to lead us in standing up to the Romans. With him as our King they wouldn't have a chance. Even the might and power of the Romans can't withstand the miraculous power of God's son the Messiah!"

Others also began to shout. "Yes, he *is* the Messiah! Let's make Jesus our King . . . Jesus our King . . . Jesus our King!"

The throng of people began to thrust themselves forward, and I feared we might all be trampled in the rush. I scampered to Jesus's side, and pushed him and the disciples toward the gates. We all managed to get inside just in the nick of time, but once we had the gates shut we realized we had left a couple of my guards outside, so I had my men throw ropes down and pull them up the walls.

Jesus said he wanted to sit by the bonfire in our courtyard, so I asked Mary and Martha to attend to his needs for food and drink, and I hurried away to make sure the gates were secure.

Before I could get to the gates, Judas Iscariot discreetly grabbed me and pulled me to the side. "We need to talk."

"Can't it wait? I really need to make sure the gates are secure."

"No. We need to talk now!"

I motioned for Horus to join us. "Horus, please inspect the gates before retiring for the night. I'd do it myself, but Judas seems to think he needs my attention, if you know what I mean."

"I'm on it. Go take care of business." Horus replied.

Judas led me to the outskirts of the gardens where two other disciples waited for us in the shadows. I was expecting Simon the Zealot because, after all, he was such a fervent Zealot, that everyone had taken to calling him 'Simon the Zealot'. He was also a part of our little inside-circle of co-conspirators. At first this was helpful because there was another man named Simon who was also one of the twelve principle disciples. He was Simon the fisherman. But now Jesus had solved the confusion by renaming that Simon and giving him the name Peter.

I was surprised to find Peter waiting there with Simon the Zealot, and I didn't hesitate to voice my displeasure, "What's he doing here?"

Judas tried to calm me down. "It's okay. He wants to help us, and he believes in what we're trying to accomplish."

"Does he understand our ideals?"

Peter pulled back the folds of his outer robe to reveal a dagger, which was the preferred weapon of the Zealots, since we were an underground paramilitary force. He patted the dagger for effect and said, "I understand we must be willing to fight for what we believe, and I believe Jesus is the Messiah."

I turned back to Judas. "We don't need him or his dagger. We've got all the help we need. Besides, the more people we involve the more likely we are to be found out. Have you forgotten so quickly what the Romans did to me?"

Judas said, "Well, it's too late now, anyway. He accidentally overheard Simon and me discussing our plans, and he approached us and asked to join us. Maybe it's good that it's worked out this way. The other disciples look up to him and respect him. If this comes down to some kind of joint decision among them he can use his influence to sway them to our perspective on things."

I didn't offer any further objections, so he continued, "For the moment we need to put our differences aside and pull together because we have bigger issues to deal with."

I sneered, "What could be bigger than trying to avoid getting flogged or crucified?"

"Well, as you know, after you debriefed us last night on your meeting with Barabbas, we decided I should make a trip into Jerusalem today to see what I could find out about the outcome of the meeting of the Great Sanhedrin."

"So, I take it you learned something worth calling this meeting?"

Judas nodded, "Yes, being the nephew of Caiaphas has its advantages sometimes. It's true that they met last night, and as Barabbas feared, they're making planes to arrest Jesus at their first opportunity."

"Will they be so bold as to come here?"

"No. They're not that brave, or that stupid, but if Jesus sets foot in Jerusalem, or anywhere near the temple, you can bet they'll do their best to take him into custody."

"So what do you suggest we do? There's no way we can keep him from going into Jerusalem, and there's no way we can keep him from going to the temple. He's stubborn as a mule when it comes to his insistence that he be out and about with the common people. He keeps referring to the people as his sheep, and he calls himself the Good Shepherd. Today, we nearly had a riot on our hands when they wanted to force him to be their king."

Simon the Zealot offered, "If we can just keep him here until Passover week it won't matter what the Sanhedrin or their temple cronies pull. We'll have all our resources and people in place by then. Can't we just keep him here till then?"

I shook my head at Simon, "Haven't you been following him around for three years? Well, then you should know, you can't tell him what to do. No, our only hope is to convince him to go into hiding for the next week or so."

Peter said, "He's not exactly prone to keeping a low profile, much less to go into hiding. I don't think he'll agree. Besides that, you've got 10,000 people camped outside your gates who will go nuts when they see him, and you'll never convince them to not follow us wherever we may choose to go. We've had crowds like this follow us for three days in the desert, and they're more charged up now than ever before."

I held my hand up. "Look, everything you guys are saying is true. I don't know if he'll agree, but let me talk to him. I'm closer to him than anyone here. I've got some out-of-the-way barracks on some of my caravan trails that would accommodate all of us in a discreet fashion. Maybe he'll listen to reason. If he does, we'll send a few people out at a time through the back gates, and we'll all meet up down the road a ways. Hopefully, if we're careful, we can slip away in the night, without the people who are camping outside being any the wiser. While I'm talking to him, you guys should be talking to the rest of his followers. Peter, if you have the confidence of the others, then use your influence to convince them this is the best course of action. Judas, you and Simon support him in his overtures. If I don't have any luck talking to him, it may take all of us to convince him."

Luckily, it didn't take long to find Jesus. He was still sitting by the fire, and seemed to be well recovered from the day's events. I watched him for a moment and was moved by his obvious enjoyment as he listened to the banter of his friends. I hated to bother him at such a moment, but eventually I made my way over, and asked him to accompany me to the gardens. We went back to the same place we had talked on the night of my resurrection, and I couldn't help but marvel at all the things that had transpired since that miraculous day.

Jesus interrupted my musing with a chuckle, "Lazarus, do you even realize you're whistling that annoying song again?"

"Oops, sorry. I was just thinking about all the things that've happened since we met here two nights ago. It's hard to believe that was only 48 hours ago."

"Yes, it's hard to believe all right. We've done a lot of good for a lot of deserving people these last two days. But I have a feeling you didn't invite me out here to talk about our successes. What's really on your mind?"

I immediately dove in, "The Great Sanhedrin met last night, and they've decided to arrest you."

"So, what do you want me to do?"

"I know you're not going to like this, but we need to go into hiding for the next week."

Jesus replied, "Okay."

I blurted, "I knew you'd say that, but just listen to me for once. . . . Wait a minute. Did you say . . . 'Okay'?"

"Yes. Okay! If you say we should go into hiding, then I'm all for it. In fact, I've got just the place for us to go."

"You do?"

"Yes, we should go to the Ephraim wilderness."

"Wait, did you say you want to go to Ephraim, or to the Ephraim wilderness?"

"To the wilderness, of course, after all, you just said we need to go into hiding, and what better place to hide than a wilderness?"

I shook my head, "No, that would never work. There's no place to get inside at night out there, and at this time of year it's nearly freezing in those hills and mountains."

"We'll take lots of blankets."

"No, the weather isn't the only problem. There are thieves and roving bands of hooligans waiting to ambush people who travel those trails. It's a treacherous place for even trained soldiers to travel, and your followers aren't soldiers by any stretch of the imagination. And on top of that, there are wild animals and poisonous snakes everywhere out there. I was thinking we could stay in some of the barracks along my caravan trails. Some of them are well off the beaten path, but not terribly dangerous like the Ephraim wilderness."

"Did I just hear you say you're still afraid of snakes? Surely you've outgrown that by now. As for thieves and hooligans, you're welcome to bring along some of your guards if you like, but it's got to be the Ephraim wilderness, or I'll just sit my behind down right here and refuse to go anywhere . . . until tomorrow, when I go to the temple!"

"Man, you're killing me here. Okay. We'll go to the Ephraim wilderness."

Jesus jumped to his feet as he exclaimed, "This is great. I knew you'd come around!"

"Well, I'm glad to see you so happy. You've seemed a little morose these last few days. But now I'm curious. Why are you so determined to go to this particular place? There are hundreds of places we could go, you know. And nearly all of them aren't as dangerous."

Jesus gazed up at the stars as he replied, "After I was baptized by John the Baptist I spent 40 days and 40 nights wandering in the Ephraim wilderness without a thing to eat. You may not believe it, but at the end of those 40 days I was tested by the Devil himself. It was the hardest thing I've ever had to do until now, but things are about to get even harder, so I think I need to revisit the place where I was so harshly tested in order to prepare myself for what's to come."

He took his eyes off the stars, and looked at me with his big sad eyes before he spoke again. "And besides that, I think you need to go there as well."

"Me? Why would I need to go there?"

"Let's just say you may need to pass a couple of tests yourself while we're there."

"Now you're scaring me a little. And would you mind telling me why you seem to have gone from being overly happy to overly gloomy just now?"

Jesus flashed a glowing smile as he replied, "I'm sorry about that. I'm really happy to be making this trip with you. It reminds me of the adventures we used to have as children. Say . . . do you remember the secret motto we used to say to each other when we were starting out on a new quest together?"

At that moment I swear I felt the wind pick up, and I looked around with my enhanced night vision to see if there were any dust devils forming near us, but there wasn't any dust in my gardens, henceforth, there were no dust devils to be seen.

I sheepishly replied, "Yes, I'm afraid I do remember it, and I'm embarrassed to admit I remember it quite well, in fact."

"Well, this is just the kind of event that deserves to be commemorated by repeating our motto one more time. Don't you think?"

"Well, I don't know about that . . . I mean, we're not little kids anymore . . . and, well . . . what if my men should see me?"

"Oh Lazarus, haven't I told you not to worry so much. Live a little, old friend. Now come on, say it with me!"

We faced each other, and over the shoulder of Jesus I thought I caught a glimpse of a falling star.

We put our right hands on our hearts as we shouted to the skies.

"For the weak." I thought I saw another shooting star out of the corner of my eye, but I kept my eyes locked on his.

"For the innocent." There it was again, but I dared not look away.

"FOREVERMORE!"

As we reached out to touch our fingers, there was no denying it; two stars fell from the heavens and went streaking into the night.

⥿ ⥷

I soon had everyone in our household working together to prepare the things we would need for our trip. We were going to need at least a week's worth of food and provisions. We would need plenty of blankets since we would be sleeping outdoors in what could potentially be brutal conditions. I also wanted each man to have at least one extra pair of shoes. Where we were going, the trails would be rough and treacherous. We would each be forced to walk on our own two feet, since even the donkeys that would be carrying our supplies were liable to fall in such conditions, if they were burdened with a rider. A fall like that in some of the high country we would be traversing could be dangerous for both the beast, and his human cargo.

After some argument, we agreed to not take any women. Peter and some of the other disciples were accustomed to traveling with their wives as they followed Jesus across the countryside. There were also several other women who were a part of the extended group of followers who routinely followed Jesus wherever he went. These were devout women who had been healed, or otherwise blessed by Jesus's ministry. They left everything behind, and pledged their wealth and wellbeing to him, as they traveled with him, and financed his endeavors.

My sister Mary, or as some called her, Mary Magdalene, was one of these women.

Before my father died, he gave my sisters and me a portion of his wealth. The always sensible Martha continued to live in my father's house, and managed her money well. My sister Mary, who was always more compulsive, chose to build an opulent palace in Magdala, hence the name Mary Magdalene, which means Mary of Magdala.

Mary was not a great judge of character at that stage of her life, and she soon found herself surrounded by freeloaders, miscreants, and troublemakers who slowly but surely pulled her down into the cesspool of life, while simultaneously dragging her reputation through the mud. Her home on the banks of the Sea of Galilee became a place known for raucous and scandalous parties that were a favorite subject of every gossip for miles around.

As fate would have it, her cousin Jesus came to visit her at her home in Magdala at just the right time. Her debauchery and shame had taken her to such a dark place that she appeared to be possessed, and many claimed that when Jesus laid hands on her, seven demons were cast out. In response, she sold her lavish estate and began using her remaining wealth to finance Jesus's ministry.

Her reputation had been ruined, and no self-respecting man would have anything to do with her, but Jesus treated her with respect, and she was deeply devoted to him in return. She had been by his side now for about two years, and she wasn't easily persuaded to stay behind while we traveled to the wilderness.

And then there was Iris. If convincing Mary to stay behind was a challenge, convincing Iris was almost impossible. She cried inconsolably, and told me I was going to get myself killed by a bunch of renegade bandits, which would leave her alone and without the love I had promised her. While attempting to relieve her fears, I found myself promising to marry her when we returned in a week. Somehow, I think that may have been the point of her protests all along, but in any case, we now had a solid timeframe to carry out our marriage, and that lifted her spirits to amazing heights. She ran off to begin planning our wedding with Nida, and I was left with a spinning head still trying to comprehend that I had agreed to be married in just one week. (2,000 years later I'm still trying to understand how she did that. I suspect the power of a beautiful woman may be the most underrated force on Earth.)

When all was said and done, we had 20 men who would be making the trip; Jesus and his 12 disciples, Horus and I, and five of my best guards. If we encountered a large band of renegades we would be hard pressed to repel them, since only a few of us were trained in the art of fighting, so I was hoping any potential adversaries would be impressed by our sheer numbers, and thus discouraged to mount an attack.

We divided up into small groups of five, so at least one guard would always be with each group while we travelled. Then we left through the back gate, one group at a time, with a few minutes between each group's exiting. Since it was the middle of the night, we didn't seem to attract any attention, but just in case, Jesus and I kept our faces well-hidden until we were outside the camp.

About a mile from my home, we all regrouped near the Mount of Olives. Then we fastened our eyes on the stars to the northeast and set off on the road to the wilderness. Since I could see better than anyone else in the dark, I took the lead of our small caravan, which consisted of twenty men, seven donkeys and of course my two dogs. What. . . ? You thought I would leave the dogs behind? Well, . . . I never!

I would have loved to bring my favorite horse, too, but the trails ahead were not ideally suited for a horse unless you were planning to fight. If you just wanted to travel, as was our intention, donkeys were the best beast for the job, unless you had some good camels, and unfortunately, all my camels were busy working with my trade caravans, so the donkeys would have to do.

The tiny town of Ephraim was about fifteen miles or so from Jerusalem, but the surrounding wilderness was an indistinct area that stretched for many miles in all directions from the town itself. Since we were trying to remain hidden, we needed to avoid contact with other travelers, so my goal was to travel through the night, and then make camp for the day, so we could sleep before traveling again the next night. The trick would be to find a place we could camp that was near the main trails, but also hidden from prying eyes.

The night passed without incident, and we managed to cover about nine miles before dawn, which wasn't bad considering the terrain. I had been watching for a suitable place to stop for the day, when I spotted a series of ledges jutting out from the base of a mountain in the distance. I led our small band there and found it was just what we needed. The ledges jutted out to provide shelter from the cool winds that tended to sweep through valleys such as this at this time of year. They also provided shadows that would allow us to move about without anyone on the trail seeing our movements. It wasn't as good a shelter as a cave would have provided, but it was close, and everyone was worn out except for me, so we made camp.

We ate a rough meal, and then everyone made a bed so they could sleep in peace throughout the day. I discreetly slipped out of my blankets and stood watch while the others snored the day away. As the sun was setting, I got everyone up and we prepared another rough meal. By sundown we were back on the trail again.

I knew we wouldn't have to travel far now to be deep enough into the wilderness to make a permanent camp for the duration of our stay here. I was hopeful to find some more accommodating ledges or possibly a cave we could use, and it would also be essential that we be within a reasonable distance of a reliable source of water.

The only problem with trying to find a cave in this wilderness is they were notorious for being the abode of crazy hermits. Most of the hermits were just insane jitterbugs and were probably more dangerous to themselves than to anyone else, but some of them were crazy like a fox and mean as a cross-eyed snake. Those were the ones you had to watch out for. You never knew when or in what direction they might strike, but sooner or later they would slit your throat and take everything you had, just because they could.

With all this in mind, I was carefully studying the surrounding terrain as we traveled. After we had covered approximately five miles, I was surprised when Jesus walked up beside me and announced, "Lazarus, we're there."

"We're where?" I looked around and saw absolutely nothing but more boring wilderness. "There's nothing here." I said.

"I recognize this place. I spent several days here after my baptism by John the Baptist. Follow me."

Without saying more, he turned left off the trail and began walking confidently into the brush. I called Horus over and handed him the reins to the donkey I'd been leading. "He thinks he knows where he is, so let me go see what he's talking about. Hold onto my critter, and watch my dogs. I'll be right back.

"Samson. . . Delilah. . . stay."

My dogs whimpered anxiously, but took a seat as commanded.

I followed Jesus several hundred yards off the trail even though I was sure he had no idea where he was going. Finally, he stopped. Then he looked at me and grinned. "Do you hear it?"

I tipped my head and aimed my right ear into the darkness and heard something indistinct in the distance. "I hear something all right, and it sounds like falling water."

Skipping away, he shouted over his shoulder, "Exactly."

I ran to keep up with him while trying to watch for snakes that might be lingering on the warm sand. I had always had a profound fear of snakes ever since one bit another boy in my village, and he blew up like a pufferfish until he looked like he would burst. I can still remember the way he screamed in the night from his anguish before he finally gave up the ghost. I didn't want to blow up, and I wasn't fond of the idea of screaming in anguish either, so throughout this trip I'd been keeping a close eye out for snakes. Honestly, I was more worried about stepping on a snake than I was encountering crazy hermits or blood-lusting bandits.

I followed him through a narrow gap between two huge boulders and suddenly we were standing in a small clearing surrounded by tall mountains and hills on all sides. There were a few scraggly trees and lots of boulders and jagged rocks but not much else to see. However, there were two features of this little gorge that made it highly attractive for our potential hiding place.

First, it had a long row of ledges jutting out from the base of the small mountain to the right that would provide excellent shelter, and second, it had a small waterfall that fell from a cliff high overhead. The water from the waterfall formed a small gurgling stream that ran for several yards before disappearing into the rocks.

I turned to Jesus and smiled. "I've got to hand it to you. When you started off the trail I thought this was going to be a wild goose chase, but you obviously really did remember this place somehow, and it's perfect for our hideout. It's far enough from the trail that no one should see or hear us while we're here. There's only one way in here unless you're a mountain goat, and that pass between the boulders, is nearly invisible and easily defendable. These overhanging ledges will provide some badly needed relief from the chilly winds, and that waterfall will provide us with water for our men and donkeys. If we're going to have to spend a week hiding out in the wilderness, I don't think we could have found a better place."

"I'm glad you approve. I especially like the waterfall. It reminds me of one I used to play in as a child. Now get everyone in here so we can set up camp, and then come see me. We need to talk."

He turned away from me and started peeling off his outer garments, so I assumed he might be intending to give himself a bit of a sponge bath by carefully wetting a rag in the waterfall, without getting soaked himself, and then using it to wipe away the dust and grime of the day.

I didn't need to see all of that, so I started walking back to our caravan, and just as I got to the hidden pass, I heard laughter behind me. I turned and saw Jesus standing nearly naked beneath the waterfall. It was practically freezing outside that night, and the water falling off the cliff had to be glacial, but he was standing there in the moonlight with his arms held out to either side while the icy water pounded his perfectly sculpted physique. He lifted his eyes to the sky and laughed like a lunatic, as if he didn't have a care in the world.

I shook my head and walked away muttering to myself, "Only Jesus. . . ."

CHAPTER TEN

It didn't take long to get everyone herded into our hiding place. Soon, each group of five had chosen an area beneath one of the ledges to serve as their campsite. Someone started a fire, and everyone gathered around to catch some of the warmth emanating from the flames. Someone else came forward with some salted meat we had brought for the trip, and it wasn't long before everyone was cooking up a dinner of sorts.

Even though I had no need to eat, I ate a few bites so no one would notice I wasn't eating my fair share anymore when we sat down to a meal. I managed to discreetly squirrel away a few choice cuts in my robes, so I called Samson and Delilah over and fed them while I wrestled with them.

Then, I noticed Jesus watching me playing with the dogs, and I remembered he had told me to seek him out once I got everyone settled into our campsite, so I made my way over to him and said, "You said you needed to talk to me."

"Yes, let's walk over by the waterfall where we can talk privately"

Once we were in there, he began to talk excitedly, "Thanks for bringing us here, but now there's something else you've got to do."

I looked all around us. "I can't imagine anything else I need to do tonight, unless you expect me to go hunt some wild game in the middle of the night."

"No, this isn't something you need to do for us; this is something you need to do for yourself."

"I have no clue what you're talking about, but you're welcome to get to the point anytime now."

"Lazarus, there are forces at work here that are greater than you and me. Our heavenly Father has designed a plan to provide salvation to our people and all of the people of the world. You and I are a part of that plan, and we must each play our part in the moments and days directly ahead of us to bring that plan to its conclusion. Your time has come to prepare yourself for the trials that await us."

"Look, I've told you I'm ready to do my part, just tell me what I need to do."

"I'm afraid the assignment I'm about to give you will make you doubt my sanity, so let me ask you something. Do you believe I have your best interests at heart?"

"Well, let's see . . . you've always been my best friend and my favorite cousin . . . we grew up practically as brothers . . . and oh, yeah . . . you raised me from the dead a few days ago, and gave me some amazing new abilities to boot. So, yeah, I'd say you kind of like me."

"He gave me a crooked smile and continued, "I need you to go on up the trail we've been traveling on tonight, until you get almost to the village of Shiloh. I believe you're familiar with it."

I laughed, "You know I'm familiar with it. That's the place my father was born, and he told me the name Shiloh means 'place of peace.' But why do you need me to go to Shiloh of all places, especially in the middle of the night?"

"You won't be going all the way into town. There's a cave just before you get there, and that's where you need to go. It'll be on your right as you follow the trail toward Shiloh. It's about halfway up a small mountain, but you can see the mouth of the cave from below if you watch carefully. I should probably warn you that it's not easily accessible, so getting there will require some climbing, but with your new abilities that shouldn't be a problem."

"And what do you need me to retrieve from this cave?"

"I'm not sending you there to get something exactly. Your first goal when you arrive will be to meet someone who abodes there."

"Someone who abodes there? You mean someone is living there?"

"Yes, his name is Enoch, and he lives in the cave. I met him when I was wondering around out here in the wilderness after my baptism."

"So what you're telling me is that you want me to travel several miles through this God-forsaken wilderness, at night, and find a cave I'll barely be able to see from the trail. Then, once I find this nearly invisible cave, I'm supposed to climb up the rocky face of the mountain, in the dark, and introduce myself to some loony cave hermit named Enoch. Is that what you're asking me to do?"

"Yes, that's it." Jesus replied.

"Well then, you're right, I do doubt your sanity. In fact, I think you've gone completely insane!"

"Oh, calm down. With your increased speed you can run there safely in just a little while. It shouldn't take you long at all. And your increased strength and agility will make climbing the hillside a breeze. As for Enoch, he's not nearly as crazy as he seems."

"Not nearly as crazy as he seems, huh? Well that gives me a lot of comfort, let me tell ya. He'll probably slit my throat the first time I turn my back on him."

"No, just tell him right away that I sent you, and he'll treat you with honor and respect. I promise."

"But why do I need to go meet this hermit? What possible good can it accomplish?"

"This is where you have to trust me. Enoch has his own role to play in the events that are unfolding. If your time with him goes well, he may choose to impart to you some very important information that will aid you in your endeavors in the future, and he may also choose to give you a mystical object that will give you a huge advantage in your fight against evil forces."

"You say 'if my time goes well with him' . . . so just how much *time* will I be spending with him?"

"Not much, it'll probably only take a couple of days."

"So a couple of days, as in two days, right?"

"Well, it could be three . . . or four . . . it just all depends."

"Four days living with a crazy hermit in a cave . . . are you kidding me?"

"Look, just do whatever he asks of you, and do your best to answer any questions he may have honestly, and everything should turn out well for you. It'll be over before you know it."

"So what if I don't do everything he asks of me, or what if I fail to answer all his questions honestly? Will everything still turn out well for me?"

"No, then he'll probably slit your throat the first time you turn your back on him."

"What?!"

"Just kidding. Everything's going to be fine. Now will you do it or not?"

I shrugged, "Yes, I'll do it, but you're gonna owe me big time for this."

He smiled and yet, somehow, still managed to look sad as he said, "Yes I will, and I promise I'll do something wonderful for you someday soon."

"Well then, I guess I'm off. Let me give Horus some instructions, and then I'll say goodbye. Just wait here for a moment, and I'll be right back."

I found Horus and pulled him aside from the other men. "Horus, Jesus has asked me to go to Shiloh and visit with someone there on his behalf. I may be gone a couple of days, or even three or four, so I need you to be in charge of security here. Keep one of our guards and one of the disciples on watch at the pass at all times. Don't let anyone leave our campsite until I return."

"You can count on me, Sir."

"You know you don't have to call me Sir, don't you? In fact, it feels really awkward to me."

"I know you don't expect it, but we're leaders of men who are warriors, and in times of war they need to know who's in charge. I'm trying to maintain the discipline of calling you Sir, so the men recognize you're my superior officer. That way, if we're ever in a battle together they won't hesitate to follow your orders."

"Well, okay then. I guess that makes sense, but it still feels awkward. Carry on."

I trotted over to Jesus. "Okay, I'm ready to go. Any final instructions?

"Yes, you can't take anything with you."

My hand went to my sword. "You mean I can't take any weapons?"

"No. No weapons."

I unbuckled my sword and laid it and my dagger at his feet. Then I pulled the necklace from my neck and handed to him.

He gave me an inquiring look as he held the ankh up. "This doesn't look like a weapon."

"Trust me. It is."

I looked around for my dogs. "Just let me find Samson and Delilah, and I'll be on my way."

He said, "You can't take anything with you."

"You mean I can't take my dogs?"

"No, no dogs."

He put his hand on my back and gently guided me to the pass between the boulders, and we stopped there and smiled at each other momentarily.

I started to walk away, and I heard him saying, "Lazarus, you can't take anything with you."

I turned and said, "I'm not taking anything. I don't need food or drink, I've given you my weapons, I've left my dogs behind, and I promise you I don't have anything hidden in my robes."

"That's just it . . . your robes."

I looked down at my clothes, and shook my head. "You can't possibly mean I've got to leave here naked . . . can you? I'll freeze to death out here without my robes."

"Sorry, I promise you won't freeze to death, but you can't take anything with you."

I turned away from him, and began to angrily strip away my clothing, and my shoes, and threw it all on the ground. When I had everything off, I turned and yelled, "I hope you're happy."

He was gone.

I looked all around and wondered how he had managed to slip away so quickly, but I was standing alone in a freezing, God-forsaken wilderness without a stitch of clothing.

So, I ran toward Shiloh. . . .

CHAPTER ELEVEN

I don't advise running through a wilderness at night without shoes. I soon found out that even though my new body had super human strength it still could feel pain, and soon I was feeling a lot of pain. First and foremost, there was the pain of running over ground that was nearly freezing, then there was the pain of thumping my toes on rocks and limbs that seemed to jump out of nowhere, and last but not least, there was the pain of stepping on sharp objects that kept finding ways to penetrate my hardened skin. I grew up not wearing any shoes or sandals for most of any given year as a boy. So by the time I was an adult, my feet were heavily calloused. In fact, even my calluses had calluses, and they stayed that way as I grew older. However, my hardened skin couldn't protect me from the hazards this terrain provided.

I stopped after a while and sat down on a boulder to look at my feet. They were both bleeding from several places, but as I watched in wonder my wounds healed themselves. Apparently, Jesus forgot to mention that my body could heal itself when he was telling me about my new abilities. This made me wonder what else he may not have told me. I looked around suspiciously, and wondered if my body could heal itself from a snake's bite. Then I jumped back up and started running again.

I also don't advise running through a wilderness naked at the speed of a horse. Not only was I freezing my butt and other unmentionables off, but I also kept running into thorn trees and thorn bushes and various species of cacti. Soon I was covered in blood from my various wounds, but thankfully, I apparently wasn't capable of bleeding to death since my injuries healed almost as rapidly as they happened.

After running several miles, I caught the smell of wood smoke wafting on the midnight air, and I realized I must be getting close to Shiloh. I slowed my pace and began looking carefully at the hillsides I was running by on the right side of the trail. And there it was. Just a smudge of black about halfway up a steep rocky hillside was all I could see from the trail, so I hopped on a huge boulder on the left side of the trail to get a better angle and the smudge became more of a blot. I was sure I was looking at a cave. As I gazed at the cave entrance someone came striding out and held a torch high up into the air. There was no doubt now. I could clearly see the cave entrance framed by the brightly burning torch. I couldn't tell much about the torch bearer, but they appeared to have an unruly head of hair.

I scouted around for a clear climbing path, but nothing looked particularly easy, so after a couple of false starts I decided I had to just bear down and keep going no matter what kind of obstacles I ran into. I was almost to the cave opening when I came face-to-face with my greatest fear. I had just pulled myself onto a ledge, and was rolling away from the edge, when I saw a huge snake lying under a rock that was jutting out over the ledge.

I knew that snakes were coldblooded, and had been taking some comfort in the fact that they normally go inside a lair or underground at night, but I also knew that sometimes they would spend the night under a rock that had been baking in the sun at the end of the day. Apparently that was the situation I had just stumbled upon. I found myself wondering again if my body was capable of healing itself from a snake's bite. I really didn't want to find out.

The snake was coiled tightly as if readying itself to strike, and I was laying helplessly on my belly staring into its eyes. My left side was facing the snake's lair and my left hand was between my face and the serpent. I decided to try to roll onto my back and away from the snake. I figured if I could quickly roll over twice I would be out of range of a strike, and could then swing my legs back over the ledge and abandon my perch.

Just as a started to roll the snake made its move. It struck directly at my face, and instinctively I snatched it out of the air by its neck with my left hand and continued rolling onto my back. I was momentarily impressed with how quickly I'd managed to snare it before it could latch onto me, but now I was laying on my back with a huge snake hissing in my face with bared fangs while it coiled around my arm and struggled with all its might to break free. Being impressed just wasn't going to get me out of this predicament. I needed to do something else.

So, I screamed bloody murder!

I screamed while I thrashed around on my back and butt, I screamed while I struggled to my feet, and I screamed when I pulled back my arm and prepared to try to throw the snake away, only to realize that would require me to let go of its head, and if it didn't let go of my arm, it would have a field day biting me at its leisure. The screaming really seemed to help . . . no, not really, but the thing that did finally help was when I pried the monster off my arm with my right hand by pulling on its tale. Once I had it pulled free from my arm, I held its head in my left hand and its tail in my right, and suddenly pulled each end in opposite directions. It snapped taunt in the middle and broke into two pieces.

I tossed the snake remains away and wiped away the bodily fluids it had left behind, but not without a good deal of revulsion. Just as I turned back to the task of finishing my climb, a big glob of something wet and sticky hit me in the face. Something that smelled suspiciously like. . . . "CRAP . . . who's throwing turds at me?"

I heard a wild cackle from above me, and a dark face encircled by a wild mane of hair poked out from the ledge just outside the cave entrance. After laughing crazily for a moment the owner of all that hair announced, "Don't worry, it's not mine, nope, it's not mine, it's just donkey dung. I collect it from the trail to share with idiots like you who try and visit my home. Yes. Yes, I do. Here, have some more."

With that said, he laughed even louder, and threw several more turds at me. I didn't have anywhere to retreat, so most of them hit their mark. I was contemplating giving up on this insanity, and heading back down to the trail when a desperate thought came to me, so I yelled, "Jesus sent me!"

My announcement didn't have the desired effect immediately, and more turds came raining down from above, so I yelled again, "Hey didn't you hear me, you crazy old fart? Jesus sent me!"

The hermit gave another wild cackle and shouted back. "Did you say Jesus sent you? Did you now? Well, who might you be?"

"I was shaking from the cold and from my encounter with the snake and half out of my own mind when I replied, "I might be Lazarus . . . I mean I'm Lazarus . . . that is . . . my name is Lazarus."

The donkey dung ceased flying, and there was a moment of welcome silence before the hermit exclaimed, "Well what are you doing hanging around on the rocks down there, fool. Come on up before you hurt yourself. Yes, you should. Yes. Yes. Yes, you should. Yes, you will."

With quivering limbs, I somehow managed to climb the last few feet to the ledge just outside the cave.

Before me stood a small one-armed man nearly as black as the night that surrounded us. About the only way to know exactly where he standing was to follow the whites of his eyes, when they occasionally peeked out from the massive mane of wild hair that bounced around crazily with his frenzied movements. He ran around me at least three times while uttering that incessant cackling sound that seemed to erupt without warning. In between cackling, he muttered repeatedly, "This is Lazarus, sent here by Jesus, oh yes, this is Lazarus, sent here by Jesus. Yes. Yes, it is. Yes. Yes, it is." A couple of times he jumped toward me, and leered at me with crazy eyes while barring his yellow teeth.

Around his midsection was a loincloth that offered the barest amount of covering. Over his shoulders and completely covering his back was a tattered fur vest of sorts, but it, too, looked barley adequate. Some type of fur, that looked suspiciously like rat hides, was tied loosely around his feet. The only other adornment he had was a bone necklace that seemed to be made up primarily of various teeth of uncertain origin, but hanging in the middle of the bones and teeth was a large sapphire jewel of obvious value. To say the least, the jewel looked strangely out of place.

I let him get a good look at me from all sides before I finally spoke. "Are you Enoch?"

He drew himself up proudly and replied, "Yes, I be. Yes, I am. Yes, I be. I'm Enoch. I'm Enoch, I am. That be me, it is."

"Pleased to meet you, Enoch. I smell smoke. Do you happen to have a fire inside your cave?"

He cackled, "Oh, I've got a fire okay. If I didn't have a fire I'd freeze to death up here. It gets cold up here, you know. Why, a man up here without a fire would . . . would . . . say . . . why are you naked?"

He drew back as if scared and moaned, "You're not in love with me are you?"

"Oh, heavens no," I think my entire body may have glowed red. "I'm naked because Jesus told me I had to come here this way."

"Well, why would he do that? Is he CRAAZZY or something?!"

"I don't know, but I'm freezing, could you take me to that fire?"

"Oh, I'll take you to my fire okay, yes I will, and I'll even give you some furs to put on, so you don't freeze your ass off, but first we need to get all that donkey dung and blood off you."

He pulled back as if he was scared again and spoke in a horrified tone, "What's that! You're . . . you're covered in blood! Oh my, covered in blood I say. Yep. Yep. Covered in blood. You've come to my home naked and covered with blood. Did you kill someone? What's wrong with you? Are you CRAAZZY or something?!"

"No, I didn't kill anyone. It's my blood. And I'm not crazy."

He looked at me like he didn't believe me, so I continued, "Okay, maybe I'm a little crazy, but not much. Not like some people anyway."

He ran around me a couple more times and asked, "If that's your blood where are your wounds. OH . . . I see, you must be bleeding from your back. Ow. Now that looks painful. You must be really hurting. Are you now?"

"No, I'm not bleeding from my back. Those are old wounds that are completely healed. They just look painful, but they actually don't hurt me at all anymore."

"Well then why are you so-o-o bloody. I don't see any other wounds. No I don't. Nope. No, I don't."

"I'm a fast healer."

He put his finger on his chin as if he was giving my claim serious thought, and then exclaimed, "Well, that explains that, now doesn't it?"

He grabbed one of my hands with his donkey dung paw, and pulled me toward the cave entrance. "Well don't just stand here all naked and bloody. Let's get you cleaned up and dressed. Yes. Let's do it. Let's do."

When we stepped inside the cave I was immediately surrounded by a warm envelope of air. I now know that the temperature in a cave is the same year-round as the average temperature of the air outside the cave, so that put the temperature inside the cave that night at around 53, which seemed balmy compared to the air I'd just ran naked through.

Nevertheless, I shuddered and shivered when he left me by the fire while he went to find some water. He returned momentarily with another torch in his hand, and a crude bucket of water clutched in the crook of his elbow just above the point where his missing arm ceased to exist. He gave me a dirty rag to clean myself with, and stood back watching me.

I motioned for him to turn away, and he finally got the message and left me with some privacy as he scurried away. Surprisingly, the remnants of my blood flaked away like dust instead of being brought back to life by adding water. It was as if I was wiping away trail dust instead of blood.

Enoch came back just as I was finishing cleaning up. He was carrying two bundles of furs and some short lengths of rope. He produced a dagger from somewhere, and suddenly jabbed it toward me before reversing the blade at the last moment and handing it to me by the hilt. "Here, you can use this to poke some holes in those hides, and then use the ropes to tie them on. Bring it all in here by the fire, and we'll get you dressed up in a hurry. Yes. Yes, we will."

He turned away casually, and left me holding the dagger, while he bent over and picked up one of the bundles of furs. In that moment, I could have easily murdered him if I had wanted to do him harm. I muttered to myself as he nearly bounced off the sides of the cave while walking away, "So far, so good. With a little luck, maybe he won't slit my throat after all."

We sat beside Enoch's fire, and he cackled and jibber-jabbered while I fitted myself with some of his rough furs. I even managed to make some makeshift sandals to give my feet some protection and comfort. He offered me some food and water of questionable origin, and I politely declined. This seemed to offend him briefly, but he quickly shook it off, and began to mutter some more incomprehensible gibberish.

I observed him out of the corner of my eye, and saw that his missing left arm was not something he had been born with. His hand, and part of his forearm, had been cleanly chopped off at some point in his life.

He shocked me when he spoke, "If you're wondering about my hand, they cut it off. Yes. Yes, they did."

"Why would anyone do that?"

He stared at the walls of the cave, as if he was trying to remember something, and then he whispered, "They said I was a thief, they did, but they lied. I'm not a thief. I only took what was mine." His hand went to the sapphire jewel hanging from his neck and he gripped it tightly. "Yes. Yes, it's true, it is. Enoch is not a thief."

"I'm sorry, who would do such a thing?"

He snatched his dagger from my hand, and waved it around angrily, as he hopped to his feet, and began to dance around the cave while jabbing his dagger at invisible enemies. "Don't you worry about those guys. If they come around here I'll slit their throats, and then I'll slit their donkey's throats, and their horse's throats. I'll slit everyone's throats! You'll see!! Yes, you will!"

"Whoa, simmer down my friend. There's no one here who wants to hurt you, so you're not going to need to slit any throats."

I gently grasped his arm, and somehow got him to settle down long enough to look him in the eye. "Trust me on this. You don't need to slit anyone's throat. Got it? Not *anyone.*"

He reluctantly nodded in agreement, so I let go of him, and he hopped around crazily again for a moment, and then the dagger disappeared inside the fur around his shoulders, and he flopped back down by the fire.

I saw a mound of blankets nearby, so I took a chance on trying to bring an end to the drama of the day. "Say, it's got to be after midnight by now, and I've had a rough day. I'm worn out, so if you've got an extra blanket or two I'd like to go to bed if you don't mind."

He bounced to his feet and began scurrying around until he had formed a crude but suitable bed on the opposite side of the fire from his own.

He gave me an annoyed look and said, "Stop that whistling, fool. That's annoying. Yes, it is."

"Oops, sorry about that. Sometimes when I'm nervous I do that without even realizing."

"What does Lazarus need to be nervous about? He has friend Enoch to protect him. Does he not?"

"You know, you're exactly right. I shouldn't be nervous at all with a brave friend like you to protect me while I sleep."

That seemed to please him immensely, and he stuck his thin chest out as he threw a couple of logs on the fire, so it would continue to provide light and warmth throughout the night, and then we both crawled into our beds.

I closed my eyes and pretended to sleep, but in reality I was waiting and watching for him to get up and come creeping toward me with his dagger.

Thankfully he never did. . . .

CHAPTER TWELVE

The next morning Enoch was up early, and I was relieved to no longer have to pretend sleeping, and to no longer have to keep watch for his dagger.

He puttered around and offered me more of his mystery meat for breakfast, but once again I politely declined. Then he took me out on the wide ledge outside the cave to help him gather some firewood from the dead trees that had fallen from above.

Once we were outside, I was amused at Enoch's obvious paranoia. He would pick up a few sticks of wood, and then stand looking up the rocky hillside as if he expected some hidden enemy to come leaping out of the boulders and brush.

I was surprised to find that in the light of day he looked younger than I had surmised in the indistinct light of last night's campfire. I had assumed he was ancient, but now I guessed him to be around 45, which was still considered pretty old in those days. I also saw that the blackness of his skin was augmented by the soot and grime he had accumulated all over his body.

As we gathered the firewood he asked me how I knew Jesus, and I told him we were cousins, and how he had raised me from the dead a few days ago. He asked me what it felt like to be dead, and he wanted to know if I'd felt any different since my resurrection.

I politely tried to answer his questions, and after we had gathered a few loads of firewood and neatly stacked them inside the cave, I posed a question of my own, "You know, when Jesus told me to come here he said I should do whatever you told me to do when I got here, so that made me think, maybe there was something you needed me to do."

He looked at me and asked, "So that's what this Jesus person says does he? That you should do whatever I say? It is, is it now?"

"Yes, that's exactly what he told me, so is there something you need me to do?"

Enoch jumped to his feet and began to bounce and jabber, "He do what I say. Yes, he do. Yes, he will. Yes, he shall. He do what I say."

He grabbed the torch from beside the fire, hooked my elbow with the crook of his crippled arm, and began to pull me outside. He left the torch in its usual place near the entrance, and continued skipping into the sunlight. When we got out on the ledge he let me go and bounced around excitedly. "He do what I say. Yes, he do. Yes, he will."

Then he threw his arms wide and proclaimed, "We play Enoch says! I say it, and you do it. Yes, I will. Yes, you do."

"Well, okay then; how does this work?'

"It EEAASY. Enoch say it, and you do it. Yes, I will. Yes, you do."

"Okay then, let's get started. Tell me what to do."

Enoch SAYS. . . pick up that rock."

He pointed to a rock about the size of a large dog. Most men couldn't have picked up a rock that big, and until now, neither could I, but now I picked it up with ease and held it in my arms. "So, what now?"

"Enoch SAYS. . . throw rock over the side."

I got a running start and heaved the rock over the side of the ledge and it tumbled down the side of the mountain.

Enoch laughed and ran around in circles.

"Okay, what's next?" By now I had resigned myself to doing stupid stuff until the sun went down. Then I was out of here. I had no idea what Jesus was thinking when he sent me here. Maybe it was just a big joke. Ha! Ha! Lazarus ran through the wilderness naked, and spent all day doing stupid stuff with a crazy cave hermit. I'd probably never live it down.

"Enoch SAYS. . . get you a present from the treasure room."

"What? I'm sorry, but I don't know what you mean."

That set him off and he started to jump around and jibber-jabber a bunch of gibberish that didn't make any sense to me. Finally he said something I could understand, "Enoch says go get you a present from the treasure room, and bring it here, so he can see. You go to treasure room, yes, yes you do."

"But I don't know where this treasure room is."

"It's in the cave just past the fire, fool. Everyone knows that. Just ask the bats. They know. Yes, yes they do."

"Okay, so you want me to go to this treasure room, and pick out a present for myself, and then bring it back for you to see?"

"Yes. Enoch says, so you do."

"Okay, just calm down I'm going. I really am."

I quickly grabbed the torch and made my way to the room where we had our fire. There was only one way in and one way out, so it wasn't like I could get lost. Once I got there I looked at the passage that continued on into the dark, and I wondered how dependable my torch was. I would hate to get stuck in a cave with no light. I took a deep breath, and stepped into the darkness. I didn't have to go far before I came to a hole in the wall to my right. It was too low down for me to walk through, even when I stooped down, so I got on my hands and knees and wiggled through the opening, until it opened up into a new room. The first thing I noticed was the smell was almost overwhelming. The second thing I noticed was the further I crawled into the room, the more my hands and knees seemed to be sinking into the stinky mud on the floor.

Wait a minute . . . . Stinky mud on the floor? I smelled one of my hands and nearly cursed, "Oh, no ... not again!" I stood and held my torch high, and the ceiling overhead seemed to move in a restless wave. There were bats everywhere. And I do mean everywhere. There were thousands of them. I looked at the floor of the cave, and realized I had been crawling in bat guano, and now I was standing in it. But on the other side of the room was a rocky ledge that poked out from the cave wall several feet, at about the height of a tall man, and under that rock, there were no bats. No, under that rock was nothing but treasure! Lots of treasure!!

There were small baskets of gold and precious jewels of all types. There were beautifully gilded swords and daggers. There were a couple of bejeweled crowns that looked fit for a king. There were garments lined with precious materials and decorated with jewels. There were golden chalices, candlesticks, and goblets.

Maybe Enoch was a thief after all. . . . Curiously, mixed in with the golden vessels there was a green cup of heavy pottery. It seemed so out of place I just had to pick it up. I held it up to the light to try and determine what would make it valuable enough to be here with items that were nearly priceless. I was surprised when the light of my torch revealed the transparent nature of the pottery. I could actually see my hand on the other side. While the material the cup was made of was curious and luminous in the torchlight, it still seemed pretty ordinary compared to the other precious items surrounding it.

Still, I considered making it my choice, but there were many other items to consider, so I decided to look further and delay my decision. I placed the cup back where I'd found it and started to look around. That's when I saw something even more curious. It was a wooden walking staff that stuck out like a sore thumb in the midst of all the other finery surrounding it.

Not that the staff wasn't well made. It had obviously been carefully hewn out of a rich wood I'd never seen before, and someone had carved the image of a snake that coiled around the bottom and climbed up until it reached about the halfway point. At that juncture there was a curious hole in the side of the staff that the image of the serpent seemed to be reaching for.

Something seemed to draw me to it, and without really thinking about what I was doing, I picked it up, and hefted it in my hand. It was surprisingly heavy, and I wondered if it had been loaded with something inside to make it useful as a cudgel. Looking closer I saw the head of the cane was made out of a bronze-like material, and formed in the shape of some type of weird looking beast I could only describe as a snake's head. The mouth of the beast was closed, and I was glad for that. I was shaking at just the thought of what the inside of that mouth might look like, and the ruby eyes of the creature seemed to sear me to the soul as they gleamed in the smoky silence.

Just then, a bat decided to do a flyby near my head, and as it flew in front of my face I jumped and squealed like a baby. I nearly dropped the staff, and my torch, which could have been a disaster, but luckily I held onto both.

I gripped both the torch and the staff a bit tighter for fear of dropping them, and when I did, the staff seemed to tremble in my hand, and I thought I heard a voice in my head in some foreign language. Although it wasn't a tongue I had ever encountered in my many travels, somehow, I could still understand it. It said, "Come to me Lazarus. Yes, you do. Yes, you should. Yes, you will."

I quickly set the staff back where I'd found it among the treasure trove and backed away. I was preparing to get the heck out of there when I remembered Enoch's instructions. I was to go to the treasure room, pick out a present for myself, and bring it back for him to see.

My eyes darted over the items before me and settled on the gilded weapons. My father's business specialized in mining rare and precious minerals, which were often mixed together and used to make fine weapons like these. They were then edged and adorned with gold by skilled craftsmen in the same way these had been made. I had seen many fine weapons made this way, but none were as fine as these. They even had jewels on their already impressive hilts. I would love to have one of these.

I was checking out the edge of one of the swords when my eye was drawn to something sticking out of the pile of treasure. It was a leather bag of some sort with a strap that could be used to carry it over one's shoulder. I wondered what such a crude piece of luggage was doing among such valuable treasure. I opened it and found something that only I, in my present predicament, would call a treasure. The bag was stuffed with writing utensils. I took a closer look at the bag and realized it was curiously very similar to the bag Jesus had given me as a present just a couple of days ago. Inside, there were several sheets of fine papyrus and even some of the strange writing material that resembled vellum just like the ones Jesus had given me. There were several bamboo reed pens and an ample supply of ink. I knew I had found my present, so I snapped it shut, tucked it inside my fur jerkin, and mucked my way back to the main passageway of the cave.

I turned left and hurried past the fire and found Enoch waiting anxiously on the ledge. He ran around me in his usual animated fashion and hammered me with questions. "So, what did you choose? Was it a jewel or a bar of gold? I don't see a crown on your silly head, so was it a pretty sword or dagger? What? What is it? What may it be?"

He finally skidded to a stop, so I slapped the remaining bat guano from my hands, and reaching inside my furs I produced the leather bag. He looked at me with a great deal of consternation at first, and then cackled, and smiled broadly as he grabbed it from my hands, and began to crow, "Oh, Lazarus is a sly man, he is. He found a bag and filled it to the brim with treasure. Why take a little, when you can take a lot. Lazarus is sly, he is."

He opened the bag, peered inside, and spoke in a bewildered tone, "What's this stuff, fool? Where's the treasure?"

"To me that is a treasure. I usually write my thoughts down every day, and I haven't been able to do that lately. I'm looking forward to catching up on my writing."

He angrily threw the bag at me, and shouted, "Writing? Who wants to write? Lazarus must be CRAAZZY or something."

I picked up the bag and hung it from my shoulder. "Look, you told me to choose a present for myself, and bring it back here to show you, so I'm playing the game just the way you told me to."

He put his finger to his chin and thought hard before saying, "Well, that explains that; but here, this will make your present better." He shuffled over and pulled a small bag from underneath the fur around his shoulders. He rudely snatched my bag open and tossed his bag in with a jingle. "There, now Enoch made your present better by adding gold and jewels. Yes. Yes, he does."

"Well, okay then. So, now it's time to tell me something else to do." I was hopeful he would move on to a new subject before he considered slitting my throat for bringing him such a pitiful choice as my present.

He strutted around me, as if considering his options, until his circuit took him near the edge of the ledge where it overlooked the trail below. He peered over the edge and bellowed, "Enoch SAYS. . . rescue the man."

I said, "What man?"

Enoch pointed down at the trail. "That man, fool."

I walked up beside him and looked where he was pointing. On the trail below was a man leading a heavy laden donkey. He was trying to get the beast to move faster, but it wasn't cooperating. Running down the trail in hot pursuit was a group of four haggard men. As I watched, the bandits closed the gap and began to joust with the traveler, as he utilized his walking staff to keep them at bay. He was valiant in his efforts, but they were coming from all sides and soon one of them tripped him up, and he went down hard. Like a pack of jackals, they rushed in and begin to kick and prod him mercilessly.

From beside me I heard Enoch say, "Enoch SAYS. . . rescue the man." As he finished his proclamation he gave me a hard shove, and suddenly I was flying through the air as the rocks below rushed up to meet me along with a sure and sudden death.

⇥ ⇤

I immediately began to scream like a wounded banshee, and seemed to fall forever before I cascaded through a tree that was growing almost sideways out of the rocky hillside. When I came out the other side, I bounced painfully a couple of times before finally rolling to a stop beside the trail. I had fully expected to die when my flight began, but now I was surprised to find that nothing appeared to be broken or badly damaged. I was bleeding from a few places, but knew from past experience that wasn't a problem.

Looking around, I realized the bandits were only a few feet away. Obviously, they had stopped battering their victim and watched in shock and wonder as an apparent madman jumped off the cliff above them and came bouncing down the hillside. They weren't sure what to do about me, and I wasn't sure what to do about them.

I looked down at my furry appearance, and decided to play the crazy cave-hermit card by saying, "You guys had better run away because I'm Enoch, and I slit the throats of bandits and hooligans like you. Yes, I do. Yes, I will. Yes, I shall. I'm crazy as a loon, and there's no telling what I'll do next. Nope, no there isn't." I bounced around a great deal, and even ran in a circle a couple of times while I was delivering my lines, but the bandits weren't buying it.

They looked at each other, and then rushed me as a group, without even conferring about it.

I hunched down, and let the lead man's weight and momentum wash over me as I grabbed him by his robe and gracefully rolled to my back while putting my right foot in his gut and flipping him nearly ten feet in the air. I continued through my backwards flip and came to my feet just in time to side-step the next man while snapping an elbow into his jaw. I heard it break like a rotten tree limb, and he went down screaming. The other two were slower on their feet, so they hadn't quite caught up to where the fight was taking place, which probably saved their lives. I was starting to warm up, and I was getting mad now, so things were only going to get worse for anyone who messed with me going forward.

They saw something in my eyes, and decided maybe they should call it a day, which was probably the smartest thing they'd done in a while, considering what I'd just done to their friends. They watched me warily while they helped their friends up. One of them ran over to the donkey and grabbed a couple of bags from its back, and then the four of them stumbled back up the trail in the direction of Shiloh.

I adjusted my bag, which was miraculously still hanging from my shoulder, and glanced over at the traveler I'd been ordered to rescue. I could hear a good heartbeat, so apparently my rescue attempt still had a chance of succeeding.

As I walked over, he began to moan and groan, which I took as a sign that he might live to travel another day. I went to his mule and found a flask of water, so I brought that to him and splashed some in his face. He sputtered, opened his eyes, and mumbled, "Would you hit a man while he's down? At least let me get to my feet, and give me a chance at a fair fight, ya bastards."

"I'm not one of the men who attacked you, friend, but I'll help you to your feet, if you think you can stay up."

He looked at me like he wasn't sure I was telling the truth, but then allowed me to pull him to his feet.

He looked down the dusty trail and saw the bandits fading into the distance. He then took the flask of water I offered and shambled over to a boulder where he sat down. "Don't know where ya came from mister, but you're an answer to my prayers, I'd say. I saw those fellows following me a ways back, and suspected they were up to no good. When they began to run after me I starting praying for deliverance, or a faster donkey. Now, a faster donkey would have been nice, *if* I was into betting on donkey races, but I'm not, so I'd say I got my top choice. Don't know how you managed to get the best of four men, but I'm much obliged."

I walked over to another nearby boulder and sat down across from him. "Do you mind telling me what you're doing traveling this trail alone? This isn't the safest place to be, you know."

He chuckled, "You can say that again. I was supposed to be traveling with a group of men, but they backed out of the trip at the last minute. I couldn't afford to wait, so I came on alone. I'm pretty sure one of those guys just now was in the group that canceled on me, so I'd say it was a setup."

"Sounds about right to me, so what was so important that it couldn't wait?'

He laughed ruefully, "Now that's a long story."

"Well it seems to me, you're going to need to recuperate a little while before you hit the trail again, and I've got nothing better to do, so why don't you entertain me with your story."

"Are you sure? Well, you asked for it, so here goes. It all started when I was a young man. My father was a fairly wealthy man who made his living loaning money to other people in the town of Jericho. Most of his loans were made to businessmen to help them expand their business ventures. When I came of age to enter the family business, I offered a loan to a shopkeeper I'd known for years. This man specialized in luxury goods, so his inventory was quite expensive to maintain. Someone broke into his shop, and stole a good deal of his goods, and he came to my father to ask for a loan to restock. I was assigned to deal with the shopkeeper, whose name was Marcus, and I saw an opportunity to take advantage of the situation. When we were sealing our deal I swore by Heaven that I wouldn't call his loan due for a full year, but oaths are not technically binding according to our religious laws unless they are made in one of several derivatives of God's holy name. As you probably know, we aren't allowed to speak the formal name of God, so our esteemed rabbis have come up with a number of substitute names we can use when we make oaths to one another.

"However, our sly and shifty rabbis had also decided that unless an oath was made on one of their approved names it wasn't binding at all. An oath sworn on Heaven wasn't a binding oath, but Marcus wasn't aware of that. He and his family were recent Jewish converts from another country who had come to make their home near Jerusalem, so they could easily take part in the religious festivals of their new faith. They didn't have any family or friends to warn them of how things were done, so I waited until he had invested my loan, and every other dime he had, in restocking his store, and then I demanded he repay me immediately.

"Of course, there was no way he could do that, so he and his family were forced out into the street to live as beggars. He and his wife were too old to work as laborers, and he only had one daughter. Her name was Miriam, and as you know, a single woman without means in our society often has to make her living as a prostitute. I had always had a crush on Miriam, but I'd been too shy to tell her of my feelings. Now, I was thinking if I offered to marry her she'd be forced to return my affection to save herself and her family.

I was young and stupid back then, and probably haven't gained a lot of wisdom in the meantime, but looking back I see how foolish I truly was. On the day her family was forced into the street I approached her and made my awkward proposal."

He looked as if he was about to burst into tears, so I had to say something to break the uncomfortable silence. "I take it that didn't go too well?"

He shook his head, "Yeah, you could say that. She laughed at me, spit in my face, and slapped me so hard I still see stars sometimes. Then she took the hands of her parents and they marched away with their heads held high. I never saw her parents again.

"Then a really strange thing happened. A couple of years ago, I was in Jerusalem for the feast of tabernacles listening to a miracle worker and teacher named Jesus teach on the steps of the temple. A group of scribes and Pharisees brought a woman and threw her at Jesus feet. One of the scribes announced the woman in question had been taken in the very act of adultery, which was a polite way of saying they'd busted a prostitute servicing a customer. Then he asked Jesus, 'Now teacher, in the law of Moses, we're commanded that a woman such as this should be stoned, but what do you say?'"

"Now let me tell you, I was a devout practitioner of our faith. I tried desperately to do everything according to our religious laws, so when I heard what they said, I assumed this Jesus guy would be all for it, so I was looking around for a rock or two. If there was going to be a stoning I was sure gonna get my licks in.

"But then Jesus did something no one expected. He squatted down and began writing in the dust, as if he didn't even hear what the scribes and Pharisees were saying. I tried to get close enough to see what he was writing, but there were too many people in the way. Apparently no one else was sure what he was writing, or else each one saw something different according to their own nature. I heard someone say he had just written, 'Where is the man?' Then someone else said he was writing something like, 'Do to others as you would have them do to you.' Another person in the crowd said he wrote, 'When you do something to the least of these, you do it to me.'"

"I don't know what he wrote, but the Pharisees were determined to try and trip him up I guess because they wouldn't shut up. They just kept pressing him for an answer, so after a while he stood up and said, 'Let he who is without sin cast the first stone.'"

"Now, by then, I had a rock in each hand, and I was ready to get down to business. I was surprised that all the other people, including the scribes and Pharisees, were just hanging their heads in shame. I had paid my tithes on time and made my sacrifices at the temple like clockwork. I was as righteous as a man could be according to the law, and if no one else was going to take care of this prostitute scum I figured I'd do it myself.

"I made my way to the front of the crowd, and wound up to make my first throw at the helpless woman lying on the ground, and about that time she looked up at me.

"And I saw . . . it was Miriam. My Miriam!"

He couldn't hold back the tears any longer, so he cried freely as he continued, "All my illusions of righteousness disappeared in an instant when I saw her face. She was still beautiful after all those years, but her beauty had been hardened by the life she'd been forced to live. She looked me in the eye, and I'm sure she recognized me. At that moment something inside my soul shattered, and I just wanted to die.

"Meanwhile, all the people, beginning with the oldest down to the youngest, had dropped their rocks, and their heads, and wandered away in shame. Jesus got up from where he'd been writing some more in the sand, and he spoke gently to Miriam, "Ma'am, where are your accusers. Has no one condemned you?"

"She hung her head and said, "No one has, Lord."

"And he said, 'Neither do I condemn you. Go and sin no more.'"

"Miriam jumped up and ran like a scalded cat to get away from the crowd before someone changed their mind, and I just sat there helplessly and watched her. My body refused to function. All I could do was think about those words Jesus had just spoken to Miriam. He'd said, 'Neither do I condemn you.' And mister, let me tell you, I would have given anything if he would have said those same words to me.

"All my delusions of grandeur regarding my righteousness were completely gone now, and I felt about as low as dirt. I was sure I was going to Hell when I died, and I didn't think there was anything I could do about it.

"Just then Jesus began to teach again, and he told us he was the light of the world. He said he'd been sent into the world by our heavenly Father to help us see the truth about how God really wanted us to live our lives. He said if we believed in him as the Son of God we could have everlasting life when this life ended. I had heard people saying he was the Messiah, but that didn't seem to be what he was getting at. He was saying there was a life beyond this life, and we could stake a claim to it if we trusted in him instead of in our puny laws and rituals, and our own ability to be righteous in the sight of God.

"Right then and there I gave up trying to be righteous by my own abilities, and I prayed to God and told him I believed he had sent Jesus his son to show us how to really please him with our lives. Now mister, you can say I'm crazy, but when I got up off my knees something had changed inside of me. I felt clean and whole like I'd never felt before. And I knew what I had to do.

"I ran around talking to the scribes and Pharisees about where they had found the prostitute, and I soon found out which pimp she was working for. I looked for them, but they had both left town in a hurry out of fear of the religious elders.

"I sold everything I had, and set out on a journey to find Miriam. For two years I've been following her, and I won't quit until I find her, buy her out of slavery, and set her free once and for all. If it's the last thing I do, I'm going to rescue her from the life *my* sin caused her to have to live."

"Do you really think you're ever going to find her? It's a big world out there, and there are prostitutes working in nearly all the towns." I said.

"I've been hot on her trail a couple of times, but she always moved on just before I got to her. This time I think I'm really going to find her. I know for sure she's owned by a slave trader and pimp named Uriah, and he's having her brought to Jerusalem to offer her services for the Passover week, which begins in just a few days. I know this whole quest I've been on probably sounds crazy, but I'm going to find her this time. I just know I am.

"And now, you're really going to think I'm crazy, but if she'll still have me, I'll marry her and make her my wife, and take care of her for the rest of her life."

"And what if she doesn't want to marry you? What you did was pretty bad. She might not be able to forgive and forget, you know."

"Then at least she'll be free, and I'll give her every last dime I have to help her on her way."

Suddenly, a look of concern darkened his features and he jumped up from his rock and rushed to his donkey. "Speaking of every last dime I have…"

He searched frantically through his belongings for something that was obviously very important and very missing. "Oh, no!! It can't be! Did you see if those fellows took anything before they ran for the hills?"

"Yeah, one of them grabbed a couple of bags before they took off."

He went to his knees, hung his head, and said, "They took all my money. Now it doesn't matter if I find her, I'll never be able to buy her freedom."

⊨+ +⊨

I looked into the distance, but there was no sign of the fleeing bandits. They were long gone. Feeling guilty I said, "I could go after them, and try to get it back."

"No I can't let you do that. You've done more than anyone could expect already. Getting you killed isn't going to help matters now."

I rested my hand on my writing bag, and was trying to think of something comforting to say, when I suddenly remembered Enoch putting something in my bag just before he pushed me over the cliff. I opened my writing bag hurriedly, and found the smaller bag Enoch had given me. I was surprised at how heavy it was.

I held it out to the traveler and said, "I think I may be able to help. Hold out your hands, sir."

The traveler was still on his knees, but he looked up at me quizzically, and then held his hands together to make a bowl of sorts. I opened the small bag and poured its contents into his hands.

Several gold bars, each about the size of a finger, poured into his hands along with an assortment of sparkling jewels. We both looked in awe at the treasure he held.

He sputtered and finally managed to speak, "Where in the world did you get this?" He looked at my rough furs and continued, "Did you steal this?"

I shook my head adamantly, "No, I promise you it was freely given to me, and now I'm giving it to you. I want you to go find Miriam, pay for her freedom, and start a new life with her. It looks like there's enough there to take care of both your needs for a long time."

"How can this be? I can never repay you. My father died some time ago, and while my mother lives in a nice big home in Jerusalem, even she doesn't have the resources to repay this amount. This is a huge fortune."

"Yes it is, so let's put it back in the bag before we lose any of it, and may I suggest you spread it around among your belongings, and on your person this time, so no one can wipe you out by just grabbing a couple of bags off your donkey."

"Good idea, that was foolish of me."

He walked over to his donkey and began to distribute his wealth in various places. While he worked, I posed a question, "If you don't mind me asking, if you find Miriam, where will you go from there, and what will you do?"

"Well, one thing's for sure. I can't take Miriam to my mother's house. She's somewhat of a snobbish socialite among the Jewish women in Jerusalem, and she would never agree to have a former prostitute living under her roof. To be honest, she's not too fond of me anymore either, since she doesn't understand this quest I've been on. I'm hoping that will change, but for now, we're somewhat estranged.

"As for what I'll do, I'd like to find Jesus, and start keeping a journal of the things he says and does. I think he's destined for big things, and someday a book about his life could be valuable."

"I think I can help you with that. Hold on for a minute or two."

I sat back down on my boulder, opened my writing bag, and spread my utensils out. Once I had everything ready. I composed a letter to Darius.

> *Darius*
>
> *Please take the man bearing this note (and his female companion) into our household. Give them suitable jobs of their liking, and pay them 2 denarii per day in wages. See that they are given clothes, and anything else they need, and treat them with the utmost respect until I return.*
>
> *Thank you for your faithful service*
> *Lazarus*

I handed the note to the traveler and said, "Once you've freed Miriam, go to Bethany just outside of Jerusalem. Ask for directions to the home of Lazarus, the caravan man. When you get there, ask for my steward Darius, and give him this note."

He read my note and said, "Mister, you don't have to give us jobs. I think the treasure you've just given me will suffice for many years to come, and besides 2 denarii a day is twice the going wage for a common laborer."

"I pay everyone in my service above average wages, and besides, you're going to be performing a special service for me. You just don't know it yet."

"I don't understand. What could I possibly do for you?"

I smiled and said, "You say you want to find Jesus, and write a book about the things he says and does. Well, I think that's a spectacular idea, and Jesus just happens to be my cousin. When I return to Bethany in a few days, he'll be with me. He plans on staying with me through Passover week, so here's your opportunity to start keeping a record of his sayings and actions. What do you say?"

The traveler beamed, "I say meeting you today has been a miraculous experience. I can't thank you enough for all you've done, and I'm more confident than ever I'm going to find Miriam. It just seems it's meant to be."

He shook my hand and said, "I hope you don't mind if I head on down the trail now, I'm feeling much better, and I'm anxious to get to Jerusalem. If I travel through the night, I can get there tomorrow."

"By all means, you should get going, and traveling by night may help you avoid bandits. Be careful, and I'll see you in a few days."

"Thank you, Lazarus."

He started to walk away, and something occurred to me, so I called after him, "Say, I just realized, I don't even know your name."

He yelled back, "Most people call me John, but my parents gave me another name of Mark also."

"Very well, then I shall call you John Mark. Go with God, John Mark. Go with God!"

And he did . . . .

CHAPTER THIRTEEN

I scrambled back up the hillside and found Enoch studying the rocks and brush on the hillside above our cave. Once he realized I was there, he bounced over and began to fire questions at me. "Did you rescue the man? Did you? Tell Enoch all about it. Tell him, you must. Tell me. Tell him now, you must! Tell us all!"

"Are you kidding? Weren't you watching? Or maybe you were too busy practicing pushing people off your cliff when they least expect it. I nearly died, you know."

He ran around me a couple of times and said, "You look good to me. You still have both your arms, and both your legs, and all your eyes, and ears, and toes, and nose. Don't be silly; you didn't almost die. No, you didn't. No, you don't."

"Well, I could have. Not only was it quite a fall, I also had to fight four men."

"You only had to fight two men, the other two ran like scared bunny rabbits. They did. Yes, they did."

"So you were watching! Then why are you asking me if I rescued the man, when you saw me rescue him?"

"You chased away the bad men, but then you talked to the other man a long time, so did you rescue him, or not? Did you, or did you not?"

"He needed help to try to buy the freedom of a woman he's been looking for over the last two years, so I gave him the bag of treasure you gave me, and I offered him a home and a job, once he finds her."

Enoch put his finger on his chin, and considered all of this, before he cackled and shouted, "Oh, you rescued him REEAAL good! Yes, yes you did. Lazarus rescued the man GOOOD. He did!" He clapped and bounced so enthusiastically I thought he might bounce off the cliff, but then he regained his composure and went on, "Lazarus did good rescuing the man, so now we can keep playing our game."

"Whoa! Now, don't you think we've played enough for one day?"

"Oh, NOOO! Lazarus has only begun. He must finish playing Enoch Says. He must."

I thought about Jesus' instructions to do whatever I was told and decided to relent. After all, how much worse could it get? I'd already crawled through bat-guano, been pushed off a cliff, and fought blood-thirsty bandits. It couldn't get any worse than that . . . could it? "Okay, then let's get on with it. What do you want me to do now?"

"Enoch SAYS. . . bring him a drink from the magic pool."

"What? What magic pool? The only water I've seen around here is in that little stream that runs down the hillside over there. I assume that's where you get your drinking water from, but there's certainly no magic pool out here."

"Magic pool is not outside, fool. Magic pool is in cave. You take this cup and bring Enoch a drink from magic pool. He reached under the fur around his shoulders and produced a cup, which he excitedly offered me.

I shook my head in wonder. "What else have you got under that fur?"

Enoch looked confused. "What's that you say?"

"Never mind, just give me the cup and tell me where to find this magic pool." I was amazed when he handed me the cup, to see that it was the same transparent green cup I'd seen in the treasure room earlier.

"Magic pool is just past treasure room. You go now Lazarus, you go."

Never one to argue with a crazy cave hermit, I grabbed the torch, that never seemed to go out from its perch at the entrance to the cave, and made my way to the entrance of the treasure room.

Standing in the main passageway, I stared into the oppressive darkness ahead and wondered again about the reliability of my torch. I'd never seen a torch that kept burning all the time, but then I'd never seen a treasure trove in a cavern full of bat guano either. It seemed my life was becoming an endless succession of absurd impossibilities piled onto one unfeasible occurrence after another. Maybe this was how my life was supposed to be now. So I put one foot in front of the other and went to find Enoch's magic pool.

I didn't have to go far to find it. The passageway kept closing in on me until my shoulders were nearly touching the sides, and I could barely stand up straight. Then the passage came to an abrupt halt. Or at least it appeared that way. I could see a wall of rock directly ahead, but upon closer examination I found the passageway continued in a sharp turn to the right. I squirmed through the tight turn and found myself standing in a room so vast I couldn't see the ceiling overhead.

I listened closely, and thought I heard water running in the distance, so I ventured a few steps further into the abyss. Now I was certain I heard running water directly ahead, so I stepped forward with renewed confidence, and there it was. Or, should I say, there *they* were. There were actually two pools. The one to my right was overflowing with water that gave off a mist of steam as it rose up from some unknown source underground and met the cool cave air. I walked closer and reached down to touch the stream of water running from this pool and found it to be surprisingly warm to the touch. The warm stream from the overflowing pool ran downhill to the other pool where it swirled about in an eerily greenish yellow whirlpool before apparently disappearing back into the ground.

I looked from one pool to the other, and wondered which one Enoch considered the magic pool. Would he even know if I brought him a drink from the wrong pool? Did the water from the two pools somehow taste differently?

I was pondering these questions when I began to notice I was hearing a voice in my head again, kind of like when I was in the treasure room holding the walking staff. Or was it two voices . . . or many voices? No, it was definitely several voices, and something about these voices filled me with a terrible sense of fear and dread. I suddenly had an overwhelming feeling I was in the presence of something horribly sinister and evil.

It seemed like the voices were far away, but in the general direction of the pool where the water was disappearing into the ground. Something about that pool was more fascinating to me, so I took a step closer and something stirred in the water.

Whatever it was, I realized it could have been there the whole time. Maybe it was a beast that had been waiting just beneath the surface for me to get closer, or maybe it wasn't underneath the water at all. Maybe it was a snake churning its way across the water before it leaped out to bite me.

With a trembling hand I raised my torch higher to get a better look, and a woman rose up out of the pool and stood there before me. As the water cascaded from her body I immediately realized three things: she was stunningly beautiful, rapturously attractive, and very naked.

I knew all of this without even seeing her face because her back was to me. Just my luck, I guess. Anyway, as the water drained away, my eyes were drawn to a brilliant tattoo emblazoned on the dark skin of her back in vivid colors. It was an image of the sun interposed within a half-moon. I also couldn't help but notice the inside of each of her hands was discolored and badly scarred.

I was entranced as I listened to the strangely alluring drumming of her heartbeat. I was trying to figure out if I should announce my presence, when she suddenly spoke, "Do you want to see more?"

Well, to tell the truth, I really did, but I was engaged to be married in just a few days, and Iris would scratch my eyes out if she ever found out. Besides that, in my travels I had heard stories of a monster named Medusa.

I'd been told Medusa was a beautiful woman with snakes in her hair, or maybe the legends said she was an extremely ugly woman, but in any case she had snakes in her hair, and if a man looked into her eyes he immediately turned to stone. I couldn't see any snakes on her head, but I wasn't going to stick around to see if they were there. I dropped the cup and ran out of the room as fast as my legs would carry me without daring to look back.

I came dashing out of the cave to find Enoch studying the hillside again. He immediately bounded over and looked at me disapprovingly. "Where's my cup, and where's my drink of water from the magic pool? Did you so soon forget what Enoch told you to do? Did you now?"

"No, I didn't forget, but there's a naked woman swimming around in your pool, and . . . and well, I think she may be a monster!"

Enoch really got a kick out of that one. He literally got down and rolled on the ground cackling and laughing. Then he got up and ran around me several times. "Lazarus saw a naked woman and nearly died of fright. Yes, he did. He say, 'she's a monster', yes, he does, yes, he do. Lazarus is CRAAZZY. Yes, he is."

He finally skidded to a stop and asked me, "What's wrong with you? You got a problem with seeing naked women? Huh, Enoch would like to see a naked woman. Yes, he would. Lazarus is a fool, yes, he is."

"It wasn't like that. It was spooky and scary. She just came up out of the water out of nowhere."

"Huh, 'naked women are spooky and scary', he say. Lazarus is cuckoo, he is." He stopped jumping around long enough to point his finger at me accusingly, and yell, "Tell the truth. You didn't see any naked woman, no you didn't. You just didn't want to play with me anymore. Lazarus is not a good friend, no, he isn't. He won't play Enoch Says like he promised. He won't bring me a drink from the magic pool, and I REEAALLY wants a drink. Yes, I do. Yes, I did."

He looked so sincerely sad at that moment it nearly broke by heart, which seemed kind of silly, since he'd just pushed me off a cliff a few hours ago, but there was a childlike innocence about this crazy hermit that was somehow really getting to me. I said, "Okay. I'll go get your drink, but only if you promise this will be the end of the game for today. I've really had about all of this I can take for one day."

He took a hard look at the sun, which was beginning to approach the western skyline, and he smiled. "Yes. Oh, yes. We can stop playing if you bring me my drink. The day is almost over anyway. You go, yes, you do."

He motioned for me to head back into the cave, so I reluctantly grabbed the eternal torch and marched to my doom.

When I got to the final turn in the passage, I hesitated and tried to figure out what I should do. I thought about it for a moment and decided to do what any brave warrior would do in such a delicate situation. I whistled for a moment to let any monsters in the vicinity have a chance to get away, and then I called out around the corner, "Uh . . . naked lady . . . if you're still in there . . . would you mind staying down in the water where I can't see you. Like *way* down low, where I can't see you at all. In fact, if you could get down low enough to where I couldn't even see your eyes that would be great. I'm going to come in there now, pick up the cup I dropped, and dip it in your pool to get a drink of water, and then I'll be gone. Once I get my drink of water I'll leave in a flash, and you'll never have to see me again. I promise."

I waited for some kind of response, or even the sound of splashing water, but I couldn't hear a thing, so I squeezed around the corner and slowly crept into the room. "Okay, I'm coming in now, and I'm just going to walk over and pick up my cup."

Thankfully, the cup was lying undisturbed just where I'd dropped it earlier, so I tiptoed over and scooped it off the ground. I listened closely for a heartbeat, but the only thing I heard was those darn voices in my head that were starting up again. I looked carefully at the ground that still lay between me and the pool and scouted out the path of least resistance.

I mouthed a quick prayer of some sort as I held my torch high and looked for any disturbance in the water, and then I sprinted for the pool in a mad rush. I slid to a stop, bent over the rocky edge, and quickly scooped up a cup of water while diverting my eyes, so I wouldn't see anything lurking in the pool.

I couldn't take the chance of spilling my water and having to do this all over again, so my retreat was more subdued, but nevertheless effective. I got to the narrow exit without spilling a drop, wiggled around the sharp turn, and strolled back toward the campfire and sleeping area.

Just as I passed by the low entrance to the treasure room, a few bats went flying by my legs and startled me. I let loose a nervous laugh and looked back to see several more bats flying out of the hole. I started to trot to the entrance, and as I ran I stuck my chin in the cup to keep the water from falling out.

It seemed that with every step I took more bats joined me in my journey, until my whole world was one mad cascade of swirling, flapping, and fluttering half-crazed bats. They were chattering to each other as they crazily bounced off me, the walls around me, and the ceiling above. Of course, all the bats wanted was to follow the call of nature and get out of the cave. I was the one getting in the way, so I finally gave up, and lay down on the floor of the cave. By now, I had dropped the torch, so I took my free hand, and covered the cup, and my precious cargo. Finally, the last of the bats went flying by, and I carefully got to my feet. Fortunately, the eternal lamp was still burning brightly, so I picked it up and stumbled out to the ledge.

Enoch waited there, and he seemed to be looking me over more carefully than ever before, as he ran in his customary fashion around me. Finally, he stopped and addressed me in a voice that sounded eerily sane, "Are you okay?"

"Well, yes, I'm fine actually. And I must say, I'm relieved to finally have this day over. Did you see all of those bats? Why didn't I see them going into the cave this morning?'

"They go out here, and they come in through another entrance."

I put my finger on my chin and paused before replying, "Oh well, I guess that explains that."

If he realized I was mimicking him he didn't seem amused, so I moved on, "Here, I got your drink of water."

I held the cup out to him, but all he did was look at it suspiciously. "Which pool did you get it from? Was it the one on the right or the one on the left? Tell me now, which one was it?!"

"I got it from the one on the left with the whirlpool in the middle. Was that not the right one?'

"No, that was the right one all right."

"Well, then here's your drink of water."

He took the cup from me, and poured the water on the ground, as he carefully scanned the hillside above us. "Game over," he said, and then he turned and strolled inside the cave without a backwards glance.

CHAPTER FOURTEEN

I stood on the ledge alone for a few minutes trying to understand what had just happened, but like everything else that had happened today, there just wasn't any logical explanation to it. I decided when you're hanging out with a crazy cave hermit, that's how life is.

After a while, I grabbed the torch, which Enoch had graciously left by the entrance for my convenience, and went to the fire to see if he wanted to talk. To my surprise, he wasn't there, so I figured he must have gone into the deeper recesses of the cave for some reason. I hung my torch behind me to provide some additional light and broke out my writing kit. I debated whether to use the papyrus or the new sheets of writing material that Jesus had said was so valuable. In the end, I was drawn to use the new stuff, and wrote the following note to be added later to my journal.

March 23rd

It's been a couple days since I've been able to write anything, and so much has happened I can't begin to summarize it all tonight, so I'll just hit the highlights.

After my last journal entry, Jesus miraculously fed several thousand of the people who had gathered outside my gates. Then he healed hundreds more. The people were so enthused by his teachings and miracles they wanted to force him to be king.

That's a welcome development for my friends and I, but there's just one problem. The Jewish elders did exactly what we feared, and put out an arrest warrant for him. After meeting with "the others" we decided it would be best to convince him to go into hiding until the week of Passover. To my relief and surprise, he agreed and even insisted on a place to escape.

At his insistence, we journeyed to the Ephraim wilderness. To pull it off, we snuck out in the middle of the night with Jesus and his 12 disciples, Horus and me, and 5 of my guards. We traveled by night for two nights until we found a perfect little gorge to hide out in.

Then to my surprise, Jesus demanded that I leave behind my weapons, dogs, and even my clothes to go running off in the wilderness on some kind of wild goose chase to find a hermit named Enoch living in a cave near Shiloh, of all places.

Against my better judgement, I ran through the wilderness in near freezing weather and found the hermit and his cave. He immediately transformed everything about my appearance by dressing me in some crude furs similar to his own. No one would recognize me now. I look, and probably smell, like a cave hermit myself.

Since I've been here, the things I've experienced have been beyond bizarre.

Enoch made me play a game with him today that he called "Enoch Says." In the course of playing the game I had to go to his treasure room and choose a present for myself. His treasure room was a room in the cave that housed a huge colony of bats, but it also contained an extraordinary hoard of real treasure. It was unbelievable!

Enoch has had his left arm amputated at some point in his life just below his elbow. I asked him about it, and he said someone did it because they accused him of being a thief. He claimed he wasn't a thief, but after seeing his treasure room, I think he must be. In fact, he may be the most prolific thief who's ever lived. But, if so, he also has a childlike innocence and charm that's endearing to say the least. I found myself really wanting to please him while playing his silly game.

I chose for my gift a writing kit, which is how I'm able to record these things tonight. There were a couple of other items I considered, but this meant more to me for some reason. But Enoch wasn't happy with my choice, so he stuffed a bag of treasures into the leather bag that contained my writing utensils.

Then he gave me my next assignment, which was to rescue a traveler who was being attacked by a band of bandits on the trail below. To help me on my way, he shoved me off the ledge without warning, and I thought for sure I would die, but luckily I hit a tree on my way down and wasn't really hurt. Then I fought off the bandits and rescued the traveling stranger.

The stranger told me a moving story of a woman, named Miriam, who was taken in adultery, and whom Jesus managed to rescue from being stoned. Turns out this woman was a love interest of the traveler. He had done some really evil things that forced Miriam and her family out into the streets years ago, and now she was apparently being forced to live as a prostitute.

The traveler had some type of transformative experience due to the words and actions of Jesus that day, and he sold everything he had and set off on a quest to find Miriam and buy her way out of slavery. For two years he had been looking for her, and now it appeared he was close to finding her. In fact, he had learned she was in Jerusalem for Passover week, and that she was owned by none other than . . . wait for it . . . Uriah. Can you believe it? I want to punch his lights out more than ever now!

After hearing the man's story I was really rooting for him, but then we discovered his quest might be over because one of the bandits had made off with all his money, and he no longer had the means to buy Miriam's freedom.

Then I remembered the bag of treasure Enoch had stuffed into my writing kit. I poured it out into the traveler's hands, and it was full of gold and huge precious jewels. It was more than enough to buy Miriam's freedom and let them start a new life. In fact, it was probably enough to take care of them for many years to come.

I insisted the man take it all, and he was thrilled beyond words. I learned from talking to him that once he rescued Miriam he intended to find Jesus and write a book about his life. That inspired me to write out a note, to be given to Darius, which instructed him to take the traveler, and his beloved Miriam, into my household as paid employees.

As he was leaving, I learned the stranger's name was John, but he said he had another name of Mark, so I intend to call him John Mark when I see him upon my return home.

Enoch was thrilled with my rescue of John Mark, and I was hopeful that the game would end at that point, but he gave me another task. This task involved going to something he called his "magic pool" to retrieve him a drink of water with a weird green cup.

When I found the room in the cave that contained Enoch's magic pool there were actually two pools, which complicated things a little bit. There was one pool that was overflowing with warm water, and the overflow ran downhill a few feet before it formed another eerie pool of water with a whirlpool in the middle. Apparently, the water in this pool was being drained away to some place below because it wasn't overflowing back into the room where I was standing.

I had decided to get Enoch's drink of water from the pool with the whirlpool, but as I approached it, a woman rose up out of the middle of the pool. And not just any woman, oh no . . . this woman was as naked at the day she was born. I was afraid she might be the monster Medusa, so I ran for the hills, but Enoch insisted I go back and try again.

Thankfully, the woman wasn't there when I went back, and I was finally successful in bringing Enoch his drink of water, but not before battling a hoard of bats trying to get out of the cave at sunset.

I was shocked, surprised, and kind of mad when Enoch contemptuously poured his drink of water on the ground after I had fought so hard to get it, but what can you expect from a crazy cave hermit, right?

After the day I've had, I shouldn't be shocked or surprised by anything, I guess.

Now Enoch has disappeared, and my account is up-to-date, so I guess I'll call it quits for now.

Who knows what will happen tomorrow.

All I know is it's creepy in here, and to tell you the truth I'm more than a little scared. . . .

⊫⊰ ⊱⊐

When Enoch didn't come back after a while, I decided to crawl into my bed and pretend to be asleep. After throwing a few logs on the fire, I settled down for the night.

Several hours passed and Enoch came creeping into our sleeping area carrying a huge bundle of items wrapped up in a blanket. He passed right by me and went outside. Several hours more passed and he still hadn't returned. Finally, my curiosity got the better of me, so I got out of bed and snuck outside. I heard his heartbeat before I saw him. Then there he was. . . .

He was sitting cross-legged on the ground and gazing steadily up at the stars that dotted the clear night sky. Occasionally, he would bend over and write something in the sand with a bone stylus. I had never seen him so still and focused, and I marveled at this new behavior. I wanted desperately to see what he was so intent on writing, but there was veneration in his demeanor that held me back from intruding.

I quietly tiptoed away and went back to my bed for the night.

⊫⊰ ⊱⊐

I waited and watched for Enoch to return all night, but he never came. The next morning, I got up to find him. I left the eternal torch at the entrance, stepped out into the sunlight, and nearly choked in amazement.

Standing before me on the ledge, as if he were waiting on me, was Enoch. I knew it was him because the man standing before me was missing his left arm just below the elbow. Other than that, there was no resemblance to the man I had come to know as Enoch.

While Enoch was dirty and rough in appearance, this man was clean and polished in every way. His hair was still long, but now it practically glowed with cleanliness, and it was neatly arranged in cornrows before being pulled back in a bun behind his head. He was wearing one of the bejeweled robes I had seen in the treasure room, and this was billowing around him as the wind blew it gently. In fact, his robe was all that moved. He wasn't jumping or moving around at all. He looked like he could hold his regal pose forever, if needed.

His good right hand rested lightly at his side on the hilt of one of the gilded daggers I had seen in the treasure room. Beneath his chin the sapphire jewel still gleamed in the sunlight, but now it was sitting alone on a golden necklace instead of being surrounded by bones and jagged teeth. On his head rested one of the crowns I'd seen in the treasure room.

His gaze was sure and steady, and there was no indication of insanity in his eyes, but the surprises didn't end there.

His amputated left arm was extended to his side, and a beautiful dark-skinned lady rested her scarred hand on his elbow with practiced elegance.

She was (and still is) one of the most beautiful women I'd ever seen. She was younger than Enoch and also taller. She too, was wearing one of the intricate gowns from the treasure room, and she also wore a crown upon her head as a vestige of her queenly heritage. I knew immediately she was the woman I'd seen in the magic pool the night before, and I was relieved to see there were no snakes beneath her crown, only a luxuriant mound of dark cascading curls could be seen there.

She had another of the gilded daggers on a belt at her side, and around her elegant neck hung a golden necklace with a sapphire jewel identical to the one Enoch wore.

She smiled at me and I nearly melted away on the spot, but I somehow recovered my wits and managed to sputter a few words, "Who are you people?"

Enoch smiled and said, "I am Enoch, the king of the ancient tribe of Issachar, and this is my mate, Queen Demetria."

I said, "Well, I'll be. . . ." I looked back and forth between them and asked, "And what did you do with the *real* Enoch?"

He laughed and replied, "I'm terribly sorry for the inconvenience, but the little ruse I pulled by assuming the role of Enoch the cave-hermit was necessary for our purposes."

To say the least, I wasn't happy with his response, and I let him know it in no uncertain terms. "Are you kidding me? Just listen to yourself." I mimicked him, "Oh, I'm terribly sorry for the inconvenience, but the little ruse I pulled was necessary for our purposes.

"You've had me running around playing *Enoch SAYS* like it was perfectly normal behavior. And in the process of doing that I had to fight four bandits, crawl through bat guano, fight off a hoard of angry bats, and suffer through a whole host of indignities. And let's not forget you pushed me off a cliff and nearly killed me. Oh . . . Oh . . . Oh yeah, and that's without even mentioning having to be scared out of my wits by seeing your wife naked . . . not that seeing you naked was such a terrible thing in and of itself ma'am . . . but . . . I mean . . . well, you still you scared me pretty bad."

Demetria smiled and seemed to blush, but she didn't say a word.

Enoch said, "Are you finished whining?"

"Whining? No, I'm not, as a matter of fact, maybe now that your little ruse is over, you'd like to tell me why Jesus made me come here naked in the first place?"

"You couldn't bring anything with you because this is a sacred place. Nothing comes here without first being sanctified."

"Sanctified? Were those *sanctified* donkey turds you were throwing at me that first night? Are you kidding me?"

"As a matter of fact, they were. Everything we bring into this place has to go through a ritual of being purified and sanctified. Even the donkey turds . . . *especially* the donkey turds."

"A sacred place, huh. I looked around me. What's so high-and-mighty, sacred, and holy about this place? All I've seen is a cave full of bats and a couple of crazy people who claim to be a king and queen. Sacred?! Hah!

"I don't know what's going on here, but just because you clean up, put on some nice clothes, and a crown, that doesn't make you a king. And what's this tribe of Issachar you claim to be king of anyway? I've traveled pretty much all over the world, and I've never heard of any place called Issachar."

"Issachar isn't a place."

"Ha! I told you so."

Enoch patiently continued, "Issachar is a people. We're one of the twelve tribes of the Jews."

I laughed and said, "Issachar. *That* Issachar? You're talking about one of the lost tribes of Israel that disappeared 700 years ago when we were invaded by the Assyrians. I've got news for you buddy, your subjects are all gone, and they've been gone for a long time. That's why they call them the lost tribes. Duh!"

"My people aren't lost. They're hidden. There's a big difference, as you will soon learn. The vast portion of our tribe departed on a great journey long ago for a faraway land. They followed the stars to their destiny, as we all do eventually. Those who remained have chosen over the centuries to remain hidden from society."

I scoffed, "Why would anyone do that?"

"The tribe of Issachar was entrusted with studying the stars to discover tendencies that might portend the future. Our wise men and elders used their knowledge of the heavens to prophesize the future. We were guardians of the oral history of our people, and we were also guardians of ancient mysterious artifacts and relics of our ancestors. Some of these artifacts and relics were rumored to be invested with great powers. In short we were the tribe entrusted with the knowledge, artifacts, and relics that were of the greatest value to our people.

"When we were invaded by the Assyrians we had no choice but to disappear with the treasures of our people, and since that time we have chosen to remain hidden. This has proven to be the best way to keep our treasures secure from those who might otherwise misuse them."

"Well, if you ask me, that all sounds a little far-fetched, but what has any of that got to do with me? Why am I here, and when can I go?"

"I have something I believe I'm supposed to give you. We are both children of Israel after all, and it may be that you are the one our ancient prophets said would come. In fact, there are a couple of things I think I'm supposed to give you, but before I could do that I had to be certain you were worthy. As you know, Jesus came here when he was wandering in the wilderness after his baptism. He spent a few days here, and like you, he refused to eat, but it was different with him. He needed the food, but refused to eat because he was fasting to prepare for a final series of tests with the Devil. You, on the other hand, don't seem to need to eat. That leads me to believe you may be the one I've been waiting for.

"When Jesus came here I thought he might be the one because of some peculiar things that happened on the night he was born, but he said there was someone else who was born on the same night as him, and that would be the person I was looking for. Is it true you were born on the same night as Jesus?"

"Yes, amazingly enough, we were born on the same night. His mother and my mother were sisters, so that makes us cousins. So, what happened on the night we were born that was so peculiar?"

Enoch looked at Demetria and she rubbed her left hand against her leg and looked as if she wanted to say something, but he didn't give her a chance. Instead, he shook his head slightly, as if to warn her not to speak. Then he said, "Now's not the time to go into all of that. The important thing for you to know right now is that he assured me you were the one I was looking for, and he told me you would be here in the days leading up to one of our Passover weeks."

"Wait, that was years ago. How could he know I'd be here in the days leading up to a Passover week?" I said.

"You'd have to ask him, but that's what he told me, so when you showed up here the other night I was waiting in my disguise. Only it's not much of a disguise these days. In order to scare away intruders, the way you've seen me the last couple of days is the way I look nearly all the time. It's a rare occasion when Demetria and I dress in our regal adornments and allow ourselves to be reminded who we really are."

Demetria spoke for the first time, and her voice had a lilt and tenor to it that was worthy of an angel. "I, for one, am thrilled you're here. It's such a pleasure to be able to clean up and put on some nicer things. Most of the time, I'm running around here like a hag, so I can try to look like a frightening cave hermit's wife."

"Ma'am, I can't imagine anyone being frightened of someone as lovely as you." I blushed when I remembered what had happened the night before. "Well, unless you pop out of a pool in a spooky cavern, that is."

We all laughed at that, and it seemed to break the tension that had been boiling beneath the surface of our conversation.

Enoch said, "You asked a moment ago when you could leave. Without your realization, we have been testing you since the moment you arrived. We have to be sure you're the one we're supposed to bestow the artifacts on, and the good news is your time of testing is almost over. There are just a few more things we must do to make our final determination. If we deem you worthy, we will give you the artifacts and train you in how to use them. Then we'll impart some knowledge to you about what to expect in the future, and after that, you'll be free to go and join back up with Jesus."

"Well, okay then, let's get on with it then. What else do I have to do?"

Enoch allowed Demetria's hand to drop from his elbow. He carefully removed his crown and set in down on a nearby boulder. Then he unbuckled his belt and handed his dagger to Demetria, with a flourish he removed his kingly robe, and handed it to her as well. Underneath he was naked except for some leather britches that fit his small frame snuggly.

He turned his back to me to pick something up from the ground, and I saw he had the same colorful tattoo on his back I had seen on Demetria's back last night. It was the sun interposed in a half-moon. When he stood back up to face me, he was holding a simple walking stick.

He whipped it up and twirled it around his head a few times with his one hand before hunching down with it tucked under his amputated arm. Then he whispered menacingly, "Lazarus, prepare to do battle."

CHAPTER FIFTEEN

I laughed uneasily and said, "What are you talking about? I don't want to fight you Enoch."

A shrill war cry erupted from Enoch's bowels, and then, without warning, he whipped his staff around in a flash and struck me on my right shin. Then he said again, "Prepare to do battle, Lazarus."

"Are you kidding me? I'm not going to fight a one-armed man."

"Oh, so the big and brave Lazarus of Bethany is afraid of a little one-armed man is he?" He twirled, and whipped his staff around again, and this time he raised his aim a bit, and slapped me hard on the right knee. "Defend yourself, Lazarus."

"Stop this nonsense, Enoch. I'm not going to fight you. It wouldn't be fair."

"Oh, you're right about that. It's not going to be fair, but I'll take it easy on you since you're slow, and puny, and a fool to boot. But I'm warning you now; you had better defend yourself because my next blow will not be as kind as the last." With that said, he jabbed his staff straight at my groin.

Instinctively, I dropped my hand without even thinking and grabbed his staff before it could make impact with my unmentionables. To my amazement, he followed through with the momentum of his strike, and pivoting off his staff, which I obligingly held steady, he leapt straight at my face and delivered a stunning head butt with his forehead.

I stumbled back, seeing stars, and he rained blow after blow on me before I could begin to get my wits about me. I went to my knees and saw blood dripping into the dirt below, but he didn't relent. The blows kept coming as swift as lightening. I was so weakened by the ferocity of his attack that I couldn't even raise my hands to try and resist. Finally, with a pitiful whimper, I crumbled to the ground.

He stood over me for a moment breathing heavily before saying, "You let yourself be beaten into the ground by a little pipsqueak of a man with one arm and a simple stick. Ha! And to think I thought *you* were *the one*. What a pity, and what a disappointment you are. Go home Lazarus, we're done here."

He turned to walk away, and I rolled over on my back and looked up into the rising sun. I spit the blood from my mouth and moaned, "No-o-o!"

He stopped and slowly turned back to take stock of my suffering, "Oh, don't take it so hard. I've never lost a fight to anyone in my life. You never really had a chance."

I spun around and balanced my aching body on my hands and knees. I somehow managed to lift my bleeding head up far enough to make eye contact with him, and I roared, "No-o-o!"

He mocked me, "No, you say. Who are you to say no to me? I'm a king and you're no one. And now you're a nobody with a bloody head to boot. Just stay down, and take your beating with some dignity, why don't you?"

I shambled from the ground, and wiped the dust and gore from my eyes with both hands. Then I took the blood and smeared it on my cheeks. I leered at Enoch and said, "Prepare to do battle Enoch, King of the Issachar."

He crouched down into his fighting stance and trilled his piercing war cry again, as I wearily approached him. As I tried to get close to him, he rapidly whipped his staff at my face and body, but this time I wasn't surprised by how quickly he struck, nor was I surprised by the gracefulness and precision of his movements and strikes. I was ready and willing to fight now, and that made all the difference.

For every blow he sent my way, I offered a counter blow, and two blows of my own with my bare hands. I was moving so swiftly everything was a blur. I didn't think about what I was doing at all, I just let my years of training, and my instinct for fighting take over. Those two things, when coupled with my new strength and speed, gave me an insurmountable advantage. It was over in less than a minute, and I pinned him to the ground by holding his own staff across his shoulders as he lay helpless beneath me.

I whispered in his ear, "What say you now, O King."

He spat and said, "I yield."

"And who do you yield to, you miserable king of donkey turds?"

"I yield to Lazarus."

"And who is Lazarus?"

"Lazarus is the supreme warrior. The warrior above all warriors."

"Oh . . . I kind of like that!"

I released some of the pressure on his back and said, "You know you asked for this don't you?"

"Yes, I know I did."

"Well, just keep that in mind when I let you up, and don't try anything funny. Agreed?"

"Agreed."

I leapt to my feet and stood back to give him ample room to regain his composure.

Until now, Demetria had been completely quiet as she watched our battle from a safe distance. Now, she hustled over and began to dab affectionately at Enoch's minor scrapes and scratches. "Are you all right, my love?" she said.

He brushed her away gently and said, "Yes, I'm hardly injured at all. I think he took it easy on me on purpose. He could have killed me if he'd wanted to."

He took a non-threatening step toward me and said, "I wasn't lying when I said I'd never been beaten in a fight before." He held up his injured arm and continued, "At least not in a fair fight against one other opponent. When they took my arm it took six warriors, and two of them died for their trouble. I've never seen anyone move as quickly or as smoothly as you just did. And I've never felt such power exuding from an opponent. That was truly magnificent!"

"So, did I pass your test?"

"Indeed, you did!"

"Then I guess you can have your stick back." I handed him his staff, and he leaned on it while continuing to catch his breath.

I asked, "You know, it just occurred to me that you said you'd been testing me ever since I arrived here. So, if you don't mind enlightening me, I'd like to know just what kind of tests you were giving me."

Enoch smiled and said, "Ah yes . . . the tests. Well, the first night you were here I gave you my dagger, and then turned my back on you to give you ample opportunity to attack me while I couldn't see it coming. You showed a sense of honor and trust by not doing me harm.

"The next day when I sent you to the treasure room you could have taken anything there, but you made a modest choice when you choose the writing kit. This demonstrated humility. Then, when I told you to rescue the stranger who was being attacked, you demonstrated toughness, in dealing with your fall, and bravery, and fighting skill when you took on the bandits. You also demonstrated a great capacity for compassion in the way you dealt with the stranger and helped him on his quest.

"You also demonstrated bravery when you were sent to bring me a drink of water from the magic pool. But most of all, that test was about purity of heart."

"Purity of heart? I don't get it. If you're talking about how I didn't try to get a better look at Demetria, that was honestly more about me being scared out of my wits, than anything having to do with me having a pure heart. Believe me; I was tempted to ask her to turn around. "

Enoch smiled, "I have no doubt that's true. She's a beautiful woman isn't she?"

"You can say that again!"

Demetria smiled and giggled, but she didn't say anything.

Enoch continued, "But the fact is, you didn't ask her to turn around, and that required more purity of heart than you may realize, due to where you were when that was all taking place. You see, the reason I say you demonstrated purity of heart is because of the nature of the magic pool itself."

He paused and locked eyes with me, "Let me ask you, do you recall hearing voices when you were near the pool?"

I nodded, "I sure did. It made me doubt my sanity at the time. What was that all about?"

"The magic pool has a tendency to attract malicious spirits, which hover by the pool waiting to possess unwitting hosts who come near. Some would call them demons. Unless a person has performed certain purifying rituals they are most likely to have a bad experience if they encounter these sprits. The only way someone can approach the pool without the proper protection is if they are a person who is pure of heart. Even then, they will hear the spirits in their minds, and if they aren't pure of heart, they will give in to the temptations in their minds. So by not asking Demetria to turn around you were demonstrating the purity of your heart by showing you had immunity to the wicked spirits by the pool. "

"I don't even know what it means to be pure of heart, so how can I possibly be someone like that?"

"Our rabbis teach that the heart is where our desires, thoughts, personal will, sense of purpose, understanding, and true character reside. So, you could say, to be pure of heart means in the core of your soul you are at peace with who you really are. I believe a person who is pure of heart has no hypocrisy, no guile, and no hidden motives. They are open and honest about who they are and what they believe."

"So are you saying a person like that can do no wrong?"

Enoch chuckled, "Oh, no. Everyone makes mistakes. The person who is pure of heart is more likely to admit their mistakes, and less likely to repeat them. Their motives are pure even if their actions don't always pass the smell test. That's all."

"How about that! Lazarus, the pure of heart. Who'd have thought that?"

"Well, before you get too proud of yourself, let me point out, I suspect when Jesus raised you from the dead he may have done something to impact the way you approach life, as well as giving you other abilities. I don't know what kind of person you were before, but there's no doubt you're an extraordinarily spiritual man now. Demetria and I have both seen evidence of that. Perhaps Jesus gave your spiritual capacity a boost along with your physical attributes."

"I suppose that's possible. I can't say I feel any different, but maybe I do have a more positive attitude since he raised me from the dead."

I saw Enoch giving Demetria some kind of weird look, and I thought perhaps, now that I had passed the fighting test, they were eager to move on to giving me the relic they had mentioned, so they could send me on my way, and have their cave paradise back to themselves.

I cleared my throat and asked, "Well, if my fighting skills passed your inspection, then I guess the testing is all over. Maybe you could give me whatever it is you're planning on giving me, so I can go join back up with Jesus."

As I was speaking, Enoch laid down his staff and fastened his dagger back around his waist. Then he motioned for Demetria to join us. He hooked his injured left arm through my right arm and I gladly allowed Demetria to take me by my left arm. The three of us started strolling in a leisurely fashion toward the entrance to the cave.

I found myself truly relaxing for the first time since I'd arrived. Here we were, walking arm-in-arm as we neared the conclusion of our time together, and I realized I would miss them when I had to leave, but for now I was completely at peace. All was well.

Enoch said, "Up until now, you've passed every test with flying colors, so there's only one more test we've got to give you."

I joyfully replied, "What would that be?"

Enoch gently pulled our procession to a stop and said, "Enoch SAYS. . . DIE!"

Simultaneously, he and Demetria pulled their daggers, and plunged them into my heart from each side!

They each held one of my arms, so I was helpless to stop either of their attacks. A searing unimaginable pain enveloped me, and, as my life ebbed away, I looked at Enoch and tried to say, "Why?"

The last thing I remembered was seeing the tears rolling down his cheeks.

And then . . . I died!

CHAPTER SIXTEEN

Almost immediately, I was back in that dark and frightening place of suffering and sadness I had visited when I died the first time. Jesus said my soul had visited Hell on that occasion, and while I had hoped to never come here again, somehow my spirit had crossed over to this accursed plane of existence once more. So, I did what any highly trained warrior should do when surrounded by monstrous beings who are stumbling around and screaming in pain and anguish. I ran.

And I would have kept running, but I didn't get far. Almost immediately, thankfully, I felt my spirit being yanked away into a realm of total blackness. In this netherworld between worlds I felt no pain, sorrow, or fright. There was just a sense of waiting on the cusp of something important to be decided. But I did hear the voices of Enoch and Demetria.

She said, "Do you think he's going to come back?"

Enoch replied, "Yes, I think he will. No, I know he will. He has to be the one."

"Are you sure there was no other way?"

"Yes, it had to be done. We had to be sure."

Demetria wept, "I pray you're right. If he does come back, I don't see how he could ever forgive us, and I can't help but love him."

"I know exactly how you feel. I love him too. Even though I've only known him for a few days. I feel as if I've known him forever. And now . . . to have to do this . . . my heart is broken."

As I was listening to their conversation, my spirit was suddenly rejoined with my body in a rush of pain and emotion, and I heard myself screaming. I screamed for a long time.

Enoch held me in his arms and rocked me, while Demetria held my thrashing hands until I calmed down. When I finally stopped lashing out she began to caress my brow.

I cried tears of pain, joy, and betrayal all at once, and she wiped them away with her hair, even as her own tears flowed freely.

When the pain subsided, I found the meager strength to ask, "Why? What did I do to you to deserve that?"

Enoch shook his head and said, "You didn't do anything to deserve what we just did, but we had to know if you could come back from the dead. Didn't Jesus tell you about this ability?"

"He told me I'd never die, but I assumed he meant I'd *never* die. I didn't know he was saying I still could die, but I wouldn't remain dead. How do you even describe what just happened to me?'

Enoch said, "Our prophets called it 'regeneration.' It's the process by which someone dies, only to have their own body reconstruct itself. Our prophets foretold that someone like you would come into the world, but no one has ever actually seen anything like this before."

"You keep alluding to some kind of prophecy, and apparently, you think I'm linked to the fulfillment of that prophecy. In light of what you've just done to me, I think I've earned the right to know the details."

"You're exactly right. It's time that we enlighten you about our beliefs and motivations, so you understand why we've done the things we've done, but more importantly, you need to understand who we believe you are. If you're feeling up to it, we'll help you up and find a place we can all sit and talk."

"Yes, I'm feeling much better now. Help me up."

Demetria pulled and Enoch lifted until they had me on my feet. I wobbled over to some nearby boulders, and we all got comfortable.

Enoch scanned the horizon and then said, "Hundreds of years ago, our prophets said there would come a time when a 'holy family' would rise up in the land of Israel to deliver the people of all the Earth from evil. Jesus says his mother, Mary, was a virgin when he was conceived. That would mean she was impregnated by means of some mysterious spiritual power. We believe she is a key part of this 'holy family.' John the Baptist is another cousin to Jesus and yourself, and he has said that he came into the world to prepare the way for Jesus. We believe John is also a part of the 'holy family.' Your uncle, Joseph of Arimathea, has also shown spiritual tendencies that may indicate he is to have an important role in things to come as well. And Jesus has a brother named James who may also have something to contribute.

"Of course, Jesus himself is the key to everything. We believe he's the promised Messiah, so he's certainly a part of the prophesized 'holy family' as well.

"And then, there's you, Lazarus. Until recently, your life as a warrior would have seemed to disqualify you for the type of kingdom Jesus seems interested in bringing forth. We have had some of our subjects following him, and they bring us reports that he preaches forgiveness, mercy, love, and peace, which all seems to be a complete contradiction to the nature of someone like you. So that may have you wondering how you fit into his plans."

"Well, now that you mention it, ever since he told me I was supposed to be some kind of eternal warrior against evil, I've been wondering how I fit into his plans. I'm confused because Jesus is usually so meek and mild in his temperament, and nearly everything he teaches is concerned with the subjects of forgiveness, mercy, love, and peace, just like you said, but he also teaches we should stand up against evil. So, I guess I'm wondering, how can someone do both?"

Enoch smiled, "That's a good question. Our tribe has a philosophy we teach each of our children that goes something like this: **I believe our first impulse should always be to offer mercy and forgiveness even to our enemies, and we should try to avoid violence and instead seek peace whenever possible, but when evil refuses to back down, someone has to be willing to fight for what's right. Even the cause of peace requires warriors, when evil forces rise up to bring death and destruction on the weak and innocent. History shows us that people are never free to live and worship in peace without warriors to guard in the night. If each of us is to have liberty to live our lives free from oppression, then each of us must be willing to fight for that freedom when evil forces are at the gate. So we are reminded to never forget these things. Just as there is no forgiveness without sacrifice, also there is no *freedom* without sacrifice.**

"Our prophets said that in the days when the 'holy family' appeared there would be 'a coming of the two.' That means there would be two individuals who would rise up to be sacrificed in accordance with God's new covenant with our world. These two individuals are identified as *'the one who must die, so that all may live,'* and *'the one who cannot die, so that all may be free.'*

"'The one who *must* die' will be exalted for the entire world to see, so they can choose to accept or reject his sacrifice for their sins. On the other hand, 'the one who *cannot* die' is to be a faceless warrior who guards in the night against the forces of evil that would strip us of our freedom.

"Lazarus, we believe you are 'the one who *cannot* die.' This means you will fight a thankless fight against evil, without recognition for your sacrifice, until the end of days."

"If you're right about me, how is my role a sacrifice? You're telling me I get to live forever with a body imbued with special powers. That doesn't sound so sacrificial if you ask me."

"Ah, at first glance, many would agree with your assessment, but you will live without the joy of sleep, you will live without having the satisfaction of eating a meal when famished, and most troubling of all, you will live on when those you love have died. Your victories may be countless, but your losses will cut to your very soul."

"I hadn't thought about outliving the people I love, but how long are we talking about here. Surely we're only talking about a few years, right?"

Enoch replied, "You may live days, years, centuries, or perhaps eons upon eons. Only God knows."

I shook my head in resignation. "Well, there doesn't seem to be a lot I can do about it, so I'll just deal with it one day at a time, but what about this other person in your prophecy? You know, 'the one who *must* die, so that all might live.' Who do you think that person is?"

"I thought you would have figured that out by now. We believe 'the one who *must* die' is Jesus!"

＊＋＋＊

When Enoch announced Jesus was going to die, I stood up in protest and said, "Now, you're just not making sense. You said you thought Jesus was the promised Messiah, so if he's to be the new King of the Jews, how can he die?"

Enoch responded, "That's where the prophecy gets a little murky. It's not clear when he will die. Most prophecies are a little sketchy when it comes to the precise timing of future events. His death may be imminent or it may be far in the future, but the prophecy says he will be exalted as a sacrifice for all the world to see, and 'Many will share the blame, some will bear the shame, and the blessed will call on his name.'"

"Well, I can accept that he might have to die eventually, but certainly not anytime too soon. We've got to declare him king and defeat the Romans first, so that's going to take a while."

"I hope you're right, but beware, prophecies have a way of delivering surprises in their day of fulfillment."

I said, "To tell you the truth, all this talk of prophecies is giving me a headache. Can we please move on to a new subject?"

Enoch nodded his agreement and said, "Yes, we can. I believe the time has come for us to give you the artifacts we've spoken of. If you'll wait here, Demetria and I will need some time to prepare."

He held out his elbow to Demetria, and she daintily placed her hand on top of it. The two of them turned away, strolled regally to the cave entrance, and left me to ponder my fate.

I waited on the ledge for a long time, but I had a lot on my mind, so I used the time to think about the prophecies Enoch had described to me earlier. Somewhere in the midst of my musings a storm blew in. Soon I was standing in a deluge of wind driven rain. Something about the storm excited me, as it seemed, with every strike of lightening my body surged with power. I had never felt so invigorated. I climbed up on the highest boulder I could find, and faced up the hillside so I could stare directly into the face of the storm. I felt as if the air around me was alive with some unseen force that was washing over me in mysteriously nourishing waves. I held my arms up to the clouds and took it all in.

I heard Enoch and Demetria calling my name, and I vaguely realized they must be back outside with me, but I couldn't bring myself to break my mystifying connection with nature, so I ignored them and held my stance.

Then something hit me . . . hard!

CHAPTER SEVENTEEN

I flew through the air from my perch atop the boulder, and rolled over and over across the ledge, completely helpless to do anything to stop rolling since I had lost all control of my extremities. I finally skidded to a stop just before tumbling over the edge of the cliff.

Enoch and Demetria were immediately hovering over me in what was becoming a much too familiar fashion. Demetria rubbed and coddled me, while Enoch looked nervously up the hillside between glances at my unmoving body.

I couldn't move, and I couldn't speak. Whatever had hit me had left me stunned and completely paralyzed.

After several minutes I began to feel my toes and fingers and soon I was able to move my arms and legs. Finally I was able to speak, "What happened to me?"

Enoch said, "You were hit by a bolt of lightning. It's a wonder it didn't blow you to bits or at least fry you to a crisp. What were you thinking standing on a boulder like that in a thunderstorm?

Has no one ever told you lightning bolts tend to hit the highest target available?"

"I wasn't thinking about that. There was something in the air that seemed to be empowering me, and I couldn't get enough of it."

"Ah, yes, I've noticed that when lightning strikes, plants in the area seem to perk up as if there's something in the air that invigorates them. We're told that when Adam and Eve were in the Garden, before the fall, their physical makeup included characteristics that were akin to plants. Perhaps when Jesus raised you from the dead your body was changed to be more like the bodies of the first humans before they fell from grace. Maybe that's why you don't need to eat or drink. Maybe you're absorbing power from the sun and from the air itself in ways we can't fathom."

"You may have something there. I've noticed when I'm in the sun awhile I feel rejuvenated, and that was the same feeling I had just now in the storm."

"Well, now we have a bit of a problem. Demetria and I are not the only members of our tribe in the vicinity. There are others who patrol the area to help us guard this sacred site and they've been watching what's been going on here since you first arrived. I've been conferring with their leaders, and not all of them are in agreement with my decision to give you the artifacts. Some don't want to believe you're 'the one who *cannot* die.' They're in no hurry to relinquish our treasures to you, and now this sign of weakness may encourage them to revolt against my decision."

"What sign of weakness? I just took on a bolt of lightning and lived to tell about it. How can that be construed as weakness?"

"You've got a point. Amazingly, not a hair on your head seems to have been singed, and your clothes are also untouched. The problem is, it knocked you for a loop and left you paralyzed awhile. My enemies will seize on this as an opportunity to seek rebellion against my leadership."

"Enemies? I thought these were your subjects, why are you referring to them as your enemies?"

"Even a king has enemies. Let's get you up, so they can see you're okay. The sooner we can get them to stop dwelling on what just happened the better."

They pushed and pulled me up again, and I walked around to demonstrate to whoever might be watching that I was perfectly fine.

I said, "Do you want me to do some cartwheels and flips to show them I'm alright?"

Enoch smiled, "No, I think that might be overdoing it a bit." He looked around at the receding storm clouds and said, "It looks like the storm is over, but I think we should go inside for what we're about to do next. I left the artifacts we want to present to you by the fire."

As we were walking inside, I tried to imagine what kind of artifact he would be giving me, and I kept coming back to the magnificent gilded swords I'd seen. Surely, I would leave with one of those fine blades.

I was surprised and disappointed, when we made the final turn and arrived at the fire, to see nothing but the walking staff with the snakehead grip propped up by the rocks we normally sat on around the fire. The ruby eyes gleamed in the semi-darkness, but that did nothing but give me the willies. I couldn't fathom why I had been put through the trials and tribulations of the last few days just to be sent away with such a crude present.

Enoch was all smiles and jubilation as he motioned for me to have a seat on one of the rocks around the fire. Demetria walked over to stand by him and she reverently picked up the staff and handed it to him. He hefted in in his hands and said, "This probably doesn't look like much to you, but this simple staff is more than it appears. We don't know exactly where it came from, or who made it. We don't know how long ago it was made, but it is certainly ancient. There is much that remains a mystery about this staff, but there's a couple of things we know for sure; it's been in the possession of the Jewish people since *at least* the time of Moses, and it has strange and legendary powers that are unmatched by any other instrument ever known to man."

Demetria motioned for me to stand. I stood to attention, and Enoch held the staff out to me as he announced, "Lazarus, by the powers invested in me by the tribe of Issachar, I present to you, THE ROD OF MOSES."

I took the staff into my hands and tried my best not to laugh, but I couldn't help thinking, "After all I've been through, this is what Jesus sent me to get? I guess the jokes on me after all. Ha! Ha! We got Lazarus to run through the desert naked, spend two days playing games with a cave-hermit, and listening to crazy prophesies, and when it was all over they gave him a stick and called it The Rod of Moses. Ha! They'll probably buy me a shirt, and have one of the women embroider a saying on it, 'I went to the wilderness and all I got was this crummy stick.' Or it could even say, 'I went to the wilderness and all I got was this crummy shirt'. . . yeah, that sounds about right."

I looked at the solemn looks on the faces of Enoch and Demetria and tried to sound serious when I spoke, "So, what you're saying is, this is the Rod of Moses I've read about in the Torah. The supernatural staff he carried around that allowed him to perform all kinds of miracles, if my memory serves me. Is that about right?"

"Yes, some called it the Rod of God, but it was used by Moses and his brother Aaron, and most people called it the Rod of Moses. He used it to cause water to flow out of a rock, to heal people who had been bitten by serpents, and to part the Red Sea when the children of Israel were escaping from the Egyptians. He also used it to help our people win a battle on at least one occasion. And there were at least two times in the Torah when we're told the rod turned into a snake only to turn back into a rod. We really don't know exactly how it works, or everything it's capable of doing, but its supernatural powers are well-founded and well-documented."

"And I guess you want me to carry this around with me while I'm going around fighting the forces of evil like you described in your prophesies. Is that the idea?"

Enoch bubbled with exuberance, "Yes! That's exactly right. It'll be an invaluable tool for you."

I bowed my head to hide my smile, and said, "Well then, I guess we're done here, and I'll be on my way. Thanks for everything."

"On your way? Oh, no. You can't leave yet, I've got to show you how to intertwine yourself with the rod, and I've got something else to give you also."

"Intertwine myself with the rod? What are you talking about?"

"Oh, we'll come back to that in a minute, but first let me make one other presentation." He motioned to Demetria and she reached inside her robes and produced an object that glimmered with a greenish tint in the light from the fire. She handed the glowing object to Enoch, and when he held it before his chest I realized I was looking at the transparent cup he had given me to bring him a drink of water with from the magic pool.

Enoch cleared his throat and continued, "This cup has also been in the possession of our people for countless ages. No one knows its origin, or what it's made of, or how it came to be made. I am not allowed to speak of its powers, but they are many. I can only tell you the cup will reveal its powers when it is ready, and to whomever it may choose."

He held the cup out to me and said, "Lazarus, by the powers invested in me by the tribe of Issachar, I present to you, The Sacred Cup of Life and Prosperity, or as some have called it, The Holy Grail."

⇌ ⇌

I solemnly took the cup from him and did my best not to smile again. "Well, thanks. I don't know how I'll ever repay you. And uh . . . how am I supposed to use this?"

"Oh, that isn't for you just yet. You should give it to Jesus. He'll know what to do with it. If it's ever meant to be yours it will come back to you in time."

"Okay, so give the cup to Jesus, and carry the stick to do battle against the forces of evil. I think I can do both of those, so now I'll just me on my way."

Demetria smiled, "Silly man! Have you forgotten? We haven't showed you how to intertwine with the rod yet. You can't leave until we've done that."

"Oh, yeah. The intertwining thing. How could I forget that? And what is that exactly?"

Enoch reached for the rod and said, "If you'll permit me to have the rod back for just a moment I'll explain what you need to do."

He took the rod and set the bottom of it on the floor of the cave. "Now, all you have to do is twist the head here on the top of the cane, and the head will pop open and hang to the side. Just put your hand over the top of the staff and hold on while the creature feeds. But I should warn you, it's going to hurt pretty badly, so be ready for that, and hold on tight until it's finished. Then you'll be fully intertwined."

I looked at him the same way I'd looked at him when I first met him. Back when I thought he was crazy as a bat, or crazy as a cave-hermit, as the case may be. "Whoa, whoa now, just slow down. I was with you right up till you said something about letting a creature *feed*. That was the word you used wasn't it? Didn't you say I was supposed to put my hand over the end of the staff and let some kind of creature *feed* on my hand? What kind of feeding are we talking about here?"

"It's just going to bite you and drink some of your blood. That's all."

164

"Oh, that's all, is it? Don't worry Lazarus, it's just going to bite you and drink some of your blood. That's all. What kind of idiot do you think I am? And what kind of creature are we talking about anyway?"

"Now, now, Lazarus I don't think you're an idiot at all. I think you're a highly honorable man, or I wouldn't be offering you this opportunity at all, but this is part of what you've got to do. It's really not as bad as it sounds, and it won't take a lot of your blood, just a bit is all. As for the creature, it's something we call a Drakon. It's really not like anything you've ever seen, but it's similar to a serpent."

"A SERPENT? So what you're saying is it's a snake. You want me to put my hand over the end of the staff and let a snake bite me and suck my blood. Oh, sure, I'll be glad to do that because, like you say, it's not as bad as it sounds, and it won't eat much. Well, in the words of Enoch the crazy cave-hermit, 'Are you CRAAZY or something?' There's no way I'm doing that."

I turned to leave the cave, and Enoch reached out to restrain me. I turned back towards him and was preparing to slug him when Demetria intervened. She hurried over and gently put her hands on each of our chests and pushed us apart. Then she put both her hands on my chest and leaned in while gazing into my eyes. "Lazarus, I've seen your bravery, and I know you're not a coward; so why are you behaving this way? Enoch speaks the truth. It's not as bad as it sounds. I've had to do it myself before, and if I can do it, I know you can do it too."

I was sure I had already turned a bright shade of red because my temper was flaring, but now I must have turned an even brighter shade of red as I stammered, "It's just . . . well . . . it's just that I'm afraid of snakes. Like . . . really afraid."

She smiled, and I melted, when she replied, "Kind of like you're afraid of naked women?"

I couldn't help but smile back, "Yes, but only when they pop out of magic pools in the dark."

I was still mesmerized by her gaze as Enoch stealthily set the staff on the ground beside me and popped it open. I was so focused on Demetria I really didn't understand what was happening when she took my right hand and placed it on the opening at the top of the staff.

When the creature struck, Demetria and Enoch both placed their hands over mine and held on, as I screamed in protest.

And the Drakon fed. . . .

CHAPTER EIGHTEEN

When Demetria clamped both of her hands over mine my first impulse was to fling her away, and with my newfound strength, I have no doubt I could have easily done it. But another part of me wanted desperately to please her, and it was this part of me that prevailed.

The creature fed, and Demetria and Enoch held onto my hand while I held onto the staff with all my might and will, as a horrible pain shot up my arm and into my skull. I felt as it my head would explode as the blinding agony tore through me in an unrelenting wave of torment. And then . . . it was over.

When the creature finally released me from its grip, the pain immediately subsided, and I nearly collapsed to the floor. In fact, if Demetria and Enoch hadn't held me up I would've fallen for sure. I felt, in that moment, as if all the strength in my body had been completely sucked away, and I was sure I was going to faint, but before I blacked out, they set me down on a rock, and I quickly regained my composure.

The only problem now was the voice inside my head.

It wasn't persistent or even annoying, but if I focused my attention it was definitely there, and even though it spoke in a tongue I had never encountered before, amazingly, I could understand everything it said.

I'll never forget the first words it spoke to me after our intertwining. "Hello Lazarus. I've been waiting for you. Now you will know me, and I will know you, and we will know each other. You may call me Drakon. Yes you will, yes you shall, and so it shall be. For the weak, for the innocent, forevermore."

I nearly fell off my rock when I heard those words. Enoch and Demetria gave me a quizzical look, and I think they knew some of what I was experiencing, but they didn't say a word. They just stood by patiently and let me come to terms with the phenomenal changes I was experiencing. I held the staff in my hands with a newfound reverence, and felt it softly pulse with an incredible energy that I sensed must be waiting to be unleashed.

I was in awe, and spoke without realizing I was speaking aloud, "The Rod of Moses."

Enoch murmured his assent, "Yes, the Rod of Moses. Only now, it's become the Rod of Lazarus."

I chuckled uneasily and said, "I kind of like the sound of that, but I just realized I don't have a clue how to make it do the things you said it's capable of doing. Is there an instruction manual or something?"

Enoch said, "No one can guide you in how to use it. When its powers are needed it will come to your aid, if able, when you reach out to it with your mind. You are intertwined now, and if it has the ability to help you, it will. However, the aid it offers may not always be what you expect, or desire. You will come to find it has a mind of its own in such matters."

"And what about the feeding thing I just did? I hate to ask, but do I ever have to do that again?"

"Yes, the feeding ritual will need to be done at least once a week. It will need to be performed more often if the creature's powers are used extensively."

"I was afraid you were going to say something like that."

Enoch glanced at Demetria and said, "Now Lazarus, there's just one more thing we need to do before we agree to let you take possession of the rod on a permanent basis. You're being given a tool with amazing powers to aid you in your fight for justice, so I need to ask you an important question."

I nodded and stood to my feet while replying, "Go ahead and ask your question."

Enoch's voice became deathly serious as he stood before me and searched my eyes while intoning, "Lazarus, do you solemnly swear before God and these assembled witnesses that you will use the Rod of Moses to protect the weak and innocent, and do you promise to come to their aid whenever you are faced with the opportunity?"

I looked steadily back into the eyes of Enoch and said the words that have guided and motivated me since that day, "Enoch, I solemnly swear before God and these assembled witnesses I will use the Rod of Moses to protect the weak and innocent, and I promise to come to their aid whenever I am faced with the opportunity."

I felt the staff tingle in my hands as I made my promise and I knew in my mind and heart I had crossed a line of some sort and there could be no going back.

Just then, a bat went flapping by our heads on its way out of the cave. We watched it go, and soon it was joined by two more.

Enoch pushed us toward the entrance. "I think we'd better get out of the way, unless you like being swarmed by bats."

We hurried to the ledge and stood back to watch the bats make their nightly exit. While we were standing there Demetria handed me my writing kit in its leather bag as she said, "I've taken the liberty of putting the Sacred Cup into your bag for safekeeping. I hope you don't mind."

I took it from her, hooked it over my shoulder, and said, "No, that's perfect. I'd probably have forgotten it otherwise, with all that's happened today."

Enoch said, "It's been a long day my friend, and unlike you, my lovely wife and I get tired. We still have a few things to explain to you before you leave, so I'm going to have to beg you to delay leaving until tomorrow. I know you were planning on leaving today, but it's taken longer to do everything we'd planned. Hopefully you won't mind spending a few more hours with us before you take your leave."

Demetria grabbed my arm and pouted, "Surely you can stand to spend a few more hours with us? Please!"

I laughed, "Demetria, if there's one thing I've learned, it's that I can never say no to you, so yes, I'll stay until tomorrow, but only on one condition."

Enoch asked, "And what might that be?"

"I am not playing Enoch SAYS. . .!"

I gave my bed to Demetria that night, since there was no longer a need to pretend I could sleep. They immediately fell into a deep sleep, so I went out on the ledge and gazed at the stars awhile, and the night passed peacefully.

The next morning Enoch and Demetria went back into the deeper recesses of the cave and came out carrying more bundles wrapped in blankets. They asked me to wait by the fire while they went outside to prepare for the events of the day. They were gone for quite a while, so I sat down and wrote an entry for my journal.

March 25ᵗʰ

I didn't get to write yesterday, so I'll try to briefly bring things up-to-date.

Yesterday morning, started off with a bang when Enoch revealed he's not a crazy cave hermit after all. He showed up looking completely different and wearing a crown. He announced he was the King of the Issachar, which turned out to one of the lost tribes of Israel. Then, to top it off, he introduced a gorgeous lady, who was also wearing a crown, and announced she was his Queen, Demetria.

It turns out she was the naked lady in the magic pool who I feared was the monster Medusa. Yeah . . . I felt pretty stupid when I learned that.

Then Enoch told me he had been testing me to see if I was worthy to receive some kind of special artifacts he wanted to give me. He told me he had a couple more tests for me, and then he challenged me to a fight.

All he had as a weapon was a walking staff, and he only has one arm, so the last thing I wanted to do was fight him, but he insisted, and when I resisted engaging him he put a beat-down on me.

Then he taunted me for being so weak that a one-armed man with a stick could completely demolish me in a fight.

That made me mad, and I fought him again, only the second time I wasn't hesitant, and I beat him pretty easily.

Then he explained the tests he'd given me and told me I was a person who was 'pure of heart.' Imagine that, Lazarus, the warrior is 'pure of heart.' Don't tell anyone!

I was just beginning to relax, when Enoch and Demetria killed me. No . . . that's not a misprint. They really killed me, but I somehow came back to life (for the second time in five days . . . now that's got to be a record of some kind).

Enoch said my body somehow reconstructed itself and he said the prophets of his tribe called it 'regeneration.' All I know is it was scary, and it hurt like hell. And that reminds me . . . I briefly went back to Hell while my spirit was absent from my body.

Enoch apologized for what they did, but he said they had to know if I was 'the one who could not die,' that their prophets had predicted would come into the world.

According to Enoch, Jesus and I, along with his mother Mary, our uncle Joseph of Arimathea, and our cousin, John the Baptist, are all part of a 'holy family' his prophets had predicted would come into the world about now. He also said that Jesus's brother, James, might be part of what was happening.

In any case, Enoch said he had decided I was 'the one who could not die,' which means I'm going to live some kind of sacrificial life fighting against evil, so people can be free. I know, it's a lot to take in. Believe me; I'm still trying to understand it all.

Then, while I was waiting for Enoch to give me the artifacts he had for me, I got hit by lightning, but I didn't die. It just knocked me on my butt and paralyzed me awhile.

Finally, Enoch and Demetria went through a formal ceremony of sorts and presented me with a walking staff they said was the Rod of Moses. I thought maybe they really were crazy then, but as it turns out they may be right. One thing's for sure, it's not like anything I've ever encountered before. When I hold it, I can definitely sense a tremendous power resides inside of it (along with something called a Drakon, but I'll get into that another time). I don't really have a clue how to use it to my advantage, but Enoch says I'll figure it out in the days to come.

They also presented me with a cup they said had supernatural powers, but they were even more cryptic about how to use it, or what its purpose is. They told me to give it to Jesus, and he'd know what to do with it.

I was ready to go join back up with Jesus last night, but they said they had some other things they needed to tell me before I left, so they asked me to stay until today.

So, today, will be my last day here, and to tell the truth, I'm a little sad to be leaving. I can't wait to get back to Jesus and go home, I'm anxious to see Iris again, and to make her my bride, but still . . . I'm going to miss Enoch and Demetria. It's weird how I feel about them after knowing them for such a short time.

Anyway, my adventure here will soon be over, and after the excitement of yesterday, I'm sure today will be quite boring.

Ah well, not every day can be full of excitement.

⇒⊦ ⊦⇐

I had just put my writing utensils back in my bag, when I heard Enoch calling my name from outside, so I slung the bag over my shoulder and picked up my new staff. Enoch had given me a leather harness to hold the staff on my back when I wasn't using it, so I slung it into its resting place, and made my way out to the ledge.

I was somewhat surprised to see that Enoch and Demetria had exchanged their regal garments and crowns for the furs of wild animals, but then I recalled they had told me this was their normal wardrobe. At first, I expected Enoch to start running in circles around me while jabbering nonsense, but the feeling soon passed.

Even in her rough furs, and with her hair in a tangled mess, Demetria was an alluring sight to behold. Despite her best efforts, there just wasn't any hiding her beauty.

Disturbingly, I couldn't help but notice they were both carrying short battle lances in addition to having daggers hanging at their sides. Enoch's lance had sharp spear points on each end, while Demetria's lance only had a spear point on one end, but it seemed to capture and reflect the sunlight with a brilliant luster that was almost blinding. There was something alluring about her lance that made me want to reach out and touch it, but I controlled the impulse.

In addition to their weapons they each wore fitted bronze plate armor on their upper bodies similar to the Greek hoplite style. They also had leather grieves tied around their lower legs.

They were obviously expecting trouble, and that made me extremely anxious for their safety.

Enoch nervously led me over to sit with them on the boulders, and he immediately began to talk. "I'm so sorry to keep you waiting so long. I didn't think it would take this long to do what we had to do. As I've told you, Demetria and I are not alone here. We went up on our little mountain here and had a meeting with our fellow tribesmen this morning. We needed to let them know that we'd concluded our testing and given you the artifacts yesterday."

He scanned the hillside and continued, "Unfortunately, our report didn't go as well as we'd hoped. To say the least, there was a good deal of disagreement with what we'd done. Some of those in attendance even threatened to come and take back the artifacts by force. I think it's best that we share a little essential information with you and then send you on your way as soon as possible. There's a secret entrance to our cave that none of them know about. I'll give you directions when we're finished talking, and you can be on your way. Just watch your back-trail until you're far away from here. I haven't told any of them who you are, or where you're from, so they won't know how to find you once you've made your escape."

He took Demetria by the hand and continued, "There's a lot to tell you and not much time for the telling, so lend me your ears my friend, and open your mind to the incredible!"

CHAPTER NINETEEN

"You know there's a pool here we call the magic pool," Enoch said, "My people call the whirlpool that swirls in the middle of that pool a *Vortex*. It's a supernatural pool that produces a fluid we call *Elixir*. When this elixir is applied to a wound it heals the wound rapidly. When I was fighting with you yesterday, Demetria had a flask beneath her robes just in case you wounded me in our scuffle. We carry one on us at nearly all times. He lifted the fur on one of his shoulders to reveal a flask strapped to his shoulder. Demetria did the same thing to reveal her own flask.

He handed me a similar flask with its own pocket and straps. "Put this in your writing bag for now, but in the future you may want to wear it just as we do. You never know when it might come in handy. Just a small amount will heal most wounds in just minutes."

As I started to take it from him, he held onto it and looked me in the eyes. "But Lazarus, let me warn you, you should never let anyone drink the elixir."

"Why not?"

"Because anyone who drinks it becomes dependent on drinking it periodically, and they will die if they can't get any."

"Well then, I'd be a fool to let anyone drink it, so that will never happen," I replied as I secured the flask in my writing bag.

"Oh, but you'll be tempted to let it happen. You see, the elixir also slows the aging process, so that anyone who drinks it regularly only ages about one year for every 12 years they live. In our tribe, only our elders are allowed to drink the elixir, so people like Demetria and I have lived for nearly 200 years, but others have lived even longer in the past. However, not everyone gets to drink the elixir, and that is another reason for the potential rebellion we're facing. Some of my enemies feel all of our tribe should have access to the vortex."

"If you have such a powerful resource that can give prolonged life to all your people, why wouldn't you allow everyone access?" I said.

"We keep this place sacred and only allow a limited number of people to come here because our history shows that when everyone is allowed to come and go as they please, someone inevitably gets lax in performing the purification rituals that are necessary to avoid possession by the malevolent spirits that lurk near such pools. Some of these spirits have enormous destructive powers and a possessed Issachar tribesman is an enemy to be truly feared. As you have seen, our training in the art of war makes us formable foes in any arena. When you couple our fighting skill with the vicious and supernatural powers of a demon you get a madman who's capable of killing hundreds of ordinary men before he's stopped.

"Our people have debated this dilemma for eons and fought battles over control of pools such as this one. Many years ago there was a rebellion against another king of the Issachar. In response to that rebellion, my forefathers met in Shiloh when it was just a nameless watering hole on the map. They agreed to rules regarding the use of vortexes and signed a treaty that brought warring factions of our tribe back together. The signing of that treaty gave birth to the name for the town now known as Shiloh. As you may know, Shiloh means 'a place of peace.'

"It appears we may be facing another rebellion here today, but I'm hopeful cooler heads will still prevail."

Enoch paused and then continued, "Now, as I was saying, the elixir can prolong life, and even heal internal wounds, but I don't think you should ever let anyone drink it. The problem is; it can only *prolong* life. They won't be able to regenerate like you, so they will eventually die from sickness, disease, physical harm, or old age. You will only be delaying their inevitable death, and when they die you will feel responsible. I gave this a lot of thought last night, and if you're going to live indefinitely, and be fighting a battle against evil, you will need to keep yourself unencumbered from being responsible for the welfare of others. Otherwise, you'll have a heart that's burdened with sadness due to the losses you endure over the years."

I thought about what he was saying about keeping my life un-encumbered, and I remembered my promise to marry Iris when I returned from the wilderness. There was no way I was breaking my promise to her. I would just have to figure out a way to live my new life without letting my relationships get in the way of what I needed to do. I nodded my acquiescence to Enoch's advice, but said nothing.

He went on with his discourse, "There's more you need to know before you leave. I've told you my tribe was entrusted with the greatest treasures of our people. Some of those treasures were the relics of our ancestors, and artifacts like the ones we've given you. But perhaps the greatest treasures we guarded were the treasures of our people's oral history and the secret knowledge our elders and prophets accumulated over our many years of existence. These elders and prophets were called *Seekers* by their fellow

Israelites since they were seekers after truth and understanding. Today we refer to all our fellow tribesmen as *Seekers.*

"Even today, our children are trained in the skills of memory, so they can recite our oral history without ever seeing it in written form. Our most skilled historians can recite our history from start to finish in about twelve hours without ever stopping.

"But there is other secret knowledge that is trusted to only a few elders, and none of our knowledge, or history, is ever written down. Our tribal law forbids us to write these things down. They exist only in our minds, and that's how we guard them against our enemies. However, there has been one exception to this practice of not writing things down.

"As I told you earlier, the vast portion of our tribe departed on a great journey long ago to travel to a faraway land. Our prophets said that God was calling us to follow a star to a new land of milk and honey, so thousands of my people left to fulfill our obligation to God's commands. They followed the star to their destiny and were never heard from again, but if they made it to their promised destination they were to build a seven hundred foot wall and inscribe it with the Torah, plus all of our history, and all our secret knowledge and prophecies."

I grinned, "It seems kind of silly for people to head off into the unknown following a star, don't you think?"

"Not at all. I believe Jesus told me there were three wise men who followed a star to his birthplace, and they gave his parents very valuable gifts, which allowed them to escape and live in Egypt awhile when King Herod tried to kill him."

"I guess you've got a point there," I said. "So, do you think your tribesmen made it to where they were supposed to go and actually built their wall?"

"Yes, I believe they did. We were given a commission much like that of Deuteronomy 27:1-3 *Now Moses, with the elders of Israel, commanded the people, saying: "Keep all the commandments which I command you today. ² And it shall be, on the day when you cross over the Jordan to the land which the LORD your God is giving you, that you shall set up for yourselves large stones, and whitewash them with lime. ³ You shall write on them all the words of this law, when you have crossed over, that you may enter the land which the LORD your God is giving you. . . .'"*

"We sent our wisest elders on the journey and our bravest warriors. So, somewhere out there, a secret wall with all our knowledge and prophesies is waiting to be discovered."

"Wait. You just called it a *secret* wall. What's so secretive about a 700 foot wall?"

"It's not 700 feet high. It's 700 feet long, and once they were done inscribing it, they were supposed to bury it, and mark its progress with a line of successive stones from above. According to the commands of God it would remain hidden until 'the fullness of time,' then at the appropriate time it would be found, and it's knowledge would be used for both good and evil, but ultimately the forces of good were prophesized to triumph . . . maybe."

"Wait. Why did you say the forces of good will triumph . . . maybe? Isn't it a given that the good guys win in the end?"

"Ah, look around at the world we live in, Lazarus. Every second of every day, there's an ongoing battle between good and evil. Sometimes good wins out, but truthfully, much of the time, the forces of evil win their own battles. If that were not the case we wouldn't have slavery, stealing, lying, cheating, and even murder. God has given us free will here on Earth, and we often choose to use our freedom in ways that support the evil forces around us.

"Those who think that God can simply impose his will on us to bring about a good ending to everything forget that our own scriptures remind us there has been war in Heaven itself at times, when angels have rebelled against the wisdom and will of God. We should never forget that angels are powerful supernatural beings who were created to fight for justice and to protect the weak and innocent, so if they can choose to go against God's will anyone can."

"So what good are prophecies if they can't tell us the exact outcome of things in the future?"

Enoch gazed at the sky and replied, "Prophesies are tricky things. You see, anyone can study the movements of the stars and heavenly bodies to try and understand how their movements may effect or even predict the future, but a prophet takes a different approach. A prophet studies the movements taking place in the celestial arena while also trying to be in tune with the mind of God. Thus the true prophet tries to paint a picture with his prophecies of what God *intends* for our future.

"The key here, is that what God intends, and what actually happens in the future can be drastically affected by how we mere mortals respond to God's plan. Do we embrace his intended plan for our lives, or do one or more key players blow their parts in the plan? Or maybe, humanity, as a whole, turns away from his intended plan, and he has no choice but to devise a new plan for us.

"You know, that's what happened when he extinguished everyone on Earth with the great flood, except Noah and his family. The people of Earth were given a second chance to create a society that pleased him, and with the covenant of the rainbow God signified he would never take such drastic measures again.

"I fear we have failed to live up to God's expectations, and the sacrificial system God instructed us to institute in our temples has been sadly corrupted. In addition, we've kept God's instructions to ourselves, and cut the other nations of the world off from finding favor with God, and redemption from their sins. I don't think this was what God intended when he gave us a new start through Noah, so I think we're on the verge of being presented with a new covenant that will give us an innovative way to interact with God, and I believe, this new covenant will be open to all the people of Earth; so everyone can freely participate. If I'm right, then we're on the verge of a new beginning in God's plan for mankind."

"I'm not following you, what kind of new beginning are you talking about?"

Enoch slid from his boulder and knelt in the sand. He drew a vertical line in the sand and said, "In the first verse of Genesis we are told that, *'In the beginning God created the heavens and the earth'.*" He drew a picture of a stick man in the sand and continued, "We are also told that God created a man named Adam and placed him in the Garden of Eden. However, Adam and his wife sinned and this led to all of mankind living under a curse.

Enoch drew another vertical line in the sand and said, "When God sent the great flood that wiped out all of mankind except for Noah and his family he struck a new covenant with mankind and hung a rainbow in the sky to seal the deal."

He drew another vertical line in the sand, and another stick man, and continued, "Then God made a covenant with Abraham and promised him he would be the father of many nations."

"It was God's intention that his chosen people would include all the people of the world in his plans for redemption, but instead we've cut them off and become an exclusive people. This was never his intention. So, now we've come to a time when a new dispensation of God's grace must be introduced into the world."

He drew another large vertical line into the sand and another stick man. Then he paused before saying, "If I'm right we're about to experience a new beginning. And if I'm right we will have new scriptures that may one day say, *'In the beginning a child was born, and they called him Jesus. And he grew in wisdom and stature, and in favor with God and man. And he became the new Adam who surrendered his will to the will of the Father and offered himself as a sacrifice for the sins of the world'.*

Enoch looked up from his lines and pictures in the sand and stared intently into my eyes. "You will have an important role in this new beginning Lazarus. And you will have an even bigger role in the things that will come afterwards. Do you understand that?"

"Sure, if you say so, but I'm not sure what all of this has to do with some secret wall buried in a faraway land. Why is it so important for me to know about that?"

"According to our prophets, you are going to live until the end of days, when the wall will be revealed. It may be important for you to understand its significance when it's finally discovered. Included in the prophecies inscribed on the wall is a prophecy of another 'holy family' that will rise up in the last days. From this family there will be another 'coming of two': 'The one who dwells in darkness, so that all may see the light,' and 'the one who dwells in silence, so that all may hear the truth.'

"Perhaps if you know the significance of the wall, you will be able to recognize these two when they come and aid them in what they must do."

"Why would they need my help?"

"Because there will be another coming at that time as well; the coming of 'The Bringer of Death and Destruction.' 'The one who dwells in silence' and 'the one who dwells in darkness' must do battle against 'The Bringer of Death and Destruction' in those days, and if you have been sent here to fight against evil, then maybe you're to be a part of this battle as well."

I took all of this in and thought about it for a moment, and then I asked, "So do you have any idea where your people were supposed to go to build their wall? I've traveled all over the world, you know. Perhaps, I can figure out where they went if you can give me a clue."

Enoch looked at the distant horizon and said, "Our prophets said they were to go to 'o ge tou eleutheria', which means 'The Land of Liberty.' And only God knows where that great land may be!"

CHAPTER TWENTY

I thought about what he'd just told me and shook my head in frustration. "Elutheria? I've never encountered a country called Elutheria, and I can't say I've heard of any of the places I've visited being referred to as 'The Land of Liberty.' I think I'd remember something like that. I'm sorry I can't shed any light on the subject of where they may have gone to build their wall."

"It's okay. Maybe someday, you'll hear about it and be able to travel there. Who knows what the future may hold?" Enoch looked up at the waning sun and said, "We spent so much time in our meeting this morning, the day is almost over. I suppose we'd better say our goodbyes and let you go on your way."

Demetria picked up a leather bag she had by her side and held it out to Enoch. "Aren't you forgetting something?" she asked.

"Ah, yes. Thanks for reminding me, my love."

Enoch took the bag, which resembled my writing kit, and addressed me again, "Demetria and I talked at length this morning as we were traveling back from our meeting, and we decided there was another artifact and a relic from one of our ancestors we should leave in your care, since we don't know what's going to happen between us and our enemies."

He stood up with the bag and began to untie the cords that held it shut as he spoke, "The first thing we want to give you is"— he stopped and gave a startled look up the hill—"They're coming!"

He thrust the bag at me, and I slung it over my shoulder with my writing kit.

Then he spoke urgently, "Go to the vortex. Behind the pool is a mud-tube that leads down to a lower passage of the cave. You'll find a stream when you get there. Turn left and follow the stream till you find the secret exit from the cave. Now go!"

While he was speaking, I was trying to listen, but my attention was really on Demetria. She had picked up her battle lance and was peeking around the boulders we had been sitting on, so she could look up the hillside.

I turned to Enoch and said, "I can't leave you."

"You have to leave us. The artifacts and relics we've given you must not fall into the hands of these rebels. If you love us, you will go!"

He shoved me in the direction of the cave entrance, and as I was passing by Demetria, I saw a flash of movement up the hill. Without thinking, I reacted to what I'd seen, and my left hand flew up and snatched an arrow out of the air just before it hit Demetria in the face.

I could hear her heartbeat galloping as she frowned and poked me in the gut with the blunt end of her lance to push me away. "They're close," she said. "Go with God Lazarus, and don't look back."

I threw the arrow angrily over the ledge and sprinted for the cave entrance. The last thing I heard as I ducked inside was Enoch's shrill war cry and the voice of Demetria shouting, "We'll never forget you, Lazarus. Never. . . ."

I grabbed the eternal torch from the entrance and dashed through the cave to the vortex pool. Just as Enoch had promised, I found a small opening in the wall of the cave directly behind the pool itself. I held the torch down to the opening, but I couldn't see more than a few feet ahead. The opening was barely big enough for me to crawl through it on my hands and knees while holding the torch with one hand. Luckily, I had the staff in its harness on my back, so it was out of the way. It was awkward, but I was making it work, until I came to the mud. One moment I was crawling down a ramp on a damp, but relatively solid surface, and the next I was starting to slide down a muddy chute. I completely lost my balance and found myself sliding on my stomach with the torch blazing in front of my face as I plummeted into the unknown.

I shot out of the mud-tube and landed in a stream of water. And that's when the eternal torch decided this would be a good time to burn out. Suddenly I found myself in complete darkness. I had never experienced darkness like this. There was absolutely no light. None!

Even my enhanced vision was useless in these conditions. I was blind.

I tried to remember what Enoch had said as he was giving me directions on how to get out of the cave. Did he say, once I found the stream I should turn left, or did he say I should turn right? I had no idea. I had been preoccupied with worrying about what was going to happen to Demetria once I was gone.

I turned to the left and reached out to find the cave wall. Then I began walking in the stream with my left hand on the wall. As I walked, the stream seeped away into the ground below me until it completely disappeared. Luckily, I chose the right direction, and I didn't have to go far before I found the secret entrance. It was just a small hole that poked out the side of the mountain. I remembered Enoch had said the bats came back into the cave through another entrance, and I wondered if this was it. It looked like it was barely large enough for me to squeeze through. I stuck my head out and saw I would have to climb down the side of the mountain to the valley below. The sun was starting to set, so if I didn't start climbing right away I'd be doing it in the dark. I remembered my encounter with the snake the night I was climbing up to the cave and I decided it was time to get moving.

I was charting a climbing path in my head when suddenly, a blood curdling scream echoed through the cave. I was sure it was Demetria, and it didn't sound like she was having tea with her visitors.

I couldn't go any further. Enoch had demanded that I leave, so the artifacts and relic he'd given me didn't fall into the hands of his enemies. Well, okay then, I'd make sure that didn't happen. I slung the harness from my back that held the Rod of Moses, and I also removed my writing kit that held the Sacred Cup. I took those two items, along with the last bag he'd given me before we were interrupted, and hid them all in a crevice in the cave wall.

I turned back into the cave barehanded just as another scream tore through the air around me and ripped into my soul. I had seen and heard some terrible things in my time on the fields of battle, and the scream I heard now was not the scream of someone being killed; it was the scream of someone being intentionally tortured. The darkness of the passage before me may have been completely black, but the only color I could see, as I ran recklessly through the stream with clenched fists, was the color of revenge.

With a good deal of effort, instinct, and blind luck, I managed to find the mud-tube, pulled myself up the slippery slope, and flopped out into the pool room. Still in total darkness, I crawled forward and nearly knocked myself out when I crashed my head into the side of the vortex pool. I rolled onto my back seeing stars and tried to get my bearings. I knew the exit from this room and the abrupt turn that led to the main entrance were somewhere directly ahead of me, but I wasn't sure how I was supposed to get there without running into more obstacles.

As I was pondering my dilemma I looked inside my mind for solutions and suddenly realized I was still intertwined with the creature in the rod. I spoke aloud as if the Drakon were there with me, "I need to figure out how to get out of here, so do you think you might be able to help me out with this?"

I listened and heard the beating of a bat's wings. Apparently the treasure room wasn't the only place in the deeper recesses of the cave that held bats. I heard one let go of its perch on the ceiling and go fluttering away from me. Then there was another. One by one they were flying right by my head as if to say, "follow me."

I knew that soon there might be a rush of bats headed for their nightly foray, so I jumped to my feet and followed the sound of the first bats that were making their way to the main passageway. When I rounded the sharp turn onto the main passage I heard a desolate moan coming from the sleeping area. I proceeded more cautiously now, and as I crept forward I heard the beating of Demetria's heart. She was alive! But there was another heart beating nearby, and it wasn't Enoch's.

Bats were coming out of the low entrance to the treasure room in twos and threes as I passed by. And then I saw her. She was tied up and hanging from the ceiling of the cave by her hands. Her armor had been removed, and a man was poking her with a hot brand from the fire and demanding that she tell him where the Rod and Sacred Cup were hidden. She wasn't saying anything . . . and neither was I.

Covering the remaining distance in a blur, I shoved her assailant's head into the wall of the cave with such force that it blew up in an instantaneous cloud of gore, but as I was shoving him with one hand, I took the liberty of relieving him of his dagger with the other. I ignored his twitching body, and the shouts I heard from outside the cave, as I used his dagger to shred the rope that held Demetria suspended in mid-air. She fell into my arms, and I turned to carry her deeper into the cave. Before I could take a step, she pointed and shouted, "My lance!"

Her battle lance was propped up against the side of the cave, so I swooped it up and prepared to run toward the back of the cave. But, when I gripped her lance for the first time a flood of thoughts and memories rushed through my mind with such intensity it threatened to bring me to my knees. I leaned against the side of the cave, while still holding Demetria in my arms, and stubbornly shook my head to clear my mind. When I regained my focus I staggered away from the fire.

As we struggled past the entrance to the treasure room the bats were still just trickling out toward the entrance. I heard a shout behind us and knew we were just moments from being under attack. I reached out with my mind to the Drakon and said, "We need more bats NOW!"

Suddenly, all the bats seemed to awaken at once, and with a mighty rush they flapped and chattered past us, but not a one of them came close to touching us. I heard our pursuers screaming and cursing and knew we would have a moment before they could reenter the cave, so I lay Demetria down and asked, "Where's Enoch?" She shook her head and wailed, "He's gone!"

I picked her up and ran into the darkness as I said, "Then we need to be leaving, too."

⊱✦✦⊰

The next few minutes are a blur of anger, sadness, frustration and joy in my mind. I was angry that I had let Enoch talk me into leaving, and I was sad that he was dead. I was also frustrated because I didn't know how many enemies still remained who were hunting us in the darkness. On the other hand, I was happy that Demetria had survived to this point, and I was determined to see that those who had attacked her and Enoch paid for their betrayal.

In my frenzied state of mind, I somehow managed to get us both down the mud-tube in total darkness without causing any more damage to Demetria. Then I carried her through the stream until I found the exit.

When I laid her down on the floor of the cave she let out a whimper, and now that I had some light to work with, I saw she had a couple of wounds on her arms and legs where she'd been cut during battle, and burn marks on her stomach and chest from her torturer.

I remembered how Enoch had said the elixir could be used to heal wounds, so I removed her flask, opened it carefully, and poured a small amount on each of her wounds. I was amazed, when almost immediately each wound began to heal itself as I watched.

So far, so good. We had found the exit, Demetria was healing, and I couldn't hear any of our pursuers getting anywhere near us, but we still had a couple of problems.

We needed to get out of this cave, climb down the side of the mountain, and travel several miles through the wilderness on our own before we could join back up with Jesus, Horus, and my guards. And to complicate matters, Demetria was spent.

The heat of battle, the agony of seeing her beloved Enoch vanquished by their enemies, and the anguish of being tortured had left her empty of emotion, and devoid of even the will to live.

She laid her lovely head in my lap, and wept for hours until she drifted off to sleep.

Holding Demetria in my arms while she slept wasn't the hardest thing I've ever had to do because I loved her . . . in a sisterly kind of way . . . of course . . . I think. . . .

In any case, I held her faithfully through the night and waited for the dawning of a new day.

And then the bats came. . . .

CHAPTER TWENTY-ONE

They came in a sudden wave of fluttering and flapping madness that I should have anticipated and been prepared for. In the back of my mind I had suspected that this was the way the bats came into the cave in the mornings, so I should have moved us to a place where the passage widened and then stayed close to the wall. But I had a lot on my mind that night, and when the light began to seep through the small opening, I didn't think about what that would portend for our future.

Unlike their nightly ritual of leaving in twos and threes until they built up a full head of steam, they seemed to all return at once. I heard them before I saw them. It sounded like a cloud of locusts descending on a crop of barley, and it gave me just a split second to pull Demetria to my chest and roll with her to the side of the passage before they were completely upon us.

I covered her with my body while the wave of chattering bats subsided, and that's how she woke up. With me straddling her and holding her close to my heart while I stared at her face. Oh, that beautiful face. . . .

Her eyes flew open, and she murmured, "Lazarus, what are you doing?"

I rolled off her and sprung to my feet, and since we were in a very constricted area of the cave, this allowed me to gracefully knock a hole in the ceiling of the cave, with the top of my head. I sunk to my knees almost as quickly as I'd bounced up, and then slumped to the side.

Demetria scooted over to me and said, "What was that all about?"

I could barely see her through the constellations, but I managed to say, "I was trying to protect you from the bats."

She looked all around us and said, "I don't see any bats."

"Well, trust me. They were here just a second ago in droves, and you would have been terrified."

She smiled, "Droves, huh? Well, whatever you say, Mister Bat-Slayer."

Then her smile disappeared, and she looked away and said, "Normally I wouldn't mind waking up to a warm embrace, but Enoch is gone now."

I spluttered, "Yes, and I'm sorry about that, I shouldn't have allowed the two of you to convince me to leave you. Maybe if I'd stayed and helped you fight, things would have turned out differently."

"You don't need to apologize. We've lived our lives in service to our people, despite what our detractors may think. Keeping the relic and artifacts out of the hands of our enemies was essential. You had to leave us and keep them safe. I don't see them here, so I assume you've hidden them nearby."

I pointed at the crevice in the wall of the cave, "They're right over there. No one would find them in a million years."

She reached over and pulled her lance close. "And you also salvaged my lance, I see."

"You insisted, so against my better judgement, I grabbed it and brought it with us. You have a way of getting what you want, you know."

She grinned, "You men have your powers, and we women have ours, I guess."

"Yes, you do."

She looked at the exit and asked, "So, what now, do we make a mad dash for freedom and go our separate ways?"

"Well, we might make a mad dash for freedom, but why would we go our separate ways?"

"There are Seekers looking for me, and they won't stop till they find me. They'll assume that finding me will lead them to you and the artifacts and relic they covet. I can't allow you to endanger the people you love by keeping company with me. As soon as we're safely away from here, I'll do my best to disappear into the night, and I'll never be a burden to you again, I promise."

"You're no burden, Demetria, you and Enoch both became dear to me in a short period of time, and now I feel responsible for his death and for your wellbeing. I want you to come back with me to Bethany and live in my fortress. You'll be safe there. Enoch said he didn't tell any of your subjects who I was or where I lived, so the Seekers won't know to look for you there. We just need to wait until dark, and then we'll try to sneak out of here and get back to my people."

"No, I've lived in this isolated place with only the company of Enoch for a long time. I can live alone in desolation if I have to. I'll find another cave and make my home there."

I said, "Don't be silly, everyone needs the help and encouragement of sharing their lives with others they love. My family and the people of my household will welcome you with open arms, and you'll soon have a home where you can bless and be blessed. You'll fit right in. Of course, no one can know you're a queen, and you won't be treated like one, but working for your living shouldn't be too tough after living in a cave. I'll have my steward find a job you enjoy doing."

"That's a very kind offer Lazarus, but there's something else you're not considering."

"What's that?"

"I'm dependent on the elixir for my life. I've been using it for nearly 200 years, and if I don't drink it at least once every week I'll begin to age very quickly and I'll die a very painful death."

"Well, obviously you can't come back here again since your enemies will be guarding this place, but I thought Enoch said your people had rules about the use of vortexes. That led me to believe there were others besides this one. Can't you just get more from another pool?"

"It's not that simple," she said. "There are other vortexes, but they're very rare, and I don't know of another one nearby. However, Enoch and I hid a supply of elixir in secret caches in several different places in the wilderness, and near Jerusalem, just in case something like this ever happened. There's probably enough stockpiled away to keep me alive for a couple of years until I can find another source."

"But how will you provide for your other needs? You're going to need a place to stay, food, and other provisions. You can't just go live in a cave on your own. A woman out here alone won't last long"

"Oh really! And I guess a man would be just fine, huh? I know you think I'm some delicate flower or something, but I'm really pretty tough, and very capable of defending myself. The elixir not only prolongs our lives, it also gives us an increase in strength, speed, and stamina. It's not nearly as great a boost as the way your own abilities have been enhanced, but it does give us an edge against most people we encounter. As for my other needs, Enoch and I were always aware of the possibility we might have to start a new life rather suddenly if we were ever forced from our sanctuary, so we were always prepared to leave, and we hid caches of elixir and treasure in several locations."

She lifted up the fur on the shoulder opposite of where she kept her flask of elixir and showed me a leather bag strapped there. "This bag is similar to the one you gave the stranger you rescued. It has enough precious jewels and gold in it to buy me all I need for a long time. There are more jewels and more gold bars in our hiding places."

"Okay, I get it. You're a tough, capable, and resourceful lady who's used to being treated like a queen. You obviously don't need the help of a bum like me, but just give some thought to the possibility of coming to live with me awhile. How can it hurt? Maybe I can help you find another vortex. After all, I've got some experience in running around in caves now."

She laughed and said, "You do have that to offer now, don't you?"

"Say, while we're on the subject, how does a vortex come to be formed anyway?"

"It's a peculiar anomaly that only happens when a hot spring forms a pool in a cave, but the water has to overflow from the hot spring and form another pool where the water swirls around and drains back into the ground. Something in that swirling causes the water to change into elixir. To find a hot spring in a cave is one thing, but to find one where the water has overflowed and formed a nearby vortex pool is even rarer. Our people have only found a few in all our days, and some of those have ceased to exist when one or both of the requisite pools dried up."

I saw her yawning, and I said, "You must be exhausted, and I woke you up prematurely this morning when the bats arrived. We've got to travel several miles through the wilderness tonight, so why don't you take a nap while I keep watch?"

She looked around at the hard floor of the cave and asked, "But what would I use as a pillow?"

I thought about offering her my lap, but decided that would probably not be wise, so instead I gave her the bag of unopened treasures to prop under her head.

She was soon fast asleep, so I broke out my writing kit and wrote awhile.

⇥⇤

March 26th

I may have been wrong when I said every day can't be a day full of excitement because yesterday was another wild day around here.

Yesterday morning, Enoch and Demetria had a meeting with their fellow Seekers that didn't go well. Some of their tribesmen weren't happy they had given me the Rod of Moses and the Sacred Cup, and they were threatening to come and take them back by force.

While we were waiting in the afternoon to see if anything would happen, Enoch told me most of his people left on a mysterious quest many hundreds of years ago to follow a star to a new land of milk and honey called Elutheria, or 'The Land of Liberty.' I've never heard of any country being described that way, but Enoch swears it's a real place.

He said once his people got to this new home they were supposed to build a wall 700 feet long and inscribe all the Torah, all of their history, and all of their secret knowledge and prophecies on it. Then they were supposed to bury it. Seems like an awful waste of time to go to all that trouble and then just bury your work, but I'm not the one in charge.

Enoch said that in the last days the wall would be discovered, and it would reveal a prophecy about another 'holy family' that was to going to appear in the last days. He said that out of this family there would be another 'coming of two' : 'The one who dwells in darkness, so that all may see the light,' and 'the one who dwells in silence, so that all may hear the truth.' Sounds like a bunch of crazy jibber-jabber to me, but Enoch seems to think it's really important.

In fact, he seems to think that one day I may have to come to the aid of these two people because of someone else who's supposed to show up in the last days.

That guy is referred to in the same prophecy as 'The Bringer'. You're probably wandering what The Bringer is supposed to bring, and I think I asked Enoch that same question. He said, "The Bringer will bring 'death and destruction.'" Sounds scary, huh? Who knows. . . ?

Also, Enoch and Demetria decided to give me another artifact and a relic of one of their ancestors for safekeeping, but before they could give them to me, and explain what they were, we were attacked by Seekers!

"What are Seekers?" you ask.

Well, turns out that's what the people of the tribe of Issachar are called these days. Their elders and prophets were called Seekers because they sought after truth and understanding, so eventually the name was adapted by the whole tribe.

Enoch insisted I retreat with the objects he'd given me to keep his enemies from getting them, so I tried to escape like he'd asked me. However, I heard Demetria screaming before I could completely get away, and I just couldn't go through with it. I hid the things I'd been given and went back to try to help.

I arrived back at the fire to find Demetria being tortured by one of the Seekers. Let's just say, that guy won't be seeking anything in the future. With a little help from the bats I rescued Demetria, but I was too late to help Enoch. He had already succumbed in battle. May he rest in peace!

I'm still trying to wrap my head around the idea that Enoch is really gone. I'll never forget the night I met him, and how afraid I was of him initially. I can still see him running in circles around me and jabbering away when he was playing the part of a crazy cave hermit. I'll always remember how surprised I was to see him cleaned up and wearing his royal robes and crown as he announced he was the King of the Issachar while Demetria stood by his side in all her regal majesty. I could go on and on listing my fondest memories. In just a few short days he made a huge impression on me with his grace, sincerity, and wisdom, and I'm sure he's changed my life in ways I can barely fathom at this point. He was a remarkable man, and I'm going to miss him!

Last night I used some of the elixir to nurse Demetria back to health from her wounds.

Oh yeah, so now you're asking, "What the heck is elixir?"

Well, that happens to be the super top-secret liquid that is somehow manufactured in the magic pool I told you about earlier. You know, the one with the whirlpool in the middle. Enoch calls the whirlpool a vortex.

Anyway, the vortex makes elixir, and if someone drinks elixir, the aging process slows down dramatically for them. Apparently, some of the Seekers have lived a long time this way, but they can't regenerate like me, so they eventually die. And if they fail to drink it once a week they age rapidly and die right away . . . or at least pretty quickly . . . I think.

Demetria was just telling me today that the elixir also enhances the user's strength, speed, and stamina, but not to the degree that my own abilities have been boosted.

Enoch gave me a small supply before he died because he said I could pour it on a person's external wounds, and it would speed the healing process dramatically, and judging from the way it worked on Demetria last night, he was right. But he cautioned me to never let anyone drink it because, if they do, they'll be dependent on it to continue living.

He seemed to think I'll eventually be tempted to share it with someone, but I don't see how that could ever happen.

Now, Demetria and I are waiting until dark to try climbing down the side of the mountain so we can make our escape from the cave.

I'm trying to convince her to come and live with me for a while. I think that would be best, at least until she can find a new source of elixir.

Oh yeah, she's been using it to extend her own life for about the last 200 years. It's hard to imagine someone as vital as she seems being that old, but that's what she claims, anyway. She's got enough stashed away to last awhile, but she's going to need to find another vortex soon.

She's sleeping now to get rested up for our big escape tonight. Hopefully, the next time I'm able to write I'll be back in the company of Jesus.

With a little luck, I'll join back up with our party and be back on the trail to Bethany before the night's over.

I can't wait to see Iris again. . . .

However, it just occurred to me that if Demetria decides to come live with us, Iris may not be too happy with the idea. Surely she won't be jealous, but who knows. We shall see. . . .

CHAPTER TWENTY-TWO

While Demetria was sleeping, and I was writing in my journal, a mysterious transformation was taking place by the vortex pool in Enoch's cave.

I wasn't there to see it happen, but I imagine it went something like this:

His spirit had fallen to Earth about 30 years ago, and since evil spirits like his couldn't see the light of day unless they inhabited a host of some type, he immediately sought shelter in a nearby cave. In his spirit form, he couldn't take the objects he'd managed to steal just before his banishment, so he had to leave them right where they'd fallen in the sand. Unfortunately, for him, he found a cave with one of the magical pools inside. The kind of pools where he, and other evil spirts like him, were sucked in and forced to helplessly wait for a living creature to come along that they could possess.

There were rules for spirits like him; rules interwoven in the fabric of creation for this particular world that most beings living here were blissfully unaware of. First, he couldn't leave the vicinity of this infernal pool unless he managed to invest his spirit in an unsuspecting host who was capable of carrying him out into the world and protecting his essence from the debilitating rays of the sun.

Second, he couldn't invest himself in a person who had a pure heart, nor could he possess someone who had taken the trouble to protect themselves with the proper cleansing rituals or talismans. However, such protections had been known to fail if the person in question had a particularly evil streak themselves.

Third, he couldn't invest himself in an animal that was nocturnal, so the bats overhead were useless. The only spirits that could possess a bat were the bloodsuckers, and thankfully, there weren't many of those. Even he was creeped-out by the bloodsuckers, and that was saying a lot.

He had been waiting here for 30 years for someone, or something, to come along that was investable, but nothing had appeared. It seemed like eternity to someone as powerful and vital as he.

The only time he'd been allowed to leave here during that thirty-year span was when an angel came and whisked him away one night, three years ago, to a remote part of the nearby wilderness. When he reached his appointed destination he was flabbergasted to find Jesus wandering around on his own.

It was disconcerting to see him in the form of an adult human, but his essence was unmistakable. Even from a distance his aura was clearly visible, and that aura still looked like the child he'd always known.

Upon closer examination, it was clear his human body was emancipated and close to shutting down. In this condition, he would be wildly susceptible to temptation, and the malicious spirit knew an amazing opportunity had just been laid at his feet. He may have been tossed out of Heaven and spent thirty years in a purgatory of sorts beside that accursed pool, but now he could use his particular powers of persuasion to prove a terrible mistake had been made in sending Jesus to be the savior of humankind. It should have been him!

He had been one of the principle leaders of the angels. Only Michael held rank above him, but Michael was an unpolished, ruffian warrior and couldn't begin to match him in cunning and skill when it came to leading and manipulating other beings.

In Heaven he was known as Satan, or Lucifer, or Beelzebub. It all depended on who you asked on any particular day. That was his nature, after all; duplicity was his power, and he was the best at what he did. He'd had a lot of names over time, but that was just a part of the job when you're the boogeyman in every culture and society under the sun. Many here on Earth referred to him as the Devil. As far as he was concerned you could call him anything, as long as you called him for supper. Ha! He really cracked himself up sometimes.

His job was testing and trying the creatures God created, to see how they'd react under pressure. He'd busted Eve big-time in the garden, and that was one indictment of which he was particularly proud. He'd taken old Noah down a notch straight off the ark, and Jonah took a one-way ride in the belly of a whale for his test (that was a good one too, by golly). There were some who got the best of him from time to time, but only Jonah got any real press in the Bible for his efforts. But, by God, he'd made him sweat and cry like a baby, and he'd paid a terrible price for it in the end (fat bastard).

Now the ultimate prize lay before him. If he could just tempt Jesus to use his powers in an unbecoming way, he could show he'd been right all along. God would have no choice but to give him back his place. And by the time Satan got done working God over with the guilt trip of a lifetime, he'd convince him to send *him* to Earth in the place of Jesus. When everything was said and done, he'd be running the show down here forever.

But first, he needed a host. Out of the corner of his eye he saw a movement and there it was. . . . A snake was crawling by. Yeah, baby . . . his favorite host of all time to the rescue! He invested his essence in the unsuspecting creature and went to work immediately.

He transformed the body of the snake into a stunningly beautiful serpent of many colors and also gave himself a couple of legs so he could stand upright. Why crawl when you can walk, right?

Then he slithered right up to Jesus and purred, "Well, hello stranger. Never imagined meeting you here."

Jesus said, "How've you been Satan?"

"Oh, you know me, dude. I've just been taking it easy, man."

"I guess you're mad at me."

"What? Me? Hell no, I'm not mad. No hard feelings on my part. You and your dad did what you thought was best, and I've come to have complete peace in my heart with your decision. Really, it's okay with me."

"Well, that's good to hear. I'm glad you're coping so well."

"Oh yeah, I'm doing great, but I've got to say, you don't look so hot yourself. When's the last time you had a decent meal, man?"

"I've not had anything to eat in 40 days and 40 nights."

"Wow, now that's just not right! Who told you to do that?"

"Our heavenly father."

"Really, what was he thinking? You know, as a part of my work down here, I've done some testing on these human bodies, and 40 days without food is about all they can take. I hate to be the one to tell you, but if you don't eat soon, you're gonna die, and that's no bullshit man. That's just the way it is. If I'm a lyin' I'm a dyin'," Satan laughed at his humor and continued, "Ya know, I'm sure the big G meant well when he told you not to eat. He was probably tryin' to see how tough you were, but I'm sure he never meant for you to starve yourself to death. Hey, now here's a thought. Maybe, he was testing you to see if you're really cut out to be 'The One,' you know what I mean. Like, are you really 'The Son of God'? I mean, can you really be 'The Sacrifice to Beat All Sacrifices'? If so, you'd have the power to turn some of these stones into bread and feed yourself, so why don't you just do that, and show Him what you're really made of. You can feed yourself and bring this whole ordeal to an end, man."

Jesus said, "I am starving, but it is written, 'Man shall not live by bread alone, but by every word that comes from the mouth of God.'"

Satan took a step back and said, "Yeah, you're so-o-o right about that, man. What was I thinking?" He paused, as if considering his options, and said, "You know what? To commemorate our reunion we should visit the Temple. Let's see if I've still got a little pizzazz left in these old bones."

Satan snapped his fingers and changed his appearance to that of a man. "Wow, didn't know if I still had it in me to pull that off. It's been a while, ya know. Now, let's try one more thing." Then he snapped his fingers again, and he and Jesus were instantly transported to the pinnacle of the temple. Below them, a crowd began to gather and point up at their precarious perch.

Satan said, "Check it out man. Do you hear those miserable cretins? Now that they've gotten over the shock of seeing us magically appear up here, they're calling for us to jump. They think we're going to commit suicide. What a bunch of losers, huh? But, you know what, if you're the 'Son of God' you could throw yourself off here and not get hurt; for it is written, 'He will give his angels charge of you,' and 'On their hands they will lift you up so you will never strike your foot against a stone.' Now that's straight outa' the holy scriptures themselves buddy, so you know it's gotta be true. And think about it. What a great way for you to prove to all these louts that you're really the Messiah. You jump, and a bunch of angels come gliding in and snatch you right out of the air. By the end of the day you'll be king of the Jews. Hell, forget that, you'll be the king of the friggin' world, man. The people will do whatever you tell them to do, so you can forget about all this talk of sacrifice and suffering. You can complete your mission without shedding a drop of blood. Dude, you won't even have to shed a tear to get this done and behind you."

Jesus said, "Again it is written, 'You shall not tempt the Lord your God.'"

Satan was forced to take another step back as he replied, "Ya know, you may have a point there. I guess it's best to not push your luck when you're in a situation like this. After all, it's a long way down from here."

Satan considered his options again and said, "Hey, there's a place I used to go every once and in a while to check out the scenery. You're gonna love it. Come with me, my friend."

He snapped his fingers and he and Jesus were instantly transported to a very high mountain. Satan said, "Wow, check out this view! You can see practically the whole known world from here. Isn't that breathtaking? Now, look into my mind and see the glory of every civilization on Earth. Satan focused his energy to project his memories of all the places he had visited on Earth before his fall from grace. In the span of just a few moments Jesus' mind was bombarded with infinite images of beauty, power, and prestige.

Satan let it all sink in and then he triumphantly said, "As you know, I've been cast out of Heaven and this is *my* domain now, so I tell you what . . . I'll give you all of these things I've just showed you if you'll only get down on your knees and worship me."

Satan held his breath and waited for Jesus to reply. He didn't really have the power to give anybody, anything, but Jesus didn't know that. It seemed like Jesus was wavering in his stance. Was it the wind here on this high mountain, or was his starving body finally giving out, or could it be that he was really going to bow down? If he did, Satan would have won and everything would change in his favor.

Just as it seemed Jesus might lose his footing and fall to the ground, he pulled himself up and said, "Give up and go away Satan! For it is written, 'You shall worship the Lord your God, and him only shall you serve.'"

As soon as Jesus said those last words, they were transported back to the wilderness where they'd met. Immediately, Satan found his essence being ripped out of the serpent he'd possessed a while earlier and his spirit was whisked back to this god-forsaken pool.

That was three years ago. Since then, he'd only seen the man named Enoch and his wife Demetria, and their hearts were far too pure for him to ever hope to touch them. Then a few nights ago, a man he'd never seen came to the pool. At first, Satan thought this was the chance he'd been waiting for. The man wore no talisman on his back like the Seekers, and he hadn't undergone any cleansing ceremonies. He wasn't even wearing a sapphire to ward away the lesser spirits. He would be easy prey. But once he got close enough to see inside his heart Satan knew he'd never have a chance with this one. It made him want to puke to see how pure his heart was. What a shame!

He went back to waiting, and now, his wait may finally be over. From the chatter he was hearing, it appeared Enoch had been taken down, and now some of his fellow Seekers were talking about checking out the pool.

A man they called Mathias was the first to come into the pool room. It was immediately clear he hadn't performed any cleansing ceremonies. Apparently, he felt secure knowing he had his sapphire jewel hanging from his neck, and, of course, he also had the talisman on his back. The sapphire jewel would deter nearly all of the spirits here, and the talisman would cause the others to retreat in most cases, but Satan was not like the others. He was far more powerful; there was really no comparison. Unless this arrogant fool had a heart as pure as Enoch and Demetria he was in far more trouble than he could possibly imagine.

Satan waited for him to come closer and slowly reached out with his essence to explore the heart of his intended victim. What he found was a heart so black and cold even he was a little disgusted. Armed with this knowledge, he rushed him, and in a moment, it was all over.

He took a moment to explore the memories of Mathias and to make himself comfortable in his new home. Then he calmly walked out into the sunlight. His minions waited for him on the ledge, and he took his time looking each one over and reading their thoughts and hearts. Yes, these would do just fine, for a start. He looked up at the sun and spread his arms wide to take it all in. He smiled and broke out into a guttural laugh that sounded disturbingly more like the roar of a lion than the laugh of a man.

The time of waiting was over, now the Great Dragon would prowl the Earth seeking to see whom he might devour!

CHAPTER TWENTY-THREE

Before the sun began to set, I woke up Demetria and had her stick her head out the exit from the cave. I tried to explain the path I'd mapped out in my head that we would need to follow as we climbed down the side of the mountain once the sun went down. I wanted her to create a picture in her head of what she would need to do when the time came.

We went over our plan several times, and then I asked her, "How many Seekers are still looking for you?"

She replied, "Well, that's hard to say. It depends on how many pairs decided to revolt."

"What are pairs?"

"When a child is born among my people they are taken away almost immediately to be raised along with other Seeker children at a place we call *The Academy* until they come of age. When they reach adulthood they're assigned a mate. We call that 'being paired.' Each pair becomes a team that works together to carry on our work. If someone should die, the survivor is mated with another tribesman; so theoretically, we're always working with someone else."

"When we come of age each pair is given a matching blue sapphire to show our allegiance to each other."

"Why a sapphire?"

"Because that's the jewel that signifies the tribe of Issachar, and sapphires also have other mystical powers."

"What else happens when you become an adult Seeker?"

"You are given your talisman."

I said, "I'm sorry. You're given a tail-of-what-man? I've no idea what you're talking about."

She laughed, "Our talisman is the tattoo you saw on my back when I rose up out of the magic pool, and on Enoch's back when you fought him. The sun interposed inside the half-moon is the symbol of the tribe of Issachar because we were tasked with studying the movements of the moon, stars, and other heavenly bodies to try and understand what the future might hold. Each adult Seeker is given their talisman as a symbol of their birthright and as a protective shield against evil spirits. It gives us an extra layer of protection when we go near vortexes to help keep us from being possessed by the spirits that hover there, but it's not foolproof in that regard, so we still need to do our purification rituals."

"So how many pairs were helping you guard this place?"

"There were a total of twelve pairs assigned to help us guard the vortex. Some of them were in close proximity, and others were scattered further out in the wilderness, but all of them could be easily summoned. I don't think all of them will have joined the revolt, but it's impossible to say for sure. I certainly didn't see that many when they attacked yesterday."

"How many would you say you saw?"

"Probably 6 pairs."

"That would be 12 people. Do you know if Enoch was able to kill any of them before he died?"

"I saw him kill one male and one female before they surrounded and overcame him. I killed one female myself, and then you killed one male when you rescued me."

208

I nodded, "That would leave a minimum of 8 still looking for us."

She looked away and said, "There could be others helping them as well."

"What are you talking about? Other Seekers?"

"No. Other men. Some of our tribesmen have infiltrated bands of brigades who attack and rob people who travel through the wilderness. They pose as hoodlums themselves, and once they've won the confidence of the other bandits, they live with them without ever giving away their true identities. It's a way to increase our manpower, and it's an effective source of revenue. Our tribesmen skim the best of the loot taken from their victims and give it to us to store here in our treasure room."

"I hate to ask, but was Enoch okay with your people joining up with common bandits to waylay innocent strangers in the wilderness? That doesn't sound like something he would condone."

"No, he didn't approve, but being the King of the Issachar didn't really give him a lot of authority or control over his subjects these days. There was a time when no one would have dared to go against what our king said, but sadly, those days are long gone. Some of our greatest enemies within our tribe were practically outlaws themselves, so they fit right in with the bandits they befriended."

"Obviously, that's going to complicate our escape."

"I'm afraid it will be nearly impossible to get your people back to Bethany without running into at least some of them. They'll be watching every trail to try to find us."

"That's even more of a reason for you to come with me to my home. If they find you out on your own, you won't have a chance against that many, I don't care how tough you are. At least if you're traveling with my caravan you'll be in the company of some of my guards who know how to fight."

"I promised you I would think about coming to live with you for a while, and I'm still considering it. I'll at least go with you till you rejoin your friends. Then I'll give you my decision."

I nodded, "That's fair enough." I glanced out the narrow opening at the lengthening shadows and said, "I think it time for us to gather our things and climb down a mountain."

⊷⊶

By the time we had our things ready to go, it was nearly dark enough outside to begin our descent. I was watching the last of the light fade from the skyline when I heard Demetria saying, "What's that you're whistling?"

"Oops, sorry. That's something I do sometimes when I'm nervous or in deep thought. To tell you the truth, I didn't even know I was doing it."

"It's okay. I like it. Where'd you hear that tune?"

"Oh, that's something my dad used to whistle when we were traveling together on the caravans or ships."

"Do you know the words?"

"Not really, he always just whistled it, but I once heard a drunken sailor sing along with my dad's whistling, and the words he sang said something about going off somewhere to find a witch, or wizard, or someone like that. I believe it was a traveling song of some kind because my dad would always whistle it when we were starting on a journey."

"Well, then it's appropriate for our situation because we're about to leave on a journey. You'll have to do it again for me sometime."

"And I will, but for now, we've got some climbing to do."

I went first, so I could assist Demetria as she moved from ledge to ledge and foothold to handhold, but the truth is she didn't need much assistance. She handled the climb quite well, and soon we had made it to the trail below without suffering any type of calamity.

I looked around and said, "To tell you the truth, I have no idea where we are in relation to the main trail I came in on, but for some reason it feels like we should go in that direction."

Demetria took a hard look at the stars and said, "You're right, the main trail is that way."

"Well, okay then. Here's the plan. We're going to stay close to the hillsides and mountains that form the valleys we'll be traveling through. We won't be walking on the main trails, so that should help us to move without being observed. I have exceptional eyesight on a night like this when the moon is so bright because I don't need much light to see, so I'll lead the way, and you stay close and follow my lead. Okay?"

"Yes."

We followed the natural flow of the terrain and took our time, so we wouldn't make any more noise than necessary. Occasionally I would stop and listen to the sounds of the night, but I never heard anything alarming. All things considered, we were making good time.

We weren't far from where I'd left Jesus and the others in our secret little gorge, when I saw something moving on the trail we were shadowing. We waited and watched, and I was soon able to determine it was a group of nine men and one woman, and they were all well-armed. One man and one woman were on horseback while the rest were on foot. This led me to surmise the man and woman was probably a Seeker pair, while the others were probably common outlaws.

I was hoping that if we stayed low, and didn't move, they would just pass on by. But the problem was, we were standing in a narrow pass between two steep hills, so there wasn't much room between us and the trail.

As they drew near, I watched them closely trying to determine which of them should be my first targets if it came to a fight. As I was making this assessment, I felt the Rod of Moses tingling in my grip, as if it was letting me know it was ready to be brought into play if needed.

Just when I thought they might pass on by, one of the men on foot stopped and said, "I need to take a leak Mathias."

The man on horseback pulled back on the reins of his horse and said, "Make it quick. I have a feeling they're close by."

The man who wished to relieve himself handed his spear off to one of his comrades and ambled over in our direction. Apparently he liked to have some privacy when he was doing his business because he walked all the way over to where we were lying on our stomachs. It was completely dark where we were hiding, and we must have been invisible to him because he marched right up to us and stepped on each of my hands with each of his feet. I grimaced at the pain, but didn't utter a sound. However, when he unbuckled his pants, and I calculated the trajectory his urine would be taking on its way to my head, I'd had enough.

I jerked my hands from beneath his shoes, jumped to my feet, and swung him around in the direction of his friends before he knew what was happening. I held the dagger I'd taken from Demetria's torturer to his throat and shouted, "I have a knife to your friend's throat, so if you value his life, you'll move on down the trail in the direction you're traveling and not look back. When you're out of sight, I'll let him go."

The one named Mathias turned his horse to face us, along with the woman. Meanwhile the other men leveled their spears in our direction and spread out in a loose semicircle around us.

Mathias took his time and gave his men ample opportunity to get into position before he said, "And what if we don't value his life?"

My captive sputtered and tried to speak but I increased the pressure of my knife on his throat and he thought better of it.

I growled, "Then I guess we've got a problem, but I hope you'll think long and hard about what you're going to do. I really don't want to have to kill you all."

Mathias laughed, "Kill us all, hey? Do you hear that boys? He says he's going to kill us all. I tell you what stranger, step out here where I can see you, and give us the woman and all the trinkets you stole from the cave of Enoch, and we'll let you go. What-a-ya-say?"

Clearly Mathias was trying to determine my exact location by the sound of my voice before he charged me with his horse, so I didn't say anything more.

Everything grew deathly quiet while each of us waited on the other to make a move. I was preparing to slit the throat of the man I held captive, and then go after the others, when I heard a slight rustling in the nearby brush. I listened closer and was able to isolate the sound of two heartbeats that hadn't been there just a moment ago.

I smiled at this new development and said, "Samson. . . Delilah. . . sic 'em."

Immediately, the silence of the wilderness was rudely disrupted by the sounds of men being torn to shreds. With little remorse, I quietly killed my captive and tossed his body aside. Meanwhile, I saw that Demetria had jumped into the fray and was dispatching one of the bandits to my left, so I moved in that direction to lend her support. I was able to club one of the other bandits in the head and send him home to meet his maker, and then it was over.

Mathias shouted, "Retreat!" as my dogs gave chase to his horses and sent them braying into the night in the direction of Shiloh. The four men who could still run joined him in flight, and I called Samson and Delilah back to my side.

I went to my knees, held my arms wide, and my dogs charged in wildly, and sent me rolling across the rough terrain. They licked and barked, and I laughed and wept to see them.

Demetria laughed and giggled as she watched me frolicking with my dogs. Then with obvious reluctance she said, "I hate to be the one to break up your reunion with your friends, but I doubt we've seen the last of those bastards. Mathias was one of Enoch's greatest enemies, and he's probably the mastermind behind the rebellion."

As she spoke, a war horn sounded in the night from the direction our attackers had just fled. Almost immediately other horns began to respond in the night.

Demetria said, "They're signaling the others to let them know we've been found, and they're calling them to congregate here. What should we do?"

I jumped to my feet, swooped up my staff, and grabbed her hand, as I said,

"We should run!"

And we did. . . .

CHAPTER TWENTY-FOUR

I knew we weren't far from the hidden gorge where I'd left Jesus and his disciples, so instead of trying to continue sneaking beside the trail we ran with abandon. Luckily, Demetria had above average stamina, thanks to drinking the elixir, or I don't think she could have kept pace with me. As it was, she seemed to take delight in running freely with me, so I held her hand, and we galloped down the trail in the moonlight with the freezing wilderness wind whipping through our free flowing hair. Samson and Delilah bounded over the obstacles they encountered as they ran on either side of the trail beside us, and I felt as if I was running in a dream.

Demetria was a superbly beautiful woman, and no one could deny it. But that night, as we ran through the desert together she was more beautiful than any woman had a right to be. I kept glancing at her as we ran, and what I saw truly amazed me. Her furs covered just enough of her flesh to not be immodest, but what they revealed, as she laughed and leapt by my side, took my breath away. Every muscle and curve of her body seemed to be in perfect harmony with the universe, and the sheen of sweat that glimmered in the moonlight on her luxuriant skin only added to her alluring persona.

Her long hair bounced in an erotic polyrhythmic pulse with the beating of her heart in my head, and I thought I'd died and gone to Heaven. Only . . . she wasn't mine . . . she could never be mine. I truly loved Iris, and nothing could ever change that . . . could it?

Luckily, I spotted something in our surroundings that interrupted this train of thought before it could lead me too far astray.

I slowed our pace, and gently pulled Demetria to a stop, and then I said, "This is it! We're back."

I stopped for a few minutes and listened carefully to the sounds of the night around us. When I was certain there were no sounds of pursuit, and therefore no one watching as we approached the hidden entrance to our gorge, I took Demetria's hand again, and led her through the shadows to the narrow pass between the boulders.

As soon as we stepped through the pass, Horus was there to meet us, and he didn't look happy. I immediately let go of Demetria's hand when I realized he must have been keeping watch from on top of the boulders and observed us as we were approaching. From the looks he was giving me, I figured he wasn't too happy with seeing me holding the hand of another woman besides his sister, Iris.

I mumbled something about being glad to be back, but he cut me off by saying, "Sorry about the dogs getting loose. I had them staked out, but they somehow loosed their tethers and ran off into the night. They must have sensed you were nearby."

He was talking to me, but he was looking at Demetria, and his looks were not kind, to say the least.

I said, "Horus, this is Demetria. She's the Que . . . wife of a friend of mine named Enoch. Enoch was murdered yesterday, and I'm helping her escape from the outlaws who attacked them."

That news seemed to put him at ease a little, and his look softened as the said, "Sorry for your loss, ma'am. We'll do what we can to make your stay with us comfortable until you can get where you need to go."

"She'll be going with us, or at least I'm hoping that's what she'll decide to do. She'll be safer there, considering she still has people pursuing her. I've offered to give her a job in my household."

Now, Horus gave me a knowing look and said, "Going with us, you say? Well that's mighty kind of you, sir. I'm sure everyone back home will be thrilled to meet her. I'll just be going back to keep watch."

As he walked by me he paused by my side and whispered, "I hope you know what you're doing." Then he took one more look over his shoulder at Demetria, and shaking his head, he walked back to his post.

Demetria said, "Is it just me, or does he hate me?"

I replied, "Horus is the brother of the woman I'm to marry when we get home. I don't think he was too happy to see me holding the hand of a mysterious, beautiful woman."

Demetria looked away and said, "Oh, so you're about to be married. I don't believe I'd heard you mention that before . . . well . . . congratulations! She's a lucky woman. I can't wait to meet the bride to be."

"Yes, I have a feeling that may be an event to remember," I said with a grim smile.

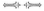

We had arrived at the gorge in the early hours of the night, yet it was late enough that everyone except the lookouts were already in bed. I woke Jesus up and introduced him to Demetria, only to be told they had met before when he visited Enoch's cave after his baptism.

He was deeply saddened when I told him of Enoch's death, and he hugged Demetria tightly while expressing his remorse.

Then he turned to me and said, "I'm sure we have a lot of catching up to do after your visit with Enoch, but we also have a lot to do back in Bethany to get ready for Passover week, so if it's alright with you I'd like to start back right away."

I nodded in agreement, "Yes, we should definitely leave as soon as possible. There are some very bad characters looking for Demetria and me. We seem to have given them the slip for now, but I don't know how long that will last, so we should travel the five miles back to the shelter we used on our first night in the wilderness and make camp there before morning. We'll shelter there during the day tomorrow and then make a run for Bethany tomorrow night."

We soon had everyone up and preparing to travel. As an added precaution, I tore up an extra robe and tied the stripes of cloth around the hoofs of our donkeys. Hopefully, this would deaden the sound of their hoofs hitting rocks as we traveled.

Jesus approached me with the clothing and weapons I'd left behind. "I thought you might like to have these back." he said, as he looked at the rough furs I was wearing.

I looked down at my appearance and replied. "I'll take my weapons and necklace back, and I'll wear my outer robe for added protection from the cold, but I think I'll keep wearing my furs until we get home. I know they make me look like a wild-man but they're really pretty effective in this kind of weather at keeping me warm."

Jesus gave me the items I'd requested and then he held out a robe and said, "Some of the men would like Demetria to wear this robe over her current attire. They find her appearance . . . distracting. I was wondering if you would mind asking her to wear it?"

I looked over to where Demetria was tying strips of clothing on the donkeys' hoofs, and realized, nearly all the men were watching her go about her work. I could understand how they were distracted. It was hard not to look at her.

I replied, "I'll see what I can do."

I took the robe and strolled over to where she was working. "Say, Jesus was wondering if you'd like to wear this robe over your furs to help you stay warm."

She kept working and said, "No, I'm comfortable in my furs, and I'll stay warm enough once we're on the trail. But, thanks anyway."

"Uh, he'd really like for you to wear it, if you don't mind."

She stood up from the hoof she'd just finished wrapping and frowned. "This isn't about me staying warm is it?"

I looked around at the men watching us and said, "No, I'm afraid it's not."

She snatched the robe from me and snapped, "You'd think they'd never seen a woman before."

I smiled, "I think the problem is they've never seen a woman like you before."

She smiled in return, "Well, okay then, I hope this makes everyone happy."

"I, for one, was perfectly happy before, but hopefully, it will please the others."

I helped her into the robe and she tied it tightly around her waist. Then she spoke just loudly enough for everyone to hear, "There now, I look just as frumpy as their wives and girlfriends. That should make them feel right at home." She laughed and went back to tying hoofs.

Once all the donkeys were packed and readied for our journey, I gathered everyone together. "We're going to have to be extra cautious on our return trip. There are dangerous people searching for Demetria and me. Once we leave here there can be no talking while we're on the trail. Get with your assigned group, and stay close to them. I'll be leading the way with my group, and Horus will bring up the rear with his group."

Horus spoke up, "And whose group will the woman be assigned to?"

I replied, "She'll be with you, Horus. Now let's move!"

Thankfully, we made it to our intended destination without seeing any signs of the Seekers. Before dawn, each of our small groups had claimed a place to make a camp under the overhanging ledges that jutted from the base of the mountain. I wouldn't allow anyone to make a fire, which angered some, but I felt we couldn't take the chance of being discovered. Without the benefit of a fire, we were forced to make meals out of jerky and other similar staples that didn't require cooking, Some complained, but then ate their meals and settled down to sleep through the day.

I sought Jesus out and said, "Before you lie down to get some sleep I'd like to bring you up to date on some things. Could we talk awhile?"

"Certainly, come with me."

He led me to a corner of his shelter that was far enough out of the way to not disturb anyone who was sleeping.

When we had found a place to sit, he asked, "So, what's on your mind?"

"I hardly know where to begin. When you sent me off running through the wilderness naked I thought you'd lost your mind. Then when I got to the cave and met Enoch I was sure you'd lost your mind. Did he give you the same mad hermit routine before he revealed he really wasn't crazy?"

"Yes, he did. But I suspect he may have carried it out a little further with you because he had to be sure you were worthy of the things he needed to give you."

I nodded, "Well, speaking of needing to give someone something. I have something to give you."

I reached into my writing bag and withdrew the green cup and held it out to Jesus. "Enoch says this is something called The Sacred Cup, and he told me to give it to you and you'd know what to do with it."

He took the cup and looked it over thoughtfully before replying, "Yes, I'll need this for what's ahead. Thanks for bringing it to me."

"If you knew everything I had to go through to get it, you'd *really* be thanking me."

He pointed at the staff in my hands and remarked, "I see you've brought something else back as well."

"Yeah, as I suspect you already know, Enoch said this was the Rod of Moses, and he told me it was meant for me to use in my battle against evil. I'm not sure if I buy the whole 'Rod of Moses' thing, but it's certainly unusual in a lot of respects, and if nothing else, it makes a good head basher. It's a lot heavier than a normal staff, and it's weighted just right for an effective cudgel. Here, see what you think."

I handed the staff to Jesus rather abruptly, and as soon as it passed into his hands the Drakon's voice exploded in my head. "The son of God! Yes, he is. Yes, he was. Yes, he shall be. The Lamb of God that takes away the sins of the world! For the weak, for the innocent, forevermore!"

I think it might have gone on incessantly if I hadn't snatched the staff back out of his hands. I could feel the power of the rod pulsing as I held it.

I shook my head to clear my mind, and Jesus asked, "What just happened?"

"Did Enoch also tell you about the creature inside the rod?"

"I'm aware of it."

"Well, my mind is intertwined with its mind, and sometimes I can hear what it's thinking, and just now, it went kind of crazy when you were holding the rod."

"Ah, I see. Now, did Enoch give you anything else?"

"Yeah, when we were getting ready to say goodbye, he gave me another bag he said contained another artifact and a relic from one of his ancestors, but he didn't have time to show them to me, or explain what they were, before he was attacked."

Jesus said, "Maybe you should ask Demetria what they are and why they're important."

"Yes, I'll do that as soon as possible. And speaking of Demetria, do you think it's going to cause a problem if she decides to come live with me?"

"Well, it's your house Lazarus, why would I have a problem with it?"

"No, I don't mean you. I mean . . . do you think it might be a problem with anyone else?"

"Why would anyone have a problem with you bringing home a gorgeous woman like Demetria to live in your house?"

"Yeah . . . I'm doomed aren't I?"

"Well, judging by the looks Horus is giving her, I suspect Iris is not going to be overjoyed to see her, either. You may have some explaining to do when you get home, but if you and Iris are truly in love, you'll work through it, and everything will be fine. You've just got to follow your heart in matters such as this."

"I'll do my best to do that." I looked up and saw Demetria walking out to the waterfall and said, "It looks like Demetria is still up and about, so this is probably a good time for me to find out the significance of the other things Enoch gave me, and maybe I can find out if she's decided to come live with me awhile. Go ahead and get some sleep. We've got a long journey ahead of us tonight. I'll stand watch and wake everyone up when it's time to leave."

I walked over to where Demetria was helping herself to a drink of water from the waterfall and said, "I was thinking this might be a good time for you to fill me in on what's in this bag you and Enoch gave me."

I handed the bag to her and she said, "Sure, let's find a place to sit down out of the wind."

She led me to the sheltering ledge her group had claimed for their campsite, and we both took seats on rocks. Then she opened the bag and took out an old ram's horn wrapped in a white cloth. It was black as a midnight sky and every surface glistened from being polished with use. She held it out to me along with the soft white cloth and laid them both in my hands. "This is the Horn of Gabriel. In ages past, the angel Gabriel used this horn to call all the other angels to battle. However, when Satan was forced out of Heaven along with the other rebellious angels, he snatched it out of Gabriel's hands just before he was cast down to the Earth. Our prophets say in the last days it will be used to call the angels to battle once more against the forces of evil."

I chuckled, "Now that's an interesting story. And what caused Satan to be cast out of Heaven?"

"Satan, or Lucifer, as some prefer to call him, was the angel who was in charge of testing and tempting humans here on Earth. Our scriptures show that he tempted Eve in the Garden of Eden, and he's also the angel who tested Job, but Job was more successful in his time of trial. Satan was one of God's favorite angels, and he was a leader among them. When God decided it was time to send the Messiah to Earth, Satan wanted to be the one who would be sent. He wasn't pleased when he found out God had decided to send his only son instead, so he led a rebellion and there was war in Heaven. One third of the angels joined him in his rebellion, and when the war was over, Satan and his followers were cast down to Earth."

"I see, and when did this war in Heaven take place?"

Demetria hesitated and then said, "On the night you and Jesus were born!"

⊫╪ ╪⊨

"Whoa! I thought this was some ancient artifact that had been in the possession of your people for a long time. If all of this happened the night Jesus and I were born, then how did you and Enoch come to have it?" I said.

Demetria looked up at the stars as if she was remembering something from long ago and then replied, "Enoch and I were outside our cave studying the stars one night about thirty years ago. We had been studying the constellations every night for weeks because we had seen signs that something important was about to happen. Suddenly there was a virtual shower of stars that streaked through the heavens and began to fall to the Earth all around us. Most all them burnt out high in the sky above us, but one kept flaming all the way to the ground. It hit not far from our cave, and we could see it glowing where it landed.

"We ran to see what it was, and as we approached, we could see something still glowing in the sand where it had crashed. When we got right up on top of it we found the imprint of a man's body in the sand, but the man himself was nowhere to be found. However, at the exact place where the imprint of the man's hands came together above his head two items still glowed brightly were they had landed. Enoch warned me not to touch them, but I couldn't help myself."

She held up her hands and I saw the terrible scars I had seen, for the first time, back in the pool room when she rose up out of the water and nearly frightened me to death. She let me get a good look at her scars and then continued, "When I picked them up they seared my flesh, and they also seared my mind with visions of what had just happened in Heaven. When I tell you about the war in Heaven that took place the night that you and Jesus were born, it's not a legend or story that someone made up. It's a memory that's been burnt into my mind. One of the objects I picked up from the wilderness sands that night was the same object you're holding in your hands right now. It's the Horn of Gabriel, and the memories I now carry in my mind are *his* memories of what happened that night when war broke out in Heaven."

"Wow, that's incredible. If anyone else was describing this to me, I'd be reluctant to believe it, but coming from you . . . well, coming from you, I have to say I believe this is something special. So you really believe this is the Horn of Gabriel?"

"No doubt about it." She replied.

I had been holding it in my hands and looking it over while she spoke, and now I noted, "It just looks like an old ram's horn to me. Has anyone ever tried to blow it?"

She smiled, "Go ahead and try."

I put it to my mouth and blew, and it didn't make a sound. I reared back and blew with more effort and still got nothing. "I think it's been blown one time too many. Looks like it's broken."

I handed it back to Demetria and she carefully wrapped it back up as she said, "No one has ever been able to make it sound out a note since it came into our possession. Our prophets say it won't be able to be blown until it's blown by Gabriel in the last days."

"But you said you picked up two items from the sand that night. What was the other one?"

She picked up her battle lance from beside her and said, "It was my lance. The reason it's so important to me is because it was once the battle lance of Michael the archangel of Heaven."

"What? You lost me there. Who is Michael, and what the heck is an archangel?"

"An archangel is the leader of all the angels. Michael was the archangel when war broke out in Heaven. He was a mighty warrior, and in charge of defending Heaven. He grappled with Satan during the battle that broke out at the birth of Jesus. Michael and Satan fought a lengthily battle, and eventually Michael subdued and defeated him. When the angels who had rebelled with Satan saw that he was beaten they all surrendered."

"And how do you know all of this? Is this all from the memories of Gabriel that you said were burnt into your mind?"

"Yes, that's part of it, but when I picked up the Lance of Michael his memories of that night were also imprinted on my mind, so I can remember everything that both of them saw that night. I see the entire battle from both of their perspectives."

"So what happened when the angels all surrendered?"

"God announced they were to be banished from Heaven. He simultaneously cast them all out at one time, and they fell from Heaven like stars falling from the sky. Satan had appeared contrite up till that point, but when he realized what was about to happen to him he angrily seized Michael's lance and thrust it into his body. Then he withdrew it and desperately rushed at God himself, but Gabriel stepped between them and clubbed Satan with his horn. Satan grabbed onto the horn just as he was being cast out of Heaven. He fell to the Earth holding Michael's lance in one hand, and Gabriel's horn in the other."

"Wow, that's amazing! You say Satan wounded Michael with his own lance. What do you think happened to him?" I asked.

"I think he died. Michael's memories go dark after he was attacked, but the memory of Gabriel goes on and shows the other angels gathering around Michael and grieving at his passing."

"And what do you think happened to the body of Satan? You said you found the imprint of a body in the sand, but the actual body had disappeared, so where'd he go?"

"That's a mystery even Enoch was unable to decipher. No one knows what became of him."

"Well, at least you managed to recover the Horn of Gabriel, and the Lance of Michael."

"Actually, Michael's lance is called The Lance of Destiny. I know from his memory that that's the name he had for it, so that's what I prefer to call it."

"The Lance of Destiny, huh? Well, if you ask me, it's a little short to be called a spear, so calling it a lance makes perfect sense, and besides, it has a nice ring to it, so that's what I'll call it, too."

Demetria lay down her lance and placed the Horn of Gabriel back in the bag in its white wrapping. Then she pulled out another smaller white cloth. She unwrapped the cloth to reveal a piece of black fabric folded up inside. She unfolded the fabric and held it up by silver hooks on each end. She took one hook and hung it in her hair on one side of her face. Then she took the other hook and placed it in her hair on the other side of her face leaving the black cloth hanging across her eyes. Then she announced, "This is the veil of Eve."

She turned her face from side to side so I could get a good look at the veil and then continued, "According to our legends, when Eve was forced to leave the Garden of Eden after succumbing to the temptations of Satan, she was ashamed for being so gullible that she allowed the beauty of the serpent, and the beauty of The Tree of Knowledge of Good and Evil, to blind her to deceit. She was also sad because she knew she had broken the heart of God and caused her husband Adam to sin as well. She made this veil to remind herself not to be fooled by beautiful things ever again, but when God saw her contrition he had mercy on her, and he touched the veil and gave it a new purpose. From that time on, when Eve wore the veil she was able to see the auras of the people she encountered, so she could discern who was telling her the truth and who was lying. Our prophets say that in the last days, the veil will once again be used to reveal the truth of God's promises and the lies of 'The Bringer.'"

I chuckled, "So, now that you're wearing it, what kind of aura do I have?"

She cleared her throat, and set up like she was taking a serious look at me, and said, "All I see is black. Oh, wait . . . that's just the blackness of your rotten heart." Then she broke out in laughter.

"Oh, you think that's funny, do you? So, what am I supposed to do with these things?"

She carefully wrapped up the veil and said, "I'm not sure what to tell you. I'll keep the lance for protection, but Enoch intended to have you hold the horn and veil for a while and then retrieve them from you when all the drama subsided, but now he's dead, and I don't know what the future holds for me, maybe you should keep them."

"Or maybe you should come and live with me until you see what the future holds. That way, if you want them back, they'll be close by when you decide to leave."

"You know, I've been thinking about your offer, and I think I'm going to take you up on it."

"Really?"

She smiled, "Yes, really. It just makes sense to try and have a safe place to stay awhile until I can figure out what I'm going to do next. Are you sure you don't mind?"

"Of course I don't mind. That's great news! It really is. Everyone is going to love you."

She glanced over at Horus, who appeared to be sleeping soundly, and said, "I don't know about that, but I can have a thick skin if needed. Hopefully it won't take long for me to figure out what I need to do, and I can move on, so I won't be a bother to anyone."

She respectfully placed the veil back into the bag and carefully fastened it shut. Then she handed the precious cargo to me and said, "For now, I want you to keep these safe until I ask for them back."

"And what if you never ask for them back?"

"If that day never comes, then I'll trust you to give them to the right person at the right time. Can I trust you to do that for me, Lazarus?"

And I said, "Forevermore!"

CHAPTER TWENTY-FIVE

A fter our talk, Demetria went to take a nap, so I broke out my writing kit.

March 27ᵗʰ

Since the last time I wrote, Demetria told me more about the Seekers and how they are paired with a mate when they come of age. She also told me when they're mated with someone they each receive a matching blue sapphire to show their allegiance to each other. And they get a tattoo on their backs of the sun interposed inside a half-moon. It's something they call their talisman, and it's supposed to provide them protection against evil spirits.

From what she's told me, it appears we've probably got somewhere between 12 and 24 Seekers looking for us, plus some of the Seekers are in cahoots with some wilderness bandits, so there's that to deal with as well.

We finally left the cave last night, and on the way to rejoin Jesus and the others, we were attacked by a pair of Seekers and 8 bandits. Luckily, Samson and Delilah showed up just in time to lend a hand, and we killed four of our attackers and sent the others running for the hills.

We ran the rest of the way to our hideout, and Horus was there to greet us.

Unfortunately, Horus saw me holding Demetria's hand as I led her through the darkness to the narrow pass into the gorge. He wasn't happy with what he saw, and if his reaction to Demetria is any indication of how Iris is going to react when she sees her, I may have a problem on my hands because Demetria has decided to come and live with us until she figures out what to do next.

I'm convinced that's for the best, so if Iris, or any of her family, should try to cause problems, I'll deal with them as needed, but that may be easier said than done.

While we had a little down-time here in our hide-out, Demetria finally had time to explain what the items were that Enoch entrusted me with right before he was attacked. Turns out I've been given the Horn of Gabriel, and the Veil of Eve. I don't have time to explain at the moment because I'm supposed to be keeping watch while everyone else sleeps. Let's just say for now, that these are pretty amazing treasures if they're really what Demetria says they are. We've agreed I'll hold on to them for now just for safe-keeping, and if Demetria wants them she can reclaim them at any time.

It will be time to wake everyone up soon, so we can travel the last nine miles back to Bethany under cover of darkness. With a little luck, we'll be home soon, and all of this wilderness adventure will seem like a distant dream. It's hard to believe all I've experienced the last few days. It's unbelievable, but you can't just make this stuff up!!

As the sun began to set, I got everyone up and had them eat a quick meal. Then we split up into our small groups again, and I gave them a final pep talk before we hit the trail. "Okay, everyone, we've only got nine more miles to cover tonight, and then we'll be home. We should be there before midnight. Just remember to stay close to the people in your group and absolutely no talking."

We filed out of the gorge in single file with me leading the way, just like the night before. My trusty dogs padded silently on either side of the trail and occasionally stopped to sniff the air. The sky was clear, and the moon was bright, so I had excellent visibility in spite of the darkness.

We had made good time, and covered several miles when suddenly Samson and Delilah went streaking to the rear of our caravan. I whistled, and they reluctantly turned and came trotting back to my side. I walked up to the nearest of my guards and whispered, "Keep the caravan moving forward and don't stop unless I tell you to."

He nodded curtly and waved for the others to follow him.

Once everyone was back on the move, I hurried to the rear and found Horus and his small group. He was standing with his spear to his side and staring intently into the darkness where we'd just been traveling.

My dogs began to growl deeply and I shushed them and said, "What do you see?"

Horus replied without taking his eyes off our back-trail, "I thought I saw someone on horseback a moment ago against the skyline, but I can't be sure." He pointed, "There, do you see it?"

"Yes, I do. There's someone coming down the trail towards us leading three donkeys, and there are several more people coming further behind him. Many are on horses and camels, and many more are on foot."

Horus looked at me unbelievingly, "How can you see all of that? I can barely make out one or two horses?"

"Trust me; I can see exactly what's coming at us."

I took the two leather bags I was carrying off my shoulders and thrust them at Horus. "I'm going to need you to keep these safe for me until I see you again."

He replied, "What do you mean, until I see you again? Where are you going?"

"Just listen to what I'm about to tell you, and don't even think about arguing with me. If any of you are to have a chance at surviving the night, you've got to do what I tell you. Take Demetria, and the rest of your group, and rejoin the other groups as soon as possible. Make them run the rest of the way to Bethany. It's only a few more miles, and the time for stealth is over. And Horus, whatever else you do tonight, make sure Jesus makes it back to Bethany alive. Do you understand?"

"If I'm to lead the others to Bethany, what are you going to do?"

"I'm going to cause a diversion and lead them astray."

He nodded, "Somehow, I don't believe you sir, but I understand, and I'll do what you've ordered, however, Demetria isn't here."

"What do you mean she isn't here?"

"When we saw the horses following us she just disappeared"

I shoved him in the direction of Jesus and the others and said, "Go home Horus, and tell Iris I'll be right behind you."

"I'll tell her sir, and sir. . . ."

"Yes?"

"Give 'em hell sir!"

He turned and herded his group down the trail, and I was left alone to face an army of Seekers and bandits!

If I had told Horus more details about what I could see on our back-trail he may have refused to leave me. There were at least 10 people on horses and camels, and probably twice that number on foot.

I peeled my outer robe off and threw it to the side of the trail. For what I needed to do now, I wouldn't need any additional fabric to keep warm, and I didn't want anything getting in my way either.

By now, the man who was leading the three donkeys was drawing even with me on the trail, as he trotted toward me while pulling his recalcitrant beasts of burden.

He panted as he approached me and said, "I don't know why you're just standing there buddy, but if I were you I'd run for it. I don't think those fellas following me just want to talk."

"Just keep moving. I've got some unfinished business with these men." I replied.

He allowed himself to look briefly over his shoulder at his pursuers, and then took a look at my furs and said, "I think you've been out here in the wilderness a little too long mister. You'd better run while you can."

"You run. I think I'll stay and see what's on their minds."

"Suit yourself, but I'm out of here."

The stranger urged his donkeys on and they trotted away in the direction of Bethany.

I said, "Samson. . . Delilah. . . guard here."

I knew that with my dogs guarding the trail, no one would pass by to pursue Jesus and my friends without paying in blood, so I paused for a moment, and touched my fingers to the ankh on my necklace while looking to the stars. Then I gripped my staff tightly in my right hand, took my dagger in my left hand, and began walking briskly to the left side of the approaching formation.

If the Seekers wanted a fight, I'd give them a fight!

The terrain was choked with brush and boulders on this side of the trail, so I marched up on them before they had time to react.

I sprinted the last few steps and clubbed the two on the end of the marching line to death before they realized what was happening. Then I ran at the nearest horse, and jumped high as I approached to run my dagger through the rider's throat. As I was flying through the air I suddenly realized my intended target was a woman, and instinctively, I almost stopped my thrust, but in a flash, I decided if she was going to attack and murder people as honorable as Enoch and Demetria she deserved to die. Needless to say, that's exactly what she did.

Then I proceeded to run in a rough semicircle back and forth at the front of the group, inflicting damage on those I encountered, but not allowing myself to get hemmed in by the throng. I was slowly whittling them down with my unorthodox tactics. With my superior speed, I could have kept it up all night, but suddenly I heard a scream from somewhere in the center of the remaining renegades, and I skidded to a stop a safe distance from the nearest attackers.

Two men came riding forward on horseback with someone being drug by ropes between them. It was Demetria. She was covered in blood, and appeared lifeless, as she hung helplessly by a rope tied to each of her wrists between the two horsemen. When they came to a stop, she slumped to her knees without making a sound, and a man came from behind, grabbed her by the hair, and pulled her to her feet.

The man holding her up was Mathias, and he grinned murderously at me, as his eyes seemed to glow with a reddish tint in the darkness. Then he shouted, "Behold the Queen of the Issachar! Soon I will make her my wench, but first, I'll let you watch her suffer a little more, unless you give me back the things you've stolen from us." To make his point, he slapped the side of her face while pulling violently on her hair, and she let out a piercing scream.

I felt the Rod of Moses vibrating in my hands, as I asked, "What do you want from me."

"I want the Rod of Moses, you idiot."

I looked down, and expected to see the staff turning a bright red, as it felt to me like it was almost on fire, but nothing about its appearance had changed.

Mathias slapped Demetria again and shouted impatiently, "Do you hear me stranger? I want the Rod of Moses, and I want it NOW!"

I roared, "Then you shall have it!!"

Without really knowing what I intended to happen, I took the staff in both hands, and pointed the snakes head at the skirmish line to the right of where Demetria was standing. I felt a pulsation of power flowing from my body into the rod, and I heard the Drakon chanting in my head, "They will die, they will, oh yes, they will."

Suddenly, the Seekers and bandits on that side of the line of battle went flying away into the wilderness. They screamed and shouted in shock and surprise, as an invisible force slammed them into the darkness. Even the horses and camels were thrown to the ground, and some of the men flew as far as fifty feet before they crashed back to the surface in bleeding heaps.

I swung the end of the Rod toward the rest of the group who were standing to the left of where Demetria was being held captive, and they turned as one and went running away in every direction. Mathias held a dagger to Demetria's throat now, so I turned the Rod, until it was pointing directly at him. He cursed me, but then laid her carefully on the ground while watching me wearily. From out of the darkness, a woman rode up on a horse, and held her hand out to him as she rode by. He grabbed her hand, and swung himself smoothly up behind her saddle, and they sped away.

I ran to where Demetria was lying on the ground, and carefully lay her head in my lap, while wiping away blood from her face. She moaned, and opened her eyes slightly, and I asked, "How'd they capture you?"

She whispered, "When I saw them following us I knew we couldn't outrun them, so I went after them, thinking I could buy you and your fiends some time to get away. I took out a couple of them before they caught mc, and you know the rest." She patted the rod and continued, "Looks like you and the Drakon are figuring out how to work together."

"I can't take any credit for what just happened. I just reacted to what was happening instinctively, and the rod did the rest."

I felt something wet underneath her and raised my right hand to the moonlight. It was soaked with blood, so I lay her down gently, and rolled her on her side to get a better look. Luckily she had abandoned her outer robe, just as I had done, so there wasn't a lot of clothing to get in my way. Once I had her on her side, I was alarmed to see a deep gash mark in her back where she was losing a lot of blood.

I took her flask from under her furs and poured elixir on all the wounds I could find, but the main wound on her back continued to ooze. I said, "I'm afraid this wound on your back has caused internal injuries. I think you need to drink some elixir."

I held the flask to her mouth, but only a few drops poured out. "Your flask is empty. Hold on, while I open mine."

I was reaching to get the flask of elixir Enoch had given me, but she grabbed my hand and said, "Don't use yours. I'm going to need more if I survive these wounds. Look around and see if you can find any dead Seekers. They'll probably have flasks like mine, now that they have access to the vortex."

I jumped up, and ran from one dead person to another, and rolled each one over and cut through their clothes to see if they had a tattoo on their back. Then I came upon a woman, and sure enough she had a tattoo and a flask on her. Beside her, was a man who also had a tattoo and a flask.

I ran back to Demetria with both flasks and helped her drink.

She stopped after drinking just a few ounces and said, "That's enough. It won't take much if it's going to work. Either I'll live now, or I'll die. Only time will tell. You should let me lie here awhile to let the elixir work its magic. Just be patient. It's in God's hands now, and he will decide my fate."

I was reaching to lift her up, so I could lay her head in my lap again, when I noticed Samson and Delilah had gone suddenly quiet. They had been barking and growing ever since our attackers had run wildly into the wilderness, and I was sure they had kept any stragglers from advancing down the trail to Bethany, but I wasn't sure if their silence was an indication the last of the Seekers and bandits were headed back to Shiloh, or if something more ominous was happening.

Then I saw the stranger with the three donkeys walking back towards me with my dogs following on either side of him. He strode up to me confidently and asked, "What's wrong with the lady?"

"She was wounded, so I'm letting her rest awhile before we catch up with our friends. Why'd you come back?"

He hung his head and replied, "I felt bad enough leaving you here alone with these renegades, and then I heard the lady screaming, and I just had to come back." He stopped, and wiped the blood from the Roman short sword he was carrying while continuing, "Your dogs were discouraging a few of these fellows from trying to follow your friends, and so I lent them a hand and mopped up a couple of stragglers they'd wounded."

I said, "Thanks for the help. Where were you going before these bandits got on your trail?"

"I'm headed to Jerusalem for Passover week. I'm a tentmaker, so I hope to ply my wares there during the festivities. There's always a lot of demand for tents during Passover, and on top of that, I'm hearing the Sanhedrin is looking to hire someone to help control some seditious heretic and his followers, so I'm thinking about applying for the job."

I gestured toward his sword. "Don't you worry about the Romans taking issue with you carrying a sword into Jerusalem?"

"Not really, I'm a Roman Citizen, and I have the papers to prove it."

He pointed at the sword hanging by my side, "What about you? Looks like you're armed to the teeth. Don't they have a problem with that?"

"No. I provide caravan services to the Romans, so they allow me and my men to go armed. They even allow me to keep a small fortress of my own in Bethany."

He looked me up and down and said, "To tell you the truth, when I first saw you on the trail, I thought you were one of the bandits, or maybe something worse, just judging by the way you're dressed. I never would have taken you for some kind of nobleman, or whatever you say you are."

I looked down at my rough furs and replied, "Yeah, I can see how my appearance may have concerned you. I've been on a bit of a pilgrimage here in the wilderness for the last few days, but I clean up pretty well when I try."

Somewhere in the darkness a battle horn sounded out from nearby. Then another sounded from further away, and then a third sounded from even further.

I said, "Mister, my name is Lazarus of Bethany. I appreciate your help here tonight, and if you ever need my help in any way, just come to Bethany and ask for me. But for now, I'd say we both need to be on our way because from the sound of those horns, the bandits we just fought are regrouping, and they'll probably be back to have another go at us soon."

He laughed, "Huh? You appreciate my help? The way I see it, if you hadn't come along when you did those filthy heathen would have killed me and stole my donkeys. I don't know how you and your lady friend managed to kill so many of them, but make no mistake, I owe you my life. So, here's the real deal, if you ever need *me* for anything, my name is Saul of Tarsus, and I'm your man."

"Thanks Saul. Maybe we'll meet again, but for now you should take your donkeys and make a run for Jerusalem. It's not far, and these fellows are really not looking for you anyway. They want me and my friend here."

He looked at Demetria and said, "How are you going to get her out of here? She doesn't look like she's ready to run."

"I'll be carrying her. Now go!"

Saul pulled his donkeys in the direction of Jerusalem and shouted over his shoulder as he trotted away, "Go with God, Lazarus. I have a feeling we'll see each other again soon."

I swung my staff into its harness on my back, hurriedly secured the flasks of elixir, and then scooped up Demetria to carry her home. When I picked her up she said, "Where are you taking me?"

"I'm taking you home."

"I can't leave without my lance."

A horn sounded nearby and I said, "It's just a lance. I'll get you another one."

She gripped my jerkin and said, "It's not just a lance, it's the Lance of Destiny, like I told you, and it's very important to me. Please find it."

I remembered how its polished surface reflected the sunlight the first time I saw it, and how I had thought then it was somehow special. "Okay, but I'm not leaving you here while I look for it. I'm going to carry you while I'm looking, and if I see Mathias, or any of his cronies coming, we're taking off without it."

"Fair enough, but please try to find it."

I began to walk rapidly over the battleground where we'd just fought, and was about to give up looking, when I saw Samson and Delilah pawing at something on the ground. When I drew near, I saw something glimmering where they were scratching. It was Demetria's lance.

I picked it up and asked my dogs, "Now how did you guys know there was something different about this thing than all the other weapons scattered around here?" They didn't say a thing. Such rude dogs!

David Beeler

I scooped the lance up and laid it across Demetria's chest, and she drew it near and said, "Thanks for finding it. You can't imagine how important it is to me. So now what?"

I raised my head and looked into the darkness, as two horns sounded nearby. "Now, we're going for another run in the wilderness." I set out at a fast trot with Demetria in my arms. "Only this time, I'll be doing all the running."

CHAPTER TWENTY-SIX

E ven while carrying Demetria, I was still able to run faster than most men, so it wasn't long before the battle horns of the Seekers and bandits faded behind me. I knew they would never expect me to be able to outdistance them so quickly, so I felt comfortable stopping to check Demetria's wounds after running awhile.

I was pleased to find that most of her minor wounds were healing nicely, but the gash on her back was still open and oozing blood. I poured more elixir on it, and I tried to get her to drink some more as well, but she was unconscious and completely unresponsive. I knew what she really needed was rest if she was going to recover, but we were still probably a mile from my home. Running with her in my arms over this unforgiving terrain was not helping matters.

Should I stay here to let her rest, while running the risk that our pursuers might find us, or should I continue carrying her, and hope I don't cause her to bleed to death in the process? That was the debate I was having with myself, when I heard the approach of horses.

Thankfully, these horses were coming from the direction of Bethany, and Horus was leading the charge!

When they drew near I saw he was leading a contingent of 10 guards from my fortress. I stepped out onto the trail to wave them down, and Horus jumped from his horse before it stopped moving.

He landed by my side and reported, "Sir, I got Jesus and his followers safely home, and brought these men to see if you needed help."

"Well done, Horus." I pointed to where Demetria lay lifelessly by the trail and continued, "Demetria is gravely wounded, so I can use your help to get her home."

He looked around and said, "How'd you get away, and how'd you get her here so quickly? Do you have a horse?"

"No, I carried her, as for how I got away, that's a story for another day. I don't suppose you brought a stretcher, did you?"

He gestured to a couple of my guards and said, "As a matter of fact, we did. I didn't know what kind of condition you'd be in when we found you. To tell the truth, I didn't expect to see you walking around on your own, much less carrying someone else."

We carefully loaded Demetria on the stretcher, and four of us picked it up and began carrying her home. I took the right hand corner and kept a sharp eye out for obstacles in the fading darkness.

Our breaths came out in puffs of vapor as we labored in the near freezing temperatures. Then as the morning sun was coloring the eastern horizon, we came within sight of my fortress. As we drew nearer, I could see several people watching from the ramparts over the front gate. I heard a shout from someone. The gates suddenly flew open, and a lone figure burst through and came running at full speed down the trail.

Horus leapt from his horse and took over my side of the stretcher, while gently moving me aside. He said, "Don't know why, but it looks like someone is glad to see you, sir."

I kept my eyes on the bouncing curls coming down the trail, and without looking at him I replied, "I'm glad to see her too, brother." I laid my staff and Demetria's lance on the ground and said, "Please see that these items and the bags I gave you earlier get to my bedroom. There's something I need to do right now."

"Samson. . . Delilah. . . come."

Then I ran to embrace my Rainbow Girl again. . . .

Iris nearly knocked me to the ground when she leapt into my arms with a shout of joy. Then she hugged me with such ferocity I wondered if she intended to ever let me go again. Finally, she released her grip on me long enough to slide to the ground and take a step back, so she could get a better look at me.

She shook her head in bewilderment and asked, "What happened to you?"

"Oh, I was in a bit of a fight last night. Sorry if I got blood on your clothes just now."

"No, I mean what happened to you that made you have to dress like a wild-man? You look like you just crawled out of a cave or something."

I ran my hands over my furs and replied, "Well, I kind of did. I spent several days and nights in a cave while we were in the wilderness."

"My brother, and Jesus, and all the others went into the wilderness with you, but none of them came back dressed like that."

"Well, that's because I went to the cave alone. It was something Jesus said I had to do."

Just then, Horus and the guards came by with the stretcher and Iris got her first good look at Demetria. Even though she was nearly dead, she was still undeniably beautiful, and I could see the wheels turning in Iris's head.

She turned and watched as they carried Demetria toward the gates, and then she asked without turning back to look at me, "Who's that strange woman, and why's she dressed just like you in those same wild furs?"

"Oh, she's the Que . . . I mean . . . she's a woman who was also at the cave where I had to stay."

She turned towards me suddenly then and sniped accusingly, "I thought you said you were at the cave alone? You mean *she* was there, too?"

I stammered, "Well, yes . . . she was there, but I went there alone . . . and she was there wit. . . ."

Before I could finish speaking, Iris threw her hands in the air and screamed, "Don't talk to me."

"But I can explain, just. . . ."

She stomped away and shouted over her shoulder, "Just don't speak to me."

Her mother Nida met her outside the gates and threw a comforting arm around her shoulders before leading her inside. Nida looked back at me and gave me the evil eye as they disappeared from sight.

I trotted toward the gate and Iris's father, Darius, came striding toward me with a murderous look of rage clouding his features. He stood in my path to stop me and thumped me in the chest. "Looks like you've got some explaining to do, Lazarus."

I looked up into his eyes and said, "That's right sir. I do have some explaining to do, but not to you. I'll explain everything to my bride-to-be. Now, if you'll excuse me, I'm on my way to find her now."

I abruptly skirted past him, and ignoring everyone else who had come to greet me, I quickly made my way inside. I knew there would be hell to pay later for not acknowledging my sisters, who were waiting just inside the gate for me, but for now, my top priority was finding Iris and soothing her wounded feelings.

It didn't take long to find her. Nida had taken her to her bedroom and closed the door. I could hear Iris crying inside, so I opened the door and boldly walked in. Nida was bending over her, and I thought at first, she was going to reveal a big spoon and start thrashing me over the head with it, but her eyes softened, and she beckoned me forward.

I came over to the bed and sat on the edge and gently put my hand on Iris's back. She was turned away from me, and when she felt my heavy hand she shuddered, but didn't pull away, so I took that to be a good sign. I spoke respectfully to her mother, "Nida, if you don't mind, I need a moment alone with Iris."

Her spine stiffened as she replied, "It's not proper for you to be alone with my daughter in her bedchamber."

"Obviously, I'm not here to try to be amorous with her. Tomorrow I intend to make her my bride, if she'll still have me, but first, I need to reassure her about some things. Could you please allow me to be alone with her for just a few moments?"

"Well, since you put it that way, I guess it'll be all right, but I'll be right outside the door, so don't try anything funny." She shook her bony finger at me as she spoke, and I kept expecting it to turn into a big spoon.

When we were finally alone, I said, "Iris, when I told you I loved you, and asked you to marry me, I meant it with all my heart and soul, and *nothing* has changed. The woman you just saw is named Demetria. Yes, she was with me at the cave Jesus sent me to visit, but so was her husband. He was there with us the whole time, until he was murdered a few days ago. The reason I'm dressed in the same furs as her is because that was how they dressed, and these were the clothes they had me wear. She and her husband, Enoch, were good to me, and I grew to consider them my friends, so when he was murdered I told her she should come here to live, at least until she can figure out what she's going to do next.

"She means nothing to me, except I consider her my friend. You, on the other hand, are my soulmate for life. You're the one I want, and the one I need, and no one can take your place. No one!

"I told you I'd marry you as soon as I returned, so if you still want to be my wife, then tomorrow, you'll become the mistress of this house, and once Demetria has recovered from her wounds, if you want her to leave, I'll have her leave."

Without turning to face me she said, "So her husband Enoch was with the two of you at the cave?"

"Right up until the moment he died. The only time I was alone with her was for a brief period of time when we were escaping from the cave to join back up with Jesus and the others"

She turned over to face me and said, "And if I'm not comfortable having her live here, you'll have her leave once she's well?"

"Yes, I'm not going to let anything, or anyone, cause you to feel insecure in your own home. You're the queen of this castle. You, and only you, are my Rainbow Girl."

"And you said you want to get married tomorrow?"

"Yes, definitely!"

She bounced up, as if nothing was ever wrong at all and kissed me passionately. Then she shoved me aside and ran to throw open the door. Nida was leaning with her ear against the door and fell into the room, but Iris caught her, flipped her to her feet, and never missed a beat, "Oh, momma! We're getting married tomorrow, so we've only got one day to get everything ready. We've got so-o-o much to do!"

Iris took her mother's hands in hers, and they danced around the room like schoolgirls. Then Nida got a panicked look on her face as she exclaimed, "I've got to plan a wedding feast!"

And Iris gleefully countered, "And I've got to figure out what I'm going to wear!"

They ran out of the room together, as if I didn't exist. Then Iris came running back, and kissed me one more time for good measure, before saying, "Tomorrow, I'm going to be Mrs. Lazarus Lazarus."

"What do you mean Mrs. Lazarus Lazarus?"

"I'm so excited to be married to you it's not going to be enough to just be called Mrs. Lazarus once, so everyone will have to call me Mrs. Lazarus Lazarus because I'm doubly proud. So you can just call me Mrs. Lazarus Lazarus."

She ran from the room again, and I laughed and said out loud, "Is she CRAAZY or something?" My imitation of Enoch was pretty good, if I do say so myself.

CHAPTER TWENTY-SEVEN

I went out to the courtyard, and Horus came over to me imme-diately and said, "Judging by the way my sister just went darting through the courtyard laughing, I take it you managed to put her mind at ease?"

"Yes, everything's fine now, and we're getting married tomor-row." I looked down at the ground and kicked a pebble before con-tinuing, "I'd appreciate it if you never said anything to Iris about seeing me holding Demetria's hand the night we came back to rejoin the rest of you. I was just helping her walk in the darkness. I know it probably looked bad, but it was really completely innocent."

"I see that now, but yes, it did look bad at the moment. I was ready to tear into you even though I love you like a brother. And no, I'll never say anything to Iris about it."

I put my arm around his shoulders and asked, "Then, would you do me the honor of standing with me tomorrow as my best man?"

"Of course, sir. I'd be honored."

"May I suggest you let some of your other duties slide for a mo-ment and go to the kitchen to see what kind of assistance your mother may require? She left in a tizzy to go and start working on a marriage feast for tomorrow, so see what she needs, and who she needs to do it, and put her mind at ease a bit."

Horus replied, "And may I suggest you find your sisters and pay your respects before they disown you. They weren't happy that you blew right past them upon your arrival, without so much as a, 'Hello.'"

"'Yikes, you're exactly right! Do you know where I'll find them?"

"Yes, they're taking care of Demetria."

"Where'd they take her?"

"Where do you think? She's in Martha's room."

I smiled, "Of course, where else would she be?"

As Horus turned to walk away he said, "Oh, those things you gave me are in your room on your bed."

"Oh, yeah, thanks for taking care of those for me."

It was no surprise that Martha would have whisked Demetria off to her room to take care of her. Ever since she was a little girl, she had been bringing home wounded creatures to try and nurse them back to health, and usually she was quite successful. As she grew older she took her concerns for sick and afflicted animals and transferred them to looking after sickly humans. Come to think of it, she seemed to have a small hint of the same healing powers our cousin Jesus had demonstrated. Martha was always happiest when she was taking care of someone else's needs. It was just her nature.

I found Martha, and my sister Mary, in Martha's bedroom. They had laid Demetria on Martha's bed and they were bending over her and gently cleaning her wounds.

I prepared myself for battle and cleared my throat to let them know I was coming in. "Ladies, I was looking for you. . . ."

Before I could continue, Mary said, "Martha, did you hear something?"

Martha replied without looking up, "Oh, it's just the wind again."

"But I thought we'd gotten rid of the wind."

"Well, yes, it blew right out of here in the middle of the night about a week ago without hardly saying goodbye, but you know how wind is; just when you think you've seen the last of it, it has a way of blowing back into your life when you least expect it," Martha said.

I snarled, "Okay ladies, I get it. I blew right past you when I got home today and didn't say a word to you, but I really had my hands full at the moment. Iris was so mad when she saw Demetria, and how we were dressed alike, she was ready to call off our wedding, so I had to track her down immediately before things got out of hand, so we could go ahead with getting married tomorrow."

My sisters both looked at each other as if they were shocked about something I'd just said. Then Martha queried, "Did he just say he's getting married *tomorrow?*"

Mary looked at her with big eyes and replied, "Yes, I believe he did!"

"Drat, then I guess we'll *have* to forgive him."

Mary nearly shouted with delight, "Yes, we will. We wouldn't want to not be invited to a wedding!"

They charged around the bed and both began to pound me playfully in the ribs and chest, while interchangeably dancing around and shouting. "You're getting married . . . he's getting married . . . our brother's getting married!"

They finally calmed down a bit, and when both of them embraced me, Mary said, "We're so happy for you and Iris. We can tell she's head over heels for you, so you'd better be good to her. "

Martha added, "Yes, better than you are to your sisters, you little brat."

"Oh, that won't be hard; she's much nicer than you two."

Martha gave me a playful swat and said, "I mean it, Lazarus of Bethany. She's a fine girl, and you'd better be good to her."

"I will; I promise. Now, how's your patient?" I walked over to get a better look at Demetria, and they followed me to the bed.

Martha said, "When I first saw how much blood she had on her clothing, I didn't think there was any way she was going to live, but all that blood must have been there awhile because her wounds are closing up nicely now, and her color's improving. I think she's going to be okay, but she definitely needs to rest, so it's good that she's sleeping so soundly. We'll get her out of these nasty furs, clean her up a bit, and put some real clothes on her. Then we'll just keep an eye on her while she rests, to make sure no complications arise. She can stay right here on my bed until she's better, and I'll set up a cot nearby, so I can check on her periodically, even at night."

"You're the best, Martha. Thanks for taking such good care of her."

Martha gave me an inquiring look, "Where did you find her anyway, and why *are* you dressed just like her in those awful furs?"

"It's a long story, and it'll have to wait for now; but the short version is, I stayed with her and her husband in a cave for a few days while we were in the wilderness, until they were attacked by some marauding bandits, and he was murdered. She and her husband were good to me, and I consider her to be a dear friend now, so I invited her to come live here until she figures out what to do next. As I said earlier, her name is Demetria, and she's a wonderful lady, so please do all you can to make her comfortable."

Mary replied, "Oh, we will. By the way, what're these flasks we found tied to her arm? You've not been trying your hand at making more of that rot-gut wine have you?"

I looked up and saw she was holding one of the flasks of elixir I had tied to Demetria's arm to keep it in place until we got home. The top was hanging open, and Mary smelled the contents, as if she was checking it out before taking a drink.

In a state of panic, I rudely snatched the flask from her hands while shouting, "Don't drink that!" I swirled the contents around and tried to judge how much was missing. "You didn't already drink any of this did you?"

"What if I did? What're you going to do about it? Spank me? I don't think so. You're my brother, not my father."

My mind was reeling with guilt as I asked, "I'm serious, Mary, did you drink any of this already?"

"No, silly. But why are you acting so crazy about it? What could possibly be so important about that stuff?"

"It's her elix . . . medicine. She'll be upset if it's not here when she wakes up, so put it in the bed beside her where she can easily find it."

I patted Demetria on the hand and turned to leave, but Martha gently held me back and said, "A couple of things happened while you were gone that I need to tell you about."

"Well, go ahead. I'm listening."

"It'll be easier to show you than to just tell you, so come with me."

I followed Martha down the hall to an oversized bedroom that was normally reserved for large parties of visitors. She knocked on the door and it was quickly opened by a young man who appeared to be around16 to 18 years old. Martha motioned to me and said, "Stephen, I'd like you to meet my brother, Lazarus. And Lazarus, please meet Stephen."

I shook his hand briskly and said, "Nice to meet you." Then I turned to Martha and inquired, "And who is Stephen?"

She looked sheepishly at her feet and answered, "Do you remember when Jesus healed that group of orphaned leper children?"

"Yes, I remember. That was one of the highlights of the day. Why do you ask?"

"Then maybe you'll also remember, there was a young man who acted as their spokesman, when Jesus asked them what they were doing here that day?"

"Yes, I remember that."

"Well, Stephen was the one who spoke up for them that day. As the oldest of the group, he was their leader. And after they left here . . . well, after they left here, they didn't have anywhere to go because orphans don't have anyone to go home to, which is what kind of makes them orphans I guess . . . so. . . ."

"So, what? What're you trying to tell me Martha?"

"They didn't have anywhere to go, or anyone to go home to, so they came back here . . . and now, this is their home, and we're their family."

With a sick feeling in my stomach, I looked back at Stephen and saw at least six pairs of little eyes peeking around him to stare at me. Upon closer inspection I could see they were all boys. Then, from the adjacent room, several little girls filed out into the hallway, and began to do their part to make me feel even more uncomfortable, with their wide-eyed, innocent stares.

I said, "Excuse us for a moment." Then, I took Martha by the hand and led her away while whispering, "How many of them are there?"

"Only 15."

I stammered, "ONLY 15?"

"Well, 16 if you count Stephen, but he's really almost an adult. It's highly commendable of him that he took it upon himself to take care of all those desperate children when no one else would have them. Don't you think?

"Oh yes, what he did is highly commendable all right, but how do you think we can take care of all those children. This isn't an orphanage you know. And have you even considered how Iris is going to feel about having all these children here? She's about to be the mistress of this house you know, and she should have a say in all this."

Martha beamed, "Oh, she's been absolutely fabulous helping us take care of the wee little ones. She's obviously going to be a wonderful mother. You really got yourself a keeper when you asked her to marry you. She's all for having the children here. In fact, she said on the day Jesus healed them and they all went running away she almost went running after them to bring them back."

I remembered the wistful look Iris gave me as the children had been running away that day and knew Martha was telling the truth about her.

I shook my head in frustration and said, "How are we supposed to even feed all of them? We've stretched ourselves to the limits trying to feed Jesus and all his followers. By now our storehouses have got to be nearly empty. In a week we'll all be starving!"

While we had been talking Mary had joined us and she now said, "Oh, don't be so dramatic. If this is what we're supposed to do, God will provide. Besides, we're rich; we'll just buy more provisions."

"Mary, no one has the amount of provisions we'd need for sale right now. Passover week is about to begin, and food is in short supply, not to mention we're still a long way from harvest time."

Martha said, "I was thinking, maybe you could ask Jesus to make us a couple of those magic baskets of fish and bread he fed the multitudes with a week ago."

"Are you serious? You invite 16 orphans to come and live with us, and your plan to feed them is to ask Jesus to make us some magic baskets to produce bread and fish. Have you lost your mind?"

"You're right, we'd probably get tired of fish and bread after a while. See if he can make some baskets that will give us some eggs and vegetables too."

Before I could even respond, Horus came practically running around the corner with a concerned look on his face. "Sir, I hate to interrupt you, but something strange has just happened that I think you need to be aware of."

I shook my head and said, "Something strange has happened here? Surely not? How could anything strange happen around here? Why, this is the most normal place on Earth. Hasn't anyone told you?"

"Sir, I'm not sure, but I think you're being sarcastic. Have I made you mad somehow? I could come back later."

"No, Horus, you haven't done anything wrong, and I'm not mad at you. I'm just a little frustrated at the moment. Go ahead and tell me what's happened. It can't be any worse, or any stranger, than the conversation I was just having with Martha."

"Well, sir, my mom sent me to check our storehouses to see what we could scrape together for your wedding feast tomorrow, and well. . . ."

"Let me guess, we're almost out of food and we need to put everyone on rations?" I looked at Mary and Martha and continued. "In fact, we're so low on food, we're all going to be eating dirt in a few days. Am I right, or am I right?"

"No, sir. Like I said before, something strange has happened. All our storehouses are full of provisions. In fact, they're bursting at the seams, sir. Everyone's calling it a miracle."

I turned back to Horus and said, "They're all full you say? All of them . . . full?"

Horus practically beamed, "That's right sir; full to the brim."

"Well, that's just . . . great. Yeah, that's fabulous news, Horus. Now, go help your mom with the feast."

Before I could get turned around Mary practically accosted me, "Hah, didn't I tell you God would provide?"

Martha said, "This is even better than magic baskets I'd say." She and Mary slipped their arms through mine and starting leading me back down the hall to where all those little eyes were waiting and watching, as Martha went on and on, "You know, you said something earlier about this not being an orphanage, and that got me to thinking, maybe it should be. . . ."

What have I done now?

CHAPTER TWENTY-EIGHT

Mary went to check on Demetria, and Martha began introducing me to all 15 of the children, but I couldn't remember a single name because my mind was still reeling with the knowledge that my home had just become an orphanage. How did that happen?

I mumbled, "Nice to meet you," as I was introduced to each child in turn, and they respectively stepped forward to politely shake my hand. They had obviously been in rough shape when Martha took them in. Some of the boys weren't wearing shirts and their ribcages were clearly visible. Nearly all of them had signs of starvation and poor nutrition.

When the children had all been introduced, they went back into their rooms, and I was left alone with just Martha and Stephen. I was still trying to think of a way out of this predicament, so I asked Stephen, "After you were healed, I saw you and your band of children running off into the distance, so what brought you back here? Didn't you have anywhere else you could go?"

Stephen said, "We were starving when we came here that day. The miraculous meal of fish and bread that Jesus provided was the first food we'd eaten in days. When you're an orphan and a leper no one wants to have anything to do with you. We'd been living by begging people to throw us money or food from a distance, and sometimes all we had were the leftovers people threw out of their houses at night, if we were lucky enough to beat the dogs to them. Once we were healed, we ran away in joy, but I soon realized we still had a lot of mouths to feed. I remembered the magic baskets of food Jesus had passed around that day, and I thought if we came back here he might give us one of them."

Martha chimed in, "Yes, Stephen came to the gates and asked for Jesus, but he'd already left with you for the wilderness, so I went out to talk to him. All he wanted was a little food for the children, and once I saw how pitiful they were, I couldn't just give them food to eat while sitting on the ground. I had to invite them in and feed them properly in our dining hall, and once I did that I couldn't send them away. It was already dark by then, and it was freezing cold that night. They were only supposed to stay here for one night, but when it came time for them to leave the next day, I just couldn't let them leave. They were filing out the gate and shaking my hand, and hugging me, and thanking me, and some of the littlest ones were crying, and . . . and . . . I just had to give them a home. I just had to, Lazarus. I've never had a child of my own, and now that I'm this old I probably never will, but some-how I feel fulfilled when I'm caring for all these kids who are so thankful for my affection. I hope you can understand and not be mad at me."

I thought of all those little faces and sad little eyes looking up at Martha, as they faced another day of living without hope or love, and I knew she never had a chance of letting them go out into the cold cruel world alone.

I put my arm around her and pulled her into my embrace, "Martha, I could never be mad at you for being true to who you are. I see now that you did the right thing, and Mary was obviously right; God will provide."

I looked at Stephen and said, "This is your home now. You and all your charges are now our children. Mary and Martha will assign you each chores, and see that your needs are met. It's going to take some getting used to, but we'll figure it out."

I turned back to Martha and said, "Now, I really have to get going. I'm getting married tomorrow, and there's a lot to be done."

She held me back and said, "Wait. Remember? I told you a couple of things happened while you were gone. I need to tell you about one other development that took place while you were away."

"Oh, great. Now what's happened?"

"Oh, I don't think this is something that's going to upset you. In fact, I think you'll be happy to hear this news."

"You mean you actually have good news for me? Well then, by all means let me hear it," I said.

"Two days ago a man came to the gates and said you had rescued him from bandits in the wilderness, and then told him he could come live here awhile. He said you knew him as John Mark. We'd never heard of him before, but he seemed to really know you and be telling the truth, so we let him in, and he's been sleeping in the courtyard with Jesus's followers."

"Why is he sleeping in the courtyard? Couldn't you give him a room? He's my invited guest."

Martha chided, "In case you haven't noticed, brother, we're running out of guest rooms. And besides, he brought a lady companion with him, so I gave her the only guest room we had left."

I smiled, "So, he had a lady with him, huh? Was her name Miriam?"

"Yes, how'd you know that?"

"He told me he was trying to find her. So why didn't you put them in the guest room together?"

"Are you kidding? Apparently, he didn't tell you everything there is to know about his lady friend. She doesn't want to have anything to do with him. It's very odd. She just sits in her room and cries and doesn't say a word. I bring her food and water three times a day and she won't even open the door for me, so I leave it in the hallway. She eats what I bring her, but she doesn't interact with any of us, and she clearly doesn't like your friend John Mark. I don't know what he did to her, but it must have been dreadful." She looked around and then whispered, "You don't think he could be a rapist do you?"

"No, it's nothing like that. He did something a long time ago to hurt her family, and he's trying to make up for it now, but apparently that's not going as well as he'd hoped. Take me to him and let me find out what's going on."

"Okay, I know which tent is his. Come with me."

Martha took me to John Mark and then excused herself to go and check on Demetria.

We stood outside his tent and I said, "Martha tells me you found Miriam and brought her here with you. That's great news, man."

A pained look crossed his face as he replied, "Not as great as I'd hoped, though. I had filled my head with all these fantasies of how much she would be grateful to me when I finally found her and rescued her out of slavery, but the truth is, she despises me. I think she's glad to be free of that piss-ant slaver Uriah, but she still hates me. I've tried to tell her how sorry I am, and I've told her how I sold everything I had and set out on a quest to find her and set her free. I've told her how I searched for her for two years and about the hardships I endured while trying to find her, and you know what she said? She said I could add up all the pain and suffering I'd endured over two years of trying to find her, and it wouldn't be equal to one day of the pain and shame my actions had caused her family, and it sure as hell wouldn't come close to even one hour of the pain, shame, and humiliation I'd caused her to endure as a slave and prostitute. Then, she slapped me and spit in my face, and she hasn't said another word to me since."

"Wow, that's pretty brutal. So, how'd you get her to come here with you?" I asked.

"After I bought her freedom from Uriah I still had a lot of the treasure left that you'd given me. I offered to let her have it all and go her own way, but I also told her about meeting you on the trail, and how you'd offered us a home for a while. I told her I was coming here, and she could come with me if she wanted to, but it wouldn't mean she owed me anything. I guess she figured she didn't have anywhere else to go because she followed me here, but she sure kept her distance while we walked from Jerusalem to Bethany. That was the longest two miles I've ever walked. I could feel her looking at my back with hatred in her eyes, and I halfway expected her to slip a dagger between my ribs, or to crack me over the head with a rock. And to tell you the truth, I guess I wouldn't have blamed her if she did."

"Well, for what it's worth, I'm glad you're here, and I'm glad you found Miriam and brought her here. Just give her some space, and maybe after a while she'll see things differently."

"I intend to stay out of her way, and so far, that's not been very hard since she's staying in her room. If she decides to stay here, I may have to move on though. It's hard to be this close, and not be able to interact with her after devoting the last two years of my life to finding her. I don't know how long I can keep doing that."

I nodded, "I understand. If you feel like you need to move on with your life, you won't hurt my feelings. In the meantime, rest assured my sisters will take good care of her."

John Mark looked me in the eye and said, "I was wondering if you might do me a favor."

"Certainly, what can I do to help you?" I quickly answered.

"Would you talk to her and let her know how sorry I am?"

I hesitated and then said, "I'm not sure I'm the best person for that job."

"Maybe not, but you're the only person I really know here; and you're the only person who knows how important she is to me. Please? Will you do it?"

The pain and emotion in his eyes caught me off guard, and I found myself saying, "Okay, I'll do it. But don't be mad at me if she hates you even more when I'm done. I'm not exactly good at this sort of thing. If you were asking me to wrestle her for her forgiveness you'd probably have a better chance of success, but if talking is what you want, then talking is what I'll do."

"Thanks man, it means a lot to me."

I excused myself and hurried off to find Martha. She led me to Miriam's door, and as we stood outside, she said, "Are you sure you want to do this? You're not exactly known for your silver tongue, you know."

"That's what I tried to tell John Mark, but he insisted, so just knock on the door and let's get on with it."

Martha shook her head and knocked on the door. There was no response, so she knocked again and said, "Miriam, I need you to open the door. I want to introduce you to my brother, since he's the head of our household."

At first there was still no response, but then we heard someone shuffling across the floor, and the door slowly opened. I followed Martha inside, and there was Miriam.

She had obviously once been a pretty woman, but her beauty had been marred by hard living and grotesque mistreatment. There were small scars on her cheeks and on her exposed arms, and there was a large scar on her forehead, which made it hard to look her in the eyes.

Martha must have sensed I was at a loss for words because she took control and said, "Miriam, this is my brother, Lazarus. Lazarus, this is Miriam."

I sputtered while trying to not look at the scar on her forehead, "Yes . . . I'm her brother . . . and. . . ."

Miriam stopped me and said, "The scar on my forehead is from where a Roman soldier head-butted me when I demanded my pay after I'd serviced him. I guess he didn't think I deserved anything for what I'd done for him."

"Wow, I'm so sorry . . . I . . . I. . . ."

"You don't have to be sorry; you didn't head-butt me. Besides you should see the scar I gave him with my dagger. Believe me, it's a lot bigger than this little thing, and it's a lot bigger than his little thing too. Ha!"

I was shocked and she could see it, but that didn't stop her from continuing, "I could show you lots of scars if that's what you'd like." She reached for the bottom of her skirt and started to raise it up.

I grabbed her hand and said, "Stop."

She smiled seductively, "What, you don't like scars? Then maybe you'd like to see my tattoos." She raised her hands and showed me the letter U that was tattooed on the back of each one. "See the U? That's the mark of my master, Uriah. He wanted to make sure everyone knew I was his property. That way, if I ever got away, everyone would know who I belonged to and bring me back to him, and you know, it worked. I must have escaped a dozen times over the last two years, and every time someone brought me back to him, and every time the bastard beat me like a dog. But if you don't like those tattoos, I've got some prettier ones I can show you." She reached for her shirt and started to raise it.

I grabbed her hands and said, "Please stop. I just want to talk to you."

"Oh, you just want to talk, huh? You must be married, that's what a lot of the married men say at first, but it's not long before they want to do more than talk."

"No, really, I just want to talk to you about my friend, John Mark."

Now her smile turned bitter and she jerked her hands away, "Yeah, that's what I figured. The coward sends another man to do his talking for him. I thought that was what this was all about. Well, don't waste your breath, I don't want to hear anything that cretin has to say. It's his fault I became a slave in the first place."

"Yes, I know, and he's really sorry for what he did. That's why he sold everything he had and went looking for you. I know what he's done to find you and set you free doesn't begin to compare with what you've been through, but he's genuinely repentant for what he did to your family. I'm sure if any of them are still alive, he'd like to help you find them and rescue them from their situation."

She seemed to soften and said, "My family . . . we were all sold into slavery years ago. I don't know where they are, or if they're even alive."

"I know for a fact that John Mark has the resources and the will to help you find them. He somehow found you, and if they're still alive, he'll be glad to help you find them, too."

"Why would he help me find my family?"

I blurted, "Because he loves you, and wants to marry you!"

"Marry me? Hah! Now that's funny! Who wants to marry a used up prostitute? He's *so* pitiful. Does he think that marrying me will absolve him of his sins? What an idiot. I wouldn't marry him if he was the last man on Earth and you can tell your *friend* I said so."

She started toward me like she meant to do me harm and Martha stepped between us and said, "Just calm down, Miriam. My brother is only trying to help. That's why he's offered you a home."

Miriam drew herself up and retorted, "I won't need your hospitality much longer. I'll be leaving soon, and in the meantime, just leave me alone."

I said, "But where will you go?"

She sneered, "That's none of your concern. And it's certainly none of John Mark's concern. I'll live my life without his help, or I'll die trying. Now, leave me alone!"

Martha took me by the arm and pulled me out of the room. The door slammed behind us, and as she led me away I said, "Well, that went well. Don't you think?"

"Yes, brother, you're sure one smooth talker when it comes to the ladies."

I grumbled, "Well, no one can say I didn't try, but that's one angry woman."

"Yes she is, but I think you may have planted some seeds of hope in her heart."

"Really?"

"Yes, really. When you mentioned finding her family that definitely had an impact on her, and I don't think John Mark had told her he wanted to marry her. That seemed to genuinely shock her. You've given her some things to think about, brother, and now we'll just have to wait and see if anything comes of it. She's had to harden her heart to survive in the world she's been living in, but deep down she's still a woman who wants to be loved."

"You really think there's hope she'll change her mind about him?"

Martha smiled, "Who knows? With the way miracles have been happening around here lately, anything's possible."

Just then, Darius called my name from behind. I turned expecting him to still be perturbed over how I'd upset Iris earlier, but the look on his face wasn't one of anger. He drew closer and said, "There's a woman at the gate who wants to come inside, and I'm not sure what I should do."

"Look around Darius. We're full to the rafters. We can't take in any more guests for now."

"But sir, she claims she's Mary, the mother of Jesus!"

CHAPTER TWENTY-NINE

I fell in beside Darius, and Martha followed behind us, as we scurried toward the main gate. I said, "Darius, have you never met our Aunt Mary?"

"I don't believe so, sir. This woman didn't look familiar to me, and she had a young man with her, whom I didn't recognize, so I thought it best I confer with you before letting strangers inside. After all, you've been hiding in the wilderness partly out of fear of assassins."

"You did the right thing, Darius, and we'll know soon enough if this is really my Aunt Mary, but it's hard to believe she'd travel all this way without notifying us beforehand." I shouted at the guards, "Open the gates."

When the gates drew open, I was surprised to see that the woman waiting outside really was my Aunt Mary, and she was also accompanied by my cousin James, the brother of Jesus.

Martha and I embraced and welcomed them all, and then I asked, "What brings you all here? Have you come for Passover?"

James answered, "We'd like to stay for Passover, but I'm afraid that won't be possible this year. We're here because we heard the Great Sanhedrin has put out a warrant for the arrest of Jesus, and we intend to take him home with us before he gets himself killed."

Mary looked at me expectantly, and I paused while trying to frame an answer that would set her mind at ease. Then I said, "Yes, we'd heard that too, so we took Jesus to the Ephraim wilderness for the last week and just got back this morning. I don't think anyone will attempt to come against him here, and next week, when he goes into Jerusalem for Passover week, we'll take precautions to see that he's never alone. He has over 100 followers and disciples here who will accompany him wherever he goes, so the temple guards won't lay a hand on him without a fight. I can promise you that."

James shook his head, "It's not enough. There's talk all across the countryside of making him the new King of the Jews. If the Romans get wind of that, it won't matter how many people are guarding him. The Roman soldiers make the temple guards look like grandmothers out for a leisurely stroll. They'll massacre anyone who tries to stop them from arresting him, and then they'll crucify him to make an example of what happens when you mess with Rome."

I responded, "Now look, Jesus is a grown man and he knows the risks involved, if he wants to. . . ."

James interrupted me, "Lazarus, I know you're close to him, but this is his mother, and I'm his brother. We're his *real* family and we want to talk to him. To tell the truth, I'm worried he may be going a little mad with all this talk of being a king or even the Messiah. Some of us think he's been spending too much time in the sun. A little peace and quiet away from the masses may be just what he needs to see things clearly again."

I hung my head, "Of course. You're right. Martha, take our honored guests to the dining hall. Darius, have Nida bring them some food. They must be famished. I'll go find Jesus and let him know you're waiting to meet with him."

I spun away abruptly and headed for the gardens, where I felt pretty certain my cousin would be soaking up the sun (just as his family suspected).

I had no idea how he would respond to my news, but I was hopeful he wouldn't shoot the messenger.

⊰ ⊱

I found Jesus right where I expected him to be, and I got right to the point. "Sorry to bother you, but your mother and your brother James are in the dining hall demanding a meeting with you."

"I'm not surprised. I've been expecting them. I guess they plan to take me home with them for my own safety."

"Yes, they think you've been spending too much time in the sun and you've lost your mind, since they're hearing talk of you being the Messiah and promised king of the Jews. Plus, they're afraid the Sanhedrin and the Romans will find a way to kill you." I said.

"And what did you tell them?"

"I tried to tell them you were a grown man, and you knew the risks and could decide for yourself what to do, but they cut me off, and insisted they were your real family, and had a right to meet with you."

Jesus stood and said, "My real family now consists of my followers. They will be the ones who will walk with me in these final days before I reach the end of my journey. Tell my family I love them and appreciate their concern, but I won't be meeting with them today, and I won't be going home with them. Encourage them to go and stay with our uncle, Joseph of Arimathea, during Passover week. He has a huge home in Jerusalem and he'll be glad to see them, and he'll happily take them in."

"And what will you do?"

"I'll sit here and soak up some more sun until I'm completely crazy."

I laughed and said, "While I've got your attention, there are a couple of things I need to ask you."

"Then go ahead and ask."

"Well, first of all, let me say thanks for filling all our storehouses."

Jesus shook his head, "I'm not sure what you're talking about."

"I was just complaining to Mary and Martha that we were about to run out of food, and Mary said not to worry, because God would provide. Then Horus showed up and informed me that all our storehouses were completely full. I just assumed a miracle like that had to be something you'd done. Am I missing something here?"

Jesus smiled, "Maybe you need to thank your sister Mary. It seems her incredible faith has once again been rewarded."

"What are you talking about?"

"Lazarus, in case you haven't noticed, you and your sisters have all been blessed with significant spiritual gifts. You have the gifts of service and helps, which inspire you to serve and protect the weak and innocent. Martha also has the gift of service, but, in addition, has the gifts of hospitality, mercy, and healing, which inspire her to nurture and heal the weak and innocent. And your sister, Mary, or as some call her, Mary Magdalene, has the incredible gifts of faith and miracles, which enable her to be a conduit of God's grace and bounty to the weak and innocent who are less fortunate."

"I have no idea what you're talking about."

"There is a manifestation of our heavenly father's spirit in this world that instills in each person various 'gifts of the spirit' that enable each person to serve God and others in unique ways. You can call that spiritual manifestation the Holy Spirit if you'd like. Anyway, you and your sisters have been given spiritual gifts that make the three of you a formidable force for good in this world when the three of you come together."

"If you say so, but I'm not sure I'm buying what you're selling. It seems to me, they stay mad at me about half the time, so I'm not sure we do much in the way of enhancing each other's strengths."

"In the days to come I think you'll see what I mean. Now, you said you had some questions for me."

"Yes, I do. When I was with Enoch, he said you were going to die."

"And?"

"And how can that be? I kind of thought you really were the Messiah, and I also thought all of this was going to lead up to you being named the new King of the Jews. Is that not going to happen?"

"In the next few days there will definitely be many who will call me the King of the Jews, and also many will recognize me as the Messiah."

I frowned, "But what good will it do to name you our king, if you just turn around and die."

"We all die eventually, Lazarus. At least, in this place we do. You're the only exception to the rule. But don't worry; our spirits live on in a new glorified body."

"What's a glorified body?"

"It's a body that's similar to the body of our heavenly father."

"So, you're saying you really are going to die soon?"

"Yes, but on the third day I'll rise again, just like you did. I won't be gone long, and then you'll have me with you forevermore."

I smiled, "Forevermore, huh? Just like our old motto?"

"Yes, just like our old motto. In fact, exactly like our old motto."

"Great, that's good to hear. Now, there's just one more thing I need to ask you. By now, you've probably heard Iris and I plan to be married tomorrow. I was wondering if you'd do me the honor of performing the ceremony?"

"Of course, I wouldn't have it any other way."

I hesitated and then dived in with my next question, "There's just one problem. Iris's family isn't Jewish. Her mom and dad still discreetly honor some of the old God's of their homeland in Egypt. I don't want to embarrass them, or Iris, by having our marriage ceremony come across as being too *Jewish* if you know what I mean."

Jesus laughed, "I see what you mean. I'll try to steer things right down the middle of the road so we don't make anyone uncomfortable. The only thing that really matters is getting you two properly hitched. Right?"

"That's exactly right. I've never been one to sweat the small details, so just get it done the best you can."

"Trust me; I'll take care of you. Now, I think you should go let my family know I won't be joining them for dinner."

"Yeah, now who's taking care of whom?

My meeting with Mary and James went about as well as could be expected. To say the least, they weren't happy, but they gathered up their pride and dignity and hurried off to my uncle's home as the sun was setting.

Now that all the drama of the day was finally settled, I found myself with nothing more to do at the end of the day, so I slyly separated myself from all our guests and made it back to my bedroom without being detected.

I shut the door and took a deep breath. It really felt good to finally be back in the comfort of my own home. I put away my staff and Demetria's lance, and then I looked around for something else to do. I decided I should update my journal in light of the big day that lay before me, but first I wanted to enter in all the notes I'd jotted down while I was in the wilderness.

I opened the bag that contained the writing kit I'd obtained in Enoch's cave and pulled out the sheets of vellum-like material I'd written on while away from home. To my dismay, they were all blank. I turned each one of them over and over and completely emptied the whole kit on my bed, but there was no denying it; the things I'd written had disappeared into thin air. I thought to myself that maybe there was something wrong with the material I'd been writing on. Maybe it soaked up the ink in some mysterious way.

Then, I remembered the writing kit Jesus had given me also had some of the same vellum-like material in it, so I found the present he'd given me and opened it up. When I pulled the vellum sheets out of the bag I was amazed to find everything I'd written in the wilderness had somehow been transcribed to these weird sheets of vellum. Every word was there just like I'd written it, only everything was in smaller print, but it was definitely my handwriting.

I didn't know what to make of it. Maybe the writing kit from Enoch's cave was an artifact or relic that had special powers like the Rod of Moses. Or maybe the writing kit Jesus had given me was somehow special, or maybe they both were. Come to think of it, they were very similar.

I'd have to ask Jesus about it later. For now, I occupied myself with just copying all the new entries into my yearly journal. When I finished, I composed a brand new entry.

March 28th

We're finally home! On the final night of traveling back to Bethany, we realized we were being followed by a large band of outlaws and Seekers. I ordered Horus to take my guards and get Jesus and his followers home safely. Then, I went back to fight, so I could try to delay the pursuit.

Unfortunately, I wasn't the only one who decided to confront our enemies. Demetria had seen the pursuit first and decided to engage them and to try to lead them away. She was captured by the Seekers and I had to use the Rod of Moses to rescue her. I managed to set her free and did enough damage with the rod to send the Seekers and their allies running for the hills, but Demetria was already badly wounded. I used elixir to speed the healing of her external wounds and had her drink some to help with things that were messed up internally. I think she almost died, but now it looks like she's going to be okay.

When I got home, Iris was really excited to see me . . . right up until she saw Demetria. When she saw how we were dressed alike in our furs she nearly lost her mind with jealousy. Luckily, I was able to explain to her how I met Demetria and how her husband had just been murdered a few days ago, and that calmed her down. Or maybe it was the realization that I intended to marry her tomorrow that calmed her down. In any case, we made up, and now Jesus will perform our marriage ceremony tomorrow.

I learned from Martha that while we were gone the orphaned leper children that Jesus healed came back looking for food. Of course Martha not only fed them, she also had them spend the night, and then she didn't have the heart to send them away. God bless her!

I was mad at first, mainly because I didn't see how we could possibly feed them. We'd used up all our resources feeding Jesus and his 100+ followers over the last couple of weeks, so it seemed crazy to me to obligate ourselves to feeding 16 children, but Mary said God would provide, and she was right.

Somehow, all our storehouses are now full again. In fact, Horus says they're fuller now than they've ever been before. Everyone said it was another miracle from Jesus, and I suspected they were right, but Jesus says it's the faith of Mary that brought about the miracle. I'm having trouble believing it, but that's what he says. Maybe there's more to my sister than I realized.

The children are led by a young man named Stephen. He seems to be a fine person, and is certainly to be commended for taking care of all those helpless, innocent kids for so long. I expect great things from him.

Now Martha is dreaming of making our home an official orphanage. Ugh. I don't know how I'll stop her from going forward with her plans, but since we've already got 16 kids living here I guess a few more won't hurt anything.

Speaking of kids, I wonder if Iris and I will ever have any of our own. Well, of course we will, and she's going to be a great mother, too. She'll certainly keep them all in line, that's for sure.

I also learned from Martha that, while we were gone, John Mark came here with Miriam. Yes! He found her and bought her freedom from Uriah. Unfortunately, she wasn't overjoyed to see him. She followed him here, but only because she didn't have anywhere else to go. Now she's locked in her room and refusing to talk to anyone.

I tried to talk to her today, but I don't know if anything I said fazed her. Martha says she thinks I may have gotten through to her, but we'll see.

Then, toward the end of the day, my Aunt Mary, Jesus's mother, showed up at the gates. She'd brought her son, James with her. They demanded to talk to Jesus because they wanted to take him back home with them for his own safety.

Jesus refused to meet with them and said his true family now was his followers. Thankfully, I learned today that he's not shying away from being called the Messiah, and he even understands that people are calling for him to be anointed the King of the Jews. That's encouraging, but he also said he would die soon, and then be raised up again on the third day just like I was raised up. I don't know what that's all about, but at least he's not backing away from being our king, and that's what's important right now.

I've been looking over some old prophecies from the scriptures, and I think it would be effective if Jesus were to come riding into Jerusalem riding on a donkey to kick off Passover week. That would seem to go along with Zachariah 9:9. We'll call it a 'triumphal entry' or something like that. It'll be the entry of the new King of the Jews into his capital city during the holiest week of the year. The common people are going to love it.

Wow, I just realized that's only two days from now. I'll have to set it up with Jesus tomorrow.

But, for now, everything's going in the right direction. I need to set up a meeting with Barabbas to make sure his people are in place later in the week for our temple gala (Ha!), and then everything will be ready to unfold just like we planned it.

Tonight, I think I'll clean up and get rid of these furs. Then I'll put on my wedding garments and go pay my gardens a visit before morning.

When I think of all that's happened these last few days, it's kind of overwhelming. Just think, nine days ago I was raised from the dead. Since then I've inherited the Rod of Moses while spending several days in a cave in the wilderness. I've met a King and a Queen, I've fought an army of bandits and Seekers, and I've become the father of 16 children in one single day, and I'm not even married yet.

But tomorrow I'll add that to my list. That's right, folks. Tomorrow, Lazarus of Bethany will be a married man. Will wonders never cease?!

Once all the excitement dies down I've got to find time to tell Iris about how my body has changed since Jesus raised me from the dead. It's a lot to take in, so I don't want to muddy the waters tonight when she's making all her wedding plans, but I've got to do it soon.

Yes, a lot has happened these last few days, but from what Enoch and Jesus have told me, a lot more is going to happen in the days to come.

Jesus says, I'm to be an eternal warrior against evil on behalf of him. Well, I can't think of anyone I'd be more honored to fight for, so . . . for the weak . . . for the innocent . . . forevermore!!

I lay my quill down and walked to my closet to try and decide what I should wear for the wedding. I was whistling up a storm and just starting to ponder the possibilities when someone began to frantically knock at my door.

After all the excitement of the last 24 hours all I wanted was a chance to take a long bath and be alone for a while, so I was somewhat hesitant about opening the door, but whoever was knocking didn't seem to be going away. I guess they had heard me whistling and they knew I was in here, so I reluctantly swung the door open.

It was Darius and he seemed more agitated and concerned than I'd ever seen him before. He nervously ran his left hand through his hair and firmly gripped the sword at his side with his right hand. It was obvious he was trying to think of what to say before speaking, and he was having a hard time with it.

I finally said, "Calm down old friend. What's got you so upset?"

He answered, "Lazarus, I'm so sorry to bother you again on the night before your wedding, and Nida is probably going to have my hide for this if it interferes with all the plans that are being made, but there's another situation at the gates that needs your attention."

"It's okay Darius. Just tell me what's going on for goodness sake."

"There's a man at the gates who says his name is Saul of Tarsus. He says he met you last night in the wilderness when you were fighting those bandits. Is that true son?"

"Well, yes. As a matter of fact that is true, but he was on his way to Jerusalem to sell tents, and I thought that by now he'd be settled down there for the night. What's he doing here?"

"He brought another fellow here with him on the back of a camel and that man is badly wounded. I don't know who got ahold of him, but what they've done to him is beyond horrible! To tell you the truth I don't think he's going to make it."

"Why would this Saul of Tarsus bring a wounded man to my house?

"Well, he says he found this fellow on the trail to Jerusalem and he claimed to know you and demanded that Saul bring him here immediately. In fact, he told Saul that only you will know how to save him."

I scratched my head in confusion and said, "If this wounded man is someone I know then what's his name?"

"Saul says his name is Enoch."

I grabbed Darius by his leather jerkin and looked up into his eyes as I nearly shouted, "Did you say Enoch?!"

"Yes son, his name is Enoch."

"Find Jesus and have him meet me at the gates. If you have to pick him up and carry him then do it, but whatever you do Darius find Jesus and bring him to me at once."

Darius stammered, "But...."

"There's no time to spare Darius. Find Jesus. Find him now!"

I shoved him away, ran back into my room, and opened my writing bag that held the flask of elixir I'd stored there earlier. I snatched the flask from the bag and sprinted for the gates. It was time to perform a miracle and I was hoping I was not too late!!

Made in the USA
Columbia, SC
13 June 2023

17819338R00157